Adrift

Praise for
How to Make Friends with the Sea

★ "Guerrero touches on many topics—anxiety, fostering, friendship, family, selective mutism, and more—seamlessly weaving them all together to create a strong, moving narrative . . . A heartbreaking, heartwarming, powerful debut novel."

—*Kirkus Reviews*, starred review

"A story for anyone who's ever asked where—and what—home is."

—Jack Cheng, author of *See You in the Cosmos*

"*How to Make Friends with the Sea* is a heartwarming story about family, friendship, identity, and finding courage within our own hearts. I know readers will have as much fun cheering for Pablo as I did."

—Dan Gemeinhart, author of *The Remarkable Journey of Coyote Sunrise*

"Touching and sweet, Tanya Guerrero's debut *How to Make Friends with the Sea* is a multilayered story with heaps of heart. Readers will root for Pablo as he finds his courage, voice, and family on this journey to self-acceptance."

—Elly Swartz, author of *Finding Perfect* and *Give and Take*

"Atmospheric and moving, *How to Make Friends with the Sea* is an impressive debut. The friendship between Pablo and Chiqui completely captured my heart."

—Jasmine Warga, author of *Other Words for Home*

Praise for
All You Knead Is Love

"*All You Knead Is Love* blended culture and cooking seamlessly into Alba's environment, showcasing food's true purpose: connection, comfort, and creativity."

—Nikki Bidun, winner of *Top Chef Junior* and *Chopped Junior*

"A heartfelt story about learning to love, trust, and thrive after trauma. This book transported me to Barcelona and made me laugh, cheer, tear up, and crave delicious bread! What a joy to get to know resilient, relatable Alba as she opens up to new experiences and becomes even more fully herself."

—Laurie Morrison, author of *Up for Air* and *Saint Ivy*

"Layered with explorations of topics such as family dynamics, abuse, and identity, Alba's first-person narrative is one of growth, forgiveness, and acceptance . . . A delightful read."

—*Kirkus Reviews*

"A cast of unique characters, beautiful surroundings, and delicious food will have readers wishing they were part of Alba's world."

—*Booklist*

ALSO BY TANYA GUERRERO

How to Make Friends with the Sea
All You Knead Is Love

Adrift

TANYA GUERRERO

Farrar Straus Giroux

New York

Farrar Straus Giroux Books for Young Readers
An imprint of Macmillan Publishing Group, LLC
120 Broadway, New York, NY 10271 • mackids.com

Our books may be purchased in bulk for promotional, educational,
or business use. Please contact your local bookseller or the
Macmillan Corporate and Premium Sales Department at
(800) 221-7945 ext. 5442 or by email at
MacmillanSpecialMarkets@macmillan.com.

Library of Congress Cataloging-in-Publication Data is available.

First edition, 2022
Book design by Aurora Parlagreco
Printed in the United States of America by Lakeside Book Company,
Harrisonburg, Virginia

ISBN 978-0-374-38965-9
1 3 5 7 9 10 8 6 4 2

*For Violet and Anika, and all the other
sister-cousins in the world*

Adrift

BON VOYAGE
Coral

THE LOBSTERS WERE ALL DEAD. WE RAN AROUND the newspaper-covered table armed with hammers, smashing the cooked crustaceans as if they were trying to escape back into the ocean.

Bang! Squirt!

"Gotcha!" my cousin Isa shouted, her hammer landing on a giant claw.

I held my hammer above the last intact lobster. "Rest in peace, *Homarus americanus*," I said with a solemn voice.

Isa snorted. "God, you're such a nerd, Coral."

"What?" I gazed at her innocently. "If we're going to eat it, the least we can do is give it a dignified send-off."

"Send-off, schmend-off . . ." Isa picked up a morsel of claw meat and dipped it in a bowl of melted butter.

For a second, I kind of felt bad about the lobsters, especially since I'd seen them crawling around, alive, in Uncle Henry's lobster trap a couple of hours ago. But ever since I could remember, our Bon Voyage Lobster-Clam

Bake was an annual tradition. And traditions were really important in the Bituin-Rousseau family.

"Kain na tayo!" Tita Sunshine announced while smacking an empty pot with a wooden spoon.

Uncle Henry sneaked up behind her and took the pot and spoon away. "I think everyone heard you, honey," he said with a wink.

All five feet and one inch of Tita Sunshine stood taller, as if she could ever reach over Uncle Henry's six-foot-three frame. It was the same move that Isa used on me whenever she tried to emphasize her seniority. I mean, she was barely a year older, yet she acted as if she were the Gandalf to my Frodo. Truth be told, she was more of a cross between Samwise and Gollum. But most of the time, I just let her believe what she wanted to believe.

For a moment, I stood there and watched the chaos that was my family. They served themselves heaps of food, joking around and laughing as the setting sun turned the sky into a molten orange.

The sisters, Tita Sunshine and Mom, gabbed with each other in Taglish as they pointed out the heads and tiny feet of lobsters, which supposedly had the sweetest meat. They were almost like twins, petite with shiny black hair, golden skin that got even more golden in the summer, and eyes that crinkled at the corners when they laughed.

Then there were the brothers, Uncle Henry and Dad, their voices booming as they talked about sailboats and the ocean and beer and whatever else they usually rambled on about. It was easy to tell they were brothers, since they shared the same coppery-blond hair, freckles, and blue eyes. But Uncle Henry was taller and beefier than Dad. It was probably the decades he'd spent working on fishing boats, while Dad designed sailboats for a living.

Most people thought it was weird that a pair of sisters would marry a pair of brothers. I mean, I guess it was kind of weird and unusual. But it only made our family closer.

One happy family. All for one. One for all.

And that made Isa and me more like sisters than cousins. Isa always liked to remind me that I was her *too-tall sister from another mister*. So much so that everyone, and I mean everyone, on Pebble Island called us the Star Sisters, because, when we were little, we went around telling anyone who would listen that *Bituin*—our mothers' maiden names—meant "star" in Tagalog.

"Are you going to eat? Or just stand there and stare at us like a psycho?" Isa asked me with a smirk.

Pfft. I was trying to make one of those sarcastic sounds, but it was just a ploy to distract Isa from seeing the tears welling up in my eyes. Because Mom and Dad and me were about to set off on a four-month-long journey by sea. Our longest one yet. And I was going to miss Isa. Like really, really miss her.

Though, I wasn't going to openly admit it. Otherwise, she would tease me about it forever.

We sat down on one of the blankets laid out on the sand, our plates in front of us. For a minute, all we did was slurp on lobster and lick the butter off our fingers. But then Isa leaned over and jabbed me with her elbow. "So . . . you're not going to forget to write to me, huh?"

I glanced at her big, honey-colored eyes, at her round face and pointy chin, at her messy top bun, at her chewed-on fingernails, and at her tiny feet, which were almost always barefoot. This was my last chance to bask in her Isa-ness, to drink in every little detail about her so she wouldn't fade from my memory too fast.

God, I was going to miss her. My sister-cousin.

I smiled. "Of course I'm going to write to you. Have I ever forgotten?"

"No." She rolled her eyes. "But there was that one time a couple of years ago when you forgot to mail me that postcard from Greece."

I rolled my eyes back at her. "And, to this day, you've never forgiven me."

"I have!" she yelled.

"Not."

"Whatever."

And then we burst out into a fit of laughter because that's what we always did whenever we disagreed.

"Seriously, though. There might be some stretches when we're, like, in the middle of nowhere, you know. I doubt some of those islands even have a post office," I said.

Isa frowned. "Well, that sucks."

"Yeah . . . ," my voice trailed off because the thought of not seeing her for four whole months made my insides hurt. It was going to be like leaving one of my limbs behind. My right arm.

I reached for the silver pendant hanging from my neck, tracing the star engraved on it with my finger. We each had the same pendant. Inside was a photo of Isa when she was eleven and a photo of me when I was ten.

The Star Sisters. That was us.

After dinner, Dad and Uncle Henry built a small bonfire to roast marshmallows. The night sky was filled with twinkling stars, so we rested our bellies and stargazed with the crashing waves as our soundtrack.

"God, your parents are perfect, you know," said Isa with the cringey expression she made whenever people were doing lovey-dovey stuff.

I glanced over to where Mom and Dad were sitting. She was leaning on his lap as he caressed her hair. The light of the bonfire flickered, casting shadows on her face, and I couldn't help but admire how serene and beautiful she was. Dad stared at the dark waters in front of them, and I knew he was daydreaming about our upcoming sailing adventures.

I smiled but didn't say anything. Because Isa was right. My parents were perfect. And so was the rest of my family— Uncle Henry, Tita Sunshine, Isa. How in the world did I get so lucky?

I leaned to the side and grabbed Isa into a side-hug. "I'm going to miss you, Little Star," I said.

"Ha! I knew it!" Isa smirked, and punched me on the arm.

I rolled my eyes.

But after a second, she placed her head into the crook of my neck, fitting perfectly like a donut that had found its missing donut hole. "I'm going to miss you, too, Big Star."

ONE
Coral

One month later.

THE STARS WERE HYPERREAL. OUR BOAT ROCKED
ever so slightly, shifting the blue-black line where the water
met the sky. It was the dead of the night, and we were
anchored in the middle of nowhere. Mom and Dad
were in the cabin conked out, navigational charts strewn
over their bodies. I, on the other hand, was stretched out
on my makeshift bed on deck—a cozy heap of cushions
and throw blankets. The breeze blew over me. I traced
the constellations with my index finger. Every time I
found one, I'd mouth its name and recite every single fact
I knew about it.

*Cassiopeia, the W-shaped constellation, named after a
queen forced into the heavenly realms for eternity because
of her vanity.*

I could picture Isa's laughing eyes. "*Nerd,*" she'd say
to me.

Suddenly, I felt lonely. Too bad Dad wasn't awake so
we could geek out over stories of ancient civilizations—
Phoenicians, Austronesians, Norsemen—using celestial

navigation to explore the unknown seas. I yawned. Pretty soon the star formations began to blur into one another and the tide lulled me into a deep sleep. That is, until I felt a jolt. I bolted upright, my heart beating fast in my chest. Was it a nightmare? I gazed left and right and then left and right again. Nothing. I looked up at the sky. The stars were as they were before I'd fallen asleep. Strange.

It was quiet. Eerily quiet.

I breathed in and out and then coughed, trying to force my heart to calm down. There. *Whew.* Better. Oh well. I must have been imagining things. Or maybe it was the enormous pile of spaghetti I'd eaten for dinner. It was in my stomach, a tangle of noodles stuck in my guts. I shouldn't have overeaten. Lesson learned. Relax. *Go back to sleep, Coral.* But for whatever reason, my body was tense.

Whoosh. The sailboat rocked. My gaze went left and then right again. At first, I saw nothing. But then . . . wait. I stood. My eyes widened. There. A big swell. No. Not big. Gigantic. Like, huge, really huge.

"Dad! Mom!" I cried out. But it came out sounding more like a croak. I cleared my throat and coughed. "Dad! Mom!" This time my voice was louder, echoing out over the dark sea.

Whooooshhh! Another swell. This one three, four, maybe five times bigger than the last one. It pushed the boat up and then down. My stomach dropped. I was dizzy all of a sudden. Everything was whirling and moving and spinning like an out-of-control carnival ride.

"Mom! Dad!" I screamed.

That's when I saw it. A wave. A series of humongous waves coming toward us. Fast. I was scared. Petrified. Panicked.

"Mom! Dad! Wake up!" I screamed again as loud as I could.

There was movement in the cabin below. Voices. Footsteps.

Whoosh. Whoosh. Whoosh . . .

The waves were getting closer. I gazed at the horizon and gasped. It was a tidal wave, twenty or thirty feet high, only a minute or two away.

Oh my god!

It felt as if my heart had leaped into my throat. My legs went weak. For a split second, time stopped. Every part of me wanted to run, to move, to do something, but my mind was somewhere else.

A flash of Mom and Dad at breakfast. Dad teasing her about the supercrispy edges of the fried eggs. *"These are Pinoy-style fried eggs,"* she said, shoving him playfully.

A flash of Isa and me riding our bikes in the rain, our clothes sopping wet as we laughed our heads off.

A flash of all of us—the Bituin-Rousseau family—Mom, Dad, Uncle Henry, Tita Sunshine, Isa, and me at the lobster-clam bake on the beach.

Was that the last time I would see them all?

No!

The thought of it scared me. I had to do something.

Anything. I wasn't ready to die. I wasn't ready to lose every single person I loved.

I stepped back toward the cabin. Part of me wanted to run down to be with Mom and Dad. But the other part of me, the one that had listened to Dad's countless, boring safety lectures, knew that I needed to grab our life vests and survival kit first.

It was dark, but I had the boat's layout memorized. *Five, four, three, two, one.* I could see the bright orange life vest and the compartment where Dad stowed the survival kit. I grabbed a vest and slipped my arms through the arm holes, snapping and adjusting it with trembling hands.

"Coral?" Dad's head poked through the hatch, searching for me with blinking eyes. After a second, he spotted me. "Coral? What are you doing?" he asked with a confused frown.

I fumbled with the survival kit, somehow managing to sling it across my chest without dropping it. "Dad! The waves!" I screamed, grabbing two more life vests.

His expression changed from confusion to shock. His eyebrows arched and his mouth rounded into a perfect circle. I looked over my shoulder.

WHOOSH!

A giant wave pummeled the side of our boat. I hurled the life vests at Dad. *Ahhhh!!!* I screamed.

"Coral!" I heard Dad calling me, but I couldn't see him anymore.

Our sailboat was tipping. My body was flying, hurtling, falling.

I hit the water hard. A woman's screams echoed into the darkness. *Mom. No! No! No! This can't be happening.*

The waves just kept on rolling over me, under me, pushing me underwater even though I had a life vest on. Everything was dark and wet and endless. My body kept on sinking, somersaulting every time another wave hit, again and again and again. Seawater pushed up my nose, into my mouth. I sputtered and choked.

Am I going to die?

Another wave pushed me under. I looked up—or was it down? I couldn't tell. For a split second, I thought I saw something—a constellation twinkling through the water's surface.

Canis Major, named after Laelaps, Orion's hunting dog.

I kicked my legs and swung my arms until my head broke through. *Hahhh* . . . I breathed and coughed and breathed again. The waves were gone. But so was our boat. And so were Mom and Dad.

I stared into the black void.

"Mom! Dad! I'm here!" I yelled. "Where are you?"

But nobody replied. I stared out into the nothingness. It was just me and the wide-open sea. For a brief moment, I imagined myself an astronaut floating away from their shuttle, only the safety tether preventing them from drifting into oblivion. This was now my oblivion. And the safety tether had snapped.

Every inch of me was numb. I tried not to panic, but the thoughts manipulated me like the current. Death. Drowning. Starving. Sharks. So many sharks could have been darting below my feet.

I shut my eyes.

Fear was my enemy.

TWO
Isa

THE GARLIC-FRIED RICE SIZZLED AS IT COOKED. Ordinarily, that smell would have made me salivate like a dog with a hunk of bacon dangling in front of its nose. But I was too busy stalking our mailbox through the kitchen window to even notice the heavenly aroma.

It had been more or less a month since Coral sailed off into the sunset, leaving pathetic ole me by my lonesome. I mean, not really by my lonesome, but you could hardly count my mom and dad as real company.

Squeak. It was the sound of the rusty gate hinges opening and closing. The mailman! I grabbed my backpack and my hoodie and rushed out of the kitchen.

"Anak! Your breakfast!" Mom shouted.

"I'm not hungry!" I shouted back.

"Hay, naku." Mom's grumbling was the last thing I heard as I slammed the door shut and leaped down the front steps.

Our mailman, Malik, smiled at me as soon as he saw

me. "That postcard you've been waiting for arrived," he said with a wink.

I gasped. "Really?"

"Yup, see for yourself." He waved and then walked off toward his red, white, and blue USPS truck.

I pounced on our mailbox, rifling through a pile of bills before I spotted it—the sharp corner of a postcard.

I shoved the bills back inside and stared at the letter. It had a green jungle that seemed to go on forever, clouds so low they almost looked like fog, and an ancient temple split in the middle by a walkway leading to god knows where. In the corner, it said, "Welcome to Bali."

Coral was in Bali, Indonesia, or at least, she had been a couple of weeks ago. *Humph.* I glanced over my shoulder at our weathered, old house in exotic, far-flung Pebble Island, New York.

Oh, well. Maybe one day . . .

I flipped the postcard over and grinned at the sight of Coral's perfect cursive handwriting.

Hey Little Star,

I bet you've been stalking the mailman for days now . . . Well, it's a good thing I was able to sneak off to one of the shops in town to send this to you before we set sail again. Bali is amazing. I mean, it's touristy and all, but the place itself is beautiful, like, beyond beautiful. Especially the temples, which kind of make you feel as if you've stepped out of a time machine into some ancient civilization. And the food, my goodness. I literally had THE BEST curry made out of jackfruit, and chicken and fish sate skewered on lemongrass sticks. So, so good. Anyway, we're touring the most remote parts of the Indonesian islands next, so you might not get a postcard from me for a while. Don't kill me! I promise, I'll send you another next chance I get. God, I really wish you were here! One day, Little Star. One day, you and me will travel the world. Just the two of us. More soon.

Lots of love,
Coral

When I was done reading the postcard two whole times, I let out a long breath. I placed the tip of my finger on the part that said, *I really wish you were here!*, rubbing the words back and forth as if I were rubbing a genie's magical lantern. Maybe if I rubbed hard enough, my wish would come true. *Zap!* I would materialize on some tropical beach with Coral.

"Anak! You're going to be late for school!" Mom yelled out the window.

Crap. I gazed at the postcard longingly.

One day. One day . . .

THREE
Coral

THE WEIGHT OF MY BODY BETRAYED ME. I HEAVED.
Something solid was behind my legs and back. I moved
my feet and felt sand between my toes. The realization
that I was still alive forced my eyes wide open. The bright
blue sky blinded me. I pushed myself up to sitting and
winced. Cramps pinched at my sand-caked limbs, which
for whatever reason reminded me of uncooked mozzarella
sticks. Maybe I was just hungry. My stomach groaned.
Yup. Hungry.

The neon orange life vest was tight against my chest,
so I took it off, breathing a sigh of relief when I found the
survival kit still clinging to me. *Thank god.*

For a good, long while, all I kept thinking was, *I'm
alive, I'm alive.* But part of me refused to believe it. Maybe
I was dead. The pain, though, the stiffness, the aches, the
cuts. They were all there. I couldn't ignore them. I really
was alive. For better or for worse.

As I wobbled and then stood, a new thought nagged

me. *I'm alone.* My stomach sank. I dropped to my knees. Scared.

A chorus of birds echoed in the distant jungle, as if they were mocking me.

Good luck surviving this place, kid . . .

You're not even going to last twenty-four hours . . .

You might as well just dig yourself a grave . . .

"No!" I shouted. "No! No! No!"

I pushed myself off the sand, took a few dazed steps toward a fallen coconut tree, and sat.

"Breathe, Coral, breathe . . . ," I said out loud to myself.

I looked around, my eyes still stinging from the salt water. It was all a bit of a blur. But in front of me was the tranquil turquoise-blue sea, hugged by a crescent-shaped beach with powdery white sand. Behind me was a row of coconut trees. And in the distance, cliffs and maybe a jungle?

What is this place?

The inside of my mouth felt as if it were coated with salty seaweed snacks. Desperate for anything to drink, I yanked open the survival kit. The contents spilled out onto the sand. My eyes zeroed in on a box of drinking water. I pounced on it, ripping the seal with my teeth. Sloppy streams trickled down my chin. It was so tempting to rip open another box. But as I knelt on the sand, I did a super-quick inventory and realized something. It wasn't enough.

Only four water boxes were left among the rest of my supplies: a straw water filter, a dozen protein bars and energy gels, a travel-size first aid kit, a mini sewing kit, a rechargeable squeeze flashlight, a box of waterproof matches, a pocket notebook and pen, a bright yellow rain poncho, and a seven-inch Tracker knife.

I stared and stared for what seemed like forever. These items would make the difference between life and death.

My life.

My death.

That's when a tidal wave of emotions hit me.

A tidal wave. How ironic.

Everything sank in all at once, twisting my stomach until the ache was unbearable. It was only then, as I stared out at the seemingly endless stretch of sea, that tears began falling down my cheeks.

Mom. Dad. There was a gaping hole in my heart.

They're not here.

Am I ever going to see them again?

What if . . . what if they're dead?

A gruesome mixture of fear and sadness gripped me. I couldn't breathe. My arms, my legs, my shoulders, my chin were trembling. It was hot, but I was cold, almost shivering. *What if they're dead? What if they're dead? What if they're dead?* That one thought kept hitting me, over and over. I was nauseated; my stomach ached. *Cough, cough.* Suddenly, my throat burned, and then I vomited all over the sand. The water I'd just drank, along with the acids from my empty stomach, formed slimy pools by my feet.

Why me? How am I supposed to go on without Mom and Dad?

I fell on my hands. I tightened my stomach muscles, trying to get all the hurt out. I pushed the tears out of my eyes, trying to rid myself of all the sadness. I swallowed hard, trying to push all the bitterness down my throat.

But none of it worked.

It wasn't until the sun beat down on me that the tears finally ran out, leaving my face puffy and raw. I may as well have been comatose. The swishing waves deepened my trance until a barely there whisper snapped me out of it, *Use what we taught you, Coral.*

I knew Dad wasn't really here. But imagining his voice stirred up a flurry of memories. It was as if shooting stars had filled my mind's sky, leaving a trail of days lived—spring mornings picking mushrooms in the forest, exploring tide pools in the summer, buckets of clams steamed in seaweed for lunch, camping in the wilderness, a blazing fire crackling at dusk.

With the back of my hand, I wiped away the tears and stood as straight as I could.

"I won't let you down, Mom and Dad."

FOUR
Isa

I WAS PRETTY SURE THAT MOST THIRTEEN-YEAR-olds slept in on weekends. But not me. Every Saturday and Sunday, I had to drag myself out of bed at the crack of dawn to help out at the Sunshine Deli and Bakery.

Yup, you guessed it. It was named after my mom, Sunshine, because nothing was cheerier and brighter than the sun. And sunny days always made everyone want to go out and buy a sandwich, a cold drink, and a dozen blueberry muffins, right?

Well, you couldn't blame me for not being a morning person. I mean, lots of people weren't morning people. Even Coral had a hard time dragging her butt out of bed, unless, of course, she caught a whiff of freshly baked croissants. Then she was sure to hurry down to the kitchen to snag one while they were still warm.

I rounded the corner onto Main Street, ringing the bell of my trusty bicycle. The only good thing about early mornings was that hardly any cars were around. I paused at the top of the hill where Main Street began and looked over the sight I'd seen my entire life—the brightly painted little buildings with shops and restaurants, the potted flowers, the colorful flags, the marina dotted with sailboats and motorboats, and, at the bottom of the hill, facing the waterfront in a red wooden building that resembled an old barn, the Sunshine Deli and Bakery.

It was all so quaint, as tourists would say.

I zoomed down the hill, *ring-ring-ringing* my bell all the way down. When I arrived, I leaned my bike against the side of the building by the parking lot, not even bothering to chain it to anything, because nobody ever stole anything on this island. Small islands were not only quaint but also extremely boring.

"Anak, is that you?" I heard Mom saying as I entered through the front door.

"No. I'm here to rob you. Give me all your money," I replied with my best gruff and tough robber impression.

Mom appeared from the back, wearing her favorite yellow apron and a scowl so deep she might as well have been wearing a mask. "It's too early for that humor of yours, Isa."

I glanced over my shoulder at the entrance. "Oh. Well, I'm happy to go back home and come back later . . ." The eye-daggers shooting across the room landed right smack in the middle of my forehead.

"Why don't you make a pot of regular and decaf, and start with setting up the pastry display," she said with puckered lips, gesturing at the baking section.

"Fine," I grumbled.

I went along my merry way, slipping on a white apron before busying myself with cleaning, arranging, and setting up for the day. I yawned. It was bad enough that I was sleepy, but then Mom began humming one of the cheesy power ballads that she loved so much.

"Near . . . far . . . mmmm . . . mmmmm . . . mmmmmm . . ."

Oh god. It was Celine Dion, that song from *Titanic* that was, like, super-duper long. *Ugh.* The morning couldn't possibly get any worse. If I was going to make it to the end of my shift, I'd need an extralarge cup of coffee with loads of sugar. Maybe two.

The landline phone by the register rang. It was probably some tourist asking if we had something gluten-free or vegan or whatever.

"I'll get it!" said Mom. She fast-walked and answered it. "Good morning, Sunshine Deli and Bakery! How can I help you?"

While she was distracted, I grabbed a coffee mug from the shelf. Mom was always getting on my case about drinking coffee. "*Anak, it will stunt your growth,*" she'd say to me with this head-to-toe glare that was meant to emphasize how short I was. Well, I mean, I was kind of short. But so was she.

I took the freshly brewed pot of regular and poured some in the mug with my back facing Mom.

"Oh. Hello . . . that's her, I mean, me. Yes, I'm Sunshine Bituin-Rousseau." Mom sounded weird all of a sudden. Her voice went from her usual cheery tone to her uh-oh-what-has-Isa-done-now tone.

I side-eyed her and noticed the deep frown etched on her forehead.

"Okay. Thank you for calling. Yes, please do update us when you know more." She hung up and stared at the wooden counter, blinking for a good minute or so.

"Mom?" I said, turning all the way around.

She looked up at me, still blinking; her face had gone pale and splotchy. It was weird, because her eyes were on me, but it was like she wasn't seeing me at all, not even the extralarge coffee in my grasp.

"Mom? What's wrong?" I asked.

Finally, her gaze seemed to focus. She stepped toward me, wobbling so much that she had to grab onto the edge of the counter for support. "There was an earthquake in Indonesia . . . It—it caused a tidal wave . . . And Uncle Jack's boat is missing."

I sucked in my breath and held it. The words she'd said, I'd heard them, but somehow what she was saying hadn't fully registered in my brain. "But they're fine. Right? Coral . . . she's okay. Right?" I uttered softly.

Mom's shoulders slumped. "Isa, they're missing. Tita Alma, Uncle Jack, Coral . . . all of them."

The coffee cup dropped from my hand, splashing hot brown liquid all over the floor, all over my pants, all over my sneakers.

"Coral!" I screamed and screamed.

FIVE
Coral

I DIDN'T WANT TO MOVE. I DIDN'T WANT TO DO ANY-thing. All I wanted was to close my eyes and magically turn back time. If we were back in Bali, I would persuade Mom and Dad to stay a bit longer, explore more temples, gorge ourselves on delicious food, and take as many ham-mock naps as we wanted.

But time machines didn't exist.

The only thing I had left from Bali were my memories.

Squack! Squack! I looked up at the sky and spotted a couple of black birds gliding down the beach toward the distant cliffs. Even from far away I could see their black feathers glistening under the sunlight. If Dad were here, we'd grab a couple of binoculars and follow them. It would be an adventure of sorts.

But Dad wasn't here. And neither was Mom.

I'd promised not to let them down. Yet I was doing absolutely nothing, like a useless glob of slime. My arms and legs were heavy. My back was slouched. My muscles were beyond sore. It was as if every ounce of energy had been sucked out of my body.

Sigh . . . My face and neck were burning all of a sudden. I knew it wasn't from the hotter-than-hot sun. No. The heat was from the utter humiliation I was feeling. Less than an hour had passed, and I was already giving up. I really was a useless glob of slime. Slime had no business on a beach full of sand. It didn't belong. And neither did I.

This place. This island. I wasn't meant to be here. I was meant to be on the boat with Mom and Dad. Three more months. And then we were supposed to go back to Pebble Island. That was the plan. Not this. Never this. Tears streamed down my cheeks. I hadn't even realized I was crying. I wiped them away with my sandy fingers. Crying would just dehydrate me more. And that was the last thing I needed.

Inhale. Exhale. Okay. Move and do something, Coral.

My legs were wobbly, yet somehow I managed to bend over and collect all the items I'd strewn all over the sand, stuffing them back into the survival kit for safekeeping. Then I stared out at the stretch of beach. It was devoid of any footsteps. There weren't any lounge chairs, no umbrellas, no fruity drinks. Nobody, not a single soul, was sunbathing or building sandcastles with their kids or throwing Frisbees at their dogs.

I took a step forward and then looked over my shoulder at the footprint I'd left behind. Me. I was on that beach.

Just me. Another step and then another and another. After a few minutes, I was a quarter of the way down the beach. I halted, my eyes following the zigzag of coconut trees, jutting here and there. Some were leaning down so far they were practically lying on the ground. To my left, beyond the trees, was a clearing with flowering shrubs in pops of red and yellow; smallish trees with huge, waxy green and orange leaves; butterflies flitting around without a care in the world. For a moment, I wished I were a butterfly. Then, maybe, I could flutter my wings and get off this island.

Except, well, there was the sea. I stared at it—a vivid turquoise blue that went on and on, eventually turning a darker blue in the distance. I was pretty sure a butterfly wouldn't make it that far anyway.

What was the point? It's not as if I could transform myself into a butterfly or a bird or a fish or something. I was stuck. And there was absolutely nothing I could do about it. My shoulders drooped in defeat.

Maybe I should just go back to the fallen coconut tree and sit there. I was sleepy, thirsty, and hungry. Maybe if I just sat there, something miraculous would happen. Maybe a boat would pass by and see me. Maybe.

Ugh. The sun was starting to bake everything on the beach. I could feel my skin beginning to burn. I had to find some shade; otherwise, I'd turn bright pink in no time.

I glanced at a small clearing. The ground was sandy, and piles of fallen leaves were scattered all over. There was also a large tree with roots sticking out that reminded me of an octopus's tentacles. It looked like a good place to sit, with the smooth roots to lean on, with the shade from the tree's leaves. I staggered over to the spot quickly so my feet wouldn't burn on the almost-too-hot-to-stand-on sand.

It immediately felt better, not being under the scorching sunlight. I plopped myself down between two of the tree roots, which sort of curved around me as if they were giving me a much-needed hug. For a moment, my mind was completely blank. Then, everything that had happened crashed into my thoughts—the waves, the boat tipping to the side, the life jackets, the water, under the water, Mom and Dad not being there. It was a lot. Too much. I slammed my eyelids shut and tried to make my mind blank again. *Whoosh, whoosh, whoosh.* The gentle sound of the waves hitting the shoreline. I listened and imagined I was back on Pebble Island. My body relaxed. So relaxed I sort of leaned into the tree's embrace, my legs digging into the soft sand beneath me.

I just needed a moment to forget. A moment to breathe. A moment to gather my strength before I was forced to consider the situation I was in. For a little while longer, I just wanted to be a kid taking a nap under the shade of a leafy tree. Just a little while longer . . .

SIX
Isa

I RAN. BECAUSE I DIDN'T KNOW WHAT ELSE TO DO.

Before I knew it, I was on my bike riding away with tears in my eyes. I didn't know where I was going. It was all a blur, Main Street passing me by like a rainbow kaleidoscope. I could still hear Mom shouting after me, "Isa! Anak! Please come back!"

But the last thing I needed was to hear more bad news, to hear Mom talking about the situation, to hear Mom telling me to calm down. I was not going to calm down. Not when Coral, Tita Alma, and Uncle Jack could be lost out there or even . . . *no.* I wasn't going to think it, because if I did, it might be true. And it wasn't. It couldn't be.

I pedaled uphill, my leg muscles burning, my vision blurred from the tears and the sweat in my eyes. My bike turned right then left then right again. I swerved past SUVs and station wagons and pickup trucks and other bikes and passersby walking their dogs. There was a kid crossing the street, too busy licking his ice cream to notice me. So I rang my bell to warn him. I may have been upset, but I wasn't about to run some kid over.

"*Isa, they're missing. Tita Alma, Uncle Jack, Coral . . . all of them . . .*" Even though I didn't want to hear them, Mom's words kept echoing softly in my mind. Reminding me, tormenting me. I tried to ignore them, instead focusing on my breathing, on the ferryboat horn blaring in the distance.

I just kept on pedaling until I suddenly found myself at the Harborview Lookout point. The wooden sign was faded by the sun and seawater, but it didn't really matter, because it was mostly only local kids who hung out there. I leaned my bike against the sign, catching my breath for a minute before heading down the dirt path. When I reached the cluster of oak trees surrounding the lookout point, I exhaled. Thank god nobody was there. I must have been quite a sight with my puffy red eyes, tears, sweat, and snot all over my face.

For a moment, I just stood there by the broken fence, gazing at the view of Main Street and the marina and the bay. I could see tiny, ant-size people wandering the streets; all the colorful flags fluttering in the breeze; sailboats and fishing boats dotting the dark blue water; and seagulls, lots of them, flying overhead searching for fish and leftover food scraps discarded by tourists. Standing there from way up high, it was as if I were looking down at another place—a beautiful, idyllic town. One I would have loved to visit if I hadn't already lived there.

Coral and I used to spend hours at the lookout making up stories about all the people below, all the strangers, all the people we knew, even the dogs. We would sit down against the gigantic oak tree, the one closest to the broken part of the fence, with our water bottles, snacking on chicharon, garlic-roasted peanuts, or Mom's legendary pastillas.

"*Holy moly, Isa! These pastillas are like heaven in food form. For real.*" I could almost hear Coral speaking, her mouth smacking as she chewed on the sugary, milky candy.

I glanced at the oak tree. It was there as it always was, staring at me with its carved trunk, covered with dozens of initials and I heart so-and-sos. For whatever reason, it looked lonely and kind of pathetic, as if it had been eons since anyone had sat there. I went over and plopped down on the patch of weeds in front of it. Then I leaned back, wanting to feel the scratchy bark through my T-shirt. The sensation was familiar and comforting. Except the space next to me was empty. I glanced at the spot where Coral used to sit with her long legs pulled up against her chest. Just thinking about her made my heart hurt—like, literally hurt, as if it had swelled so much that it was beginning to inch up my throat. Still, I didn't want to stop thinking about her.

I closed my eyes, remembering the last time we'd hung out here. It was a couple of days before their trip. Sunset. The sky was tie-dyed in shades of purple, orange, and pink. We were kind of spaced out, watching the colors change, watching the sun dip lower and lower. Coral elbowed me gently and said, "*Hey, let's stay until the stars come out.*"

"*Yeah, okay,*" I replied, even though I was pretty sure Mom would be annoyed at us for skipping dinner.

Coral scooched down and lay on the ground with her hands behind her head. "*C'mon. We can see better this way,*" she said.

I did what she did and lay next to her. For a while, it was quiet. We just stared up at the sky with our own thoughts. Dad told me once that the more you know someone, the closer you are to them, the easier it is to be silent around them. No need for small talk, no expectation of coming up with the perfect thing to say. And I believed him, because that's how it was with me and Coral. One minute we'd be chatting up a storm, the next minute silence.

"*Hey, Isa . . .*"

I turned my head to look at her. "*What?*"

"*While I'm gone, I want you to do this every night. Okay?*" She met my gaze.

I frowned at her. "*Every night?*"

"*Yes. That way I'll know we're both looking up at the same stars. In a way, we'll still be together,*" she explained.

"*Sure. As long as you don't expect me to remember ANY of the constellations. Nerd.*" I chuckled.

Coral rolled her eyes jokingly. "*And if you ever see a shooting star, make sure to close your eyes and send me a message . . .*"

"*Really? What are we, in third grade or something? Why don't we just talk to each other with two cans and a string?*" I said, trying not to laugh at her.

"*Funny. Ha ha. Whatever. Don't do it if you don't want to,*" said Coral in a huff.

I reached over for her hand and squeezed it. "*All right, all right. I'll do it. But only if you promise to tell me your deepest and darkest secrets. Then, for sure, I'll listen,*" I said with my world-famous sarcastic grin.

"*Deal.*"

Then I leaned my head on her shoulder, and we waited for the stars to appear one by one. The memory was still so fresh. If only I could go back to that day and somehow persuade Coral not to go on the trip. Then maybe she would still be here with me.

I slid down and lay on the exact same spot. It was nowhere near nighttime, but I was going to stay right there and wait. Because wherever Coral was, I wanted her to know we were still together. We were still staring up at the same stars. And maybe, just maybe, I might even be able to tell her that I was still waiting for her to come back home.

SEVEN
Coral

MY STOMACH GROWLED. I WAS FAMISHED, BUT MY stomach was the only one complaining. The rest of me wanted to stay exactly where I was—cocooned in the comfort of the tree's roots. Staying there meant I could ignore the situation I was in. Even for just a little while longer.

It felt cowardly lying there in the fetal position with a blanket of fallen leaves. Yet still, I didn't budge. *Just five more minutes* turned into *Just ten more minutes*. And pretty soon an hour, maybe two, had passed.

The sun was even brighter and hotter than it had been earlier in the day. I felt fragments of it streaming through the canopy of the tree I was lying under, hitting parts of my face and chest and arms and legs. I opened one eye and was immediately blinded by a ray of light. *Ugh*. My stomach growled again, and this time it wouldn't take no for an answer.

I reluctantly sat up, wincing at my sore muscles. The survival kit was by my feet. I reached for it and pulled out one of the protein bars, taking one bite before wrapping it back up and putting it away. As hungry as I was, I had to ration whatever I had.

Crunch. Crunch. There was a noise coming from somewhere nearby. I sat up straighter and gazed around the clearing at the patches of sand, at the piles of crispy leaves strewn all over, at the spaces between the bushes and trees and flowering shrubs.

"Hello?" I said out loud. "Is anyone out there?"

Crunch. Crunch. Crunch. I got up to my feet and hid behind the tree.

But what if it's Mom and Dad? Could they have been on the island all along?

I peeked out with one eye. A cinnamon-colored bird with longish legs hopped out of the shadows. A water hen, perhaps? It pecked at a dried leaf and then froze as if it sensed my presence.

I came out from behind the tree, and it immediately darted back into the shadows. Its long feet stomping on more leaves as it ran off. *A bird. Just a stupid bird.*

Behind me, the tree and its roots and its fallen-leaf blanket seemed to whisper, *Come back, Coral. You know you want to take another nap.* But I needed to snap out of it. I needed to do something other than lie down and feel sorry for myself.

Should I explore? For all I knew, the island might not actually be so bad. What if there were people there who could help me? Maybe I wasn't even marooned on a deserted island. I strapped the survival kit across my chest and then inhaled and exhaled as if I were preparing to run a marathon. If I was lucky, the extra oxygen would make up for the lack of food and water. Every part of me was sore, and my legs were jiggly and weak. But I had to force myself to act. My life depended on it.

One step, then another and another. Instead of walking on the beach under the scorching sun, I opted to stay under the trees. The coconut trees didn't provide much shade, but other trees, ones with layers of low-lying branches and fan-shaped leaves, offered protection from the heat. It was a weird sort of terrain, not quite the beach, with all the weeds and trees and bushes and viny plants on the ground and on tree trunks. But it wasn't quite the jungle, either, with the patches of sand and random pieces of driftwood and renegade shells that had somehow found their way inland. I scanned the debris, looking at shell after shell after shell. For a moment, I felt as if I were a little kid again, back on Pebble Island, combing the beach for treasures—unusual shells, sand dollars, and, if I was lucky, a colorful piece of sea glass.

I bent over and plucked an eyeball shell staring up at me. It wasn't really an eyeball, obviously. But that's what I used to call them before I found out what they really were, the little trapdoors of operculum shells that resembled smooth, shiny eyeballs. Mom used to call them Shiva eye shells, explaining that there was a superstition that the shells could help sharpen a person's intuition. I never really knew if all that stuff was true. But I needed every bit of help I could get. So I wiped it with my finger and stared into its greenish-brown center.

Please send me some sort of sign. Please . . .

A minute passed. And then another minute. Nothing happened, though. Not a single thing. *Ahhhhhh!* I screamed out in frustration. I didn't know I had it in me, but apparently, I did. I screamed again and again. And then I flung the Shiva eye as far as I could toward the beach. I watched it in the air, twirling a few times before landing with a bounce.

I stood for a good long while just staring at it from a distance. There was this tightness in my chest, the same tightness I got whenever I felt guilty that I was betraying someone's trust. *Whoosh. Whoosh . . .* It was as if the waves were speaking to me, telling me that as soon as high tide came, they would reach out and take the shell back. The Shiva eye. Mom's Shiva eye.

I ran fast toward the beach as if that shell were an actual piece of Mom. When I reached the spot where it fell, I scooped it up and held it against my heart. Relieved.

Maybe it was Mom's way of watching over me.

EIGHT
Isa

I STARTLED AWAKE. IT WAS NIGHTTIME, AND I WAS still at the lookout. For a second, I forgot what I was doing there. But as my vision cleared, the stars above twinkled. As if they were trying to tell me something. But what?

My mind was twisting and turning and tangling itself up with too many thoughts. And as I tried to make sense of those thoughts, my eyes wandered from star to star, trying to find answers in those constellations that Coral was always blabbing about. But it was hopeless. The only one I managed to recognize was the Big Dipper. *Big whoop.*

I shifted and my star pendant slipped across my collarbone. The Star Sisters. It was sort of cringey how childish we had been, running around the island telling everyone we knew, telling any stranger who would listen that we were *the* Star Sisters, as if we were famous or something. But I guess we were sort of famous in a way. Everyone in town knew us. They all thought we were adorable. Well, maybe more like a-dork-able. God, we really were dorks.

Things sort of changed, though, when I turned eleven and Coral turned ten. We both kind of realized how babyish we were being. Being a-dork-able was more embarrassing than anything else. Especially when the cool, older kids were around.

Christmas of that year, we were at my house, sitting around the tree—a real, live eight-foot-tall Douglas fir that Dad insisted on getting every year. If it were up to Mom, we'd have one of those reusable white plastic ones, but Dad and Uncle Jack had grown up with the tradition of going out to the forest a week before Christmas and chopping one down. So it became our tradition, too.

When it came time to open presents, Coral and I sprawled out on the rug so it would be easier to navigate around the piles of crumpled wrapping paper. And our parents were on the couch, acting like parents were supposed to act, with their straight faces pretending they had no idea what was going to be in each box and bag. "*Ohhh! Yay! Wow! Cool!*" With each present that we ripped open, we made some sort of squeal. Finally, when all the big reveals were done, everyone exhaled in relief. Uncle Jack whipped out his favorite whiskey from the liquor cabinet and poured himself a small glass. And then he and Tita Alma grinned at each other before he pulled out two small, shiny red boxes from his pocket.

"*Oh. We almost forgot . . . Santa said to make sure you open these last,*" said Uncle Jack.

Coral and I glanced at each other knowingly, because the year before we'd both decided that Santa was as legit as Bigfoot. Yet we hadn't had the heart to tell our parents, who still clung to the belief that we still thought of Santa, the Easter Bunny, and the Tooth Fairy as real.

"*What is it, Dad?*" asked Coral as he handed her one of the red boxes.

Uncle Jack's eyes lit up as bright as the Christmas lights. "*Open it up and you'll see!*"

He handed me the other box, and at the count of three, we opened the boxes at the exact same time. Inside, on velvety green cushions, were identical silver pendants with stars engraved on them. I looked at Coral and she looked at me, and we smiled. It was the cooler, more mature version of the Star Sisters. We'd truly left our a-dork-able selves behind.

"*Look! It's us!*" Coral showed me the photo of her and me inside her pendant.

I opened mine, and the same photo stared up at me from the circular silver frame. And at that moment, something strange happened. A flurry of images materialized in front of my eyes—me and Coral graduating from high school, me and Coral going off to college together, me and Coral at each other's weddings, me and Coral with our children on the beach.

We were Star Sisters for life. And nothing would ever change that.

The sound of the ferry's horn snapped me out of the memory. I let go of the pendant. There were tears on my cheeks. I hadn't even realized I was crying.

It must have been late. Really late. I glanced at my watch, the 9:47 glaring at me. Mom was probably pissed, and Dad would be worried. I leaned back and gazed up at the night sky again. Looking for something, anything. A sign. And just when I was about to give up, there it was—a shooting star. I scrambled to my feet and watched it zip across the blue-black sky. *"And if you ever see a shooting star, make sure to close your eyes and send me a message . . ."*

I closed my eyes, just as Coral had asked me to do. Then I imagined her standing with her eyes closed, wherever she was, listening. "Coral! Hang in there, Coral! Stay strong! We're going to find you!"

NINE
Coral

I GASPED, BECAUSE THE SIGHT IN FRONT OF ME WAS truly gasp-worthy. The crescent-shaped beach had ended, giving way to a different kind of terrain. The sand had transformed into something else. If it weren't for the sea, it would have looked as if I were standing on the moon or Mars. The smooth, hardened lava hugged the coastline, with the occasional rock formations jutting out. Nestled in between the crevices were craters filled with salt water, little fish darting back and forth. And in the distance, away from shore, ginormous trees reached into the sky. Some had colorful flowers and long, leathery-looking pods, others dripped with oval-shaped seeds the size of avocados.

Under normal circumstances, I would have been over-joyed to be in such a place. It was stunning and almost unreal in its untouched beauty. Like a picture-perfect postcard I would have sent to Isa. My stomach dropped at the thought of Isa and all the messages she was expect-ing from me. Did she know what had happened to us yet? Did she think I was dead? No, she couldn't. She wasn't usually an optimist, but she was stubborn, oh so stubborn. Nobody could change her mind if she believed in something strongly enough, not even me.

And I just knew she wouldn't give up on me. She would make sure Uncle Henry and Tita Sunshine kept the search party alive until I was found.

I reached to my collarbone and traced the star engraving on my pendant with my finger. Somehow, I could feel her. Not physically, but mentally, as if our thoughts were together, me thinking of her and her thinking of me. *I'm alive, Isa. I'm alive.* I kept on repeating those words, hoping she could hear me.

I *was* alive, but for how long?

Shelter. Food. Water. Getting rescued.

I knew I couldn't ignore any of those things for much longer. If Dad were with me, he would have been searching for a decent shelter already. *It's time to snap out of it, Coral.*

"Okay," I mumbled.

I forged ahead, scrambling past rocks and boulders of all sizes, my feet dipping in and out of the pools, until I reached a gently sloping cliff covered with grooves and ripples. From below, it looked as if there were ledges, maybe even caves, hiding between the jagged curves of limestone, or whatever the cliff was made of. I had to see what was up there. My toes and fingers clung to the grooves as I attempted to climb. But the layer of sweat all over my body made it hard to get a firm grip. My clammy palms and wet soles were too slick. Cuts and scrapes sliced into my skin as I stumbled. I paused for a moment and closed my eyes. I pictured Isa scowling. "*Pain-Schmain*," she would have said to me with an exaggerated eye roll.

I inhaled and exhaled and then opened my eyes. About ten feet up, a rock shelf morphed into a limestone alcove. I pushed myself up farther so I could reach it. I pushed and pushed and pushed some more, until finally, I spotted the entrance to a small cave. I wasn't sure if it was just luck or some otherworldly intervention that brought me there, but as I bent down to peek inside, I mumbled, "This is it, Mom and Dad. This will be home for now . . ."

It took a moment for my eyes to adjust. When I could finally see, I wasn't disappointed. The cave was just a tad bigger than my reading nook at home. With a little tidying up, it would do. I hunched over, feeling like giant Alice in front of the too-small door. I got down on all fours, crawling so I could sweep the sand and all the other crap into a small pile. A while passed; my sweat-soaked shorts and T-shirt were filthy, my knees clobbered, blood oozing down my arms and legs. But eventually, the cave floor was clean enough. Objects that had probably been inching their way in from the outside, for god knows how long, were swept aside into a neat pile.

Phew. I caught my breath. Success! But as I admired my handiwork, waiting for my pride to emit that warm and fuzzy feeling, all I got was a hollow drop in my stomach and the vacant hum of the cave.

I'm still alone.

I grabbed the protein bar from earlier and went outside, hoping the chocolate would do something to fill that void in my gut. With my bloodstained legs dangling off the ledge, I nibbled on it, waiting for some sort of satisfaction. Something other than pain and fear and loneliness. But it was only when my thoughts drifted that the warm tingles finally radiated, happier memories preventing me from feeling so lost.

I thought about that last night on Pebble Island with the lobsters and s'mores and endless pitchers of ice-cold calamansi juice. I thought about Mom lying on Dad's lap as he caressed her hair, which had looked almost blue from the moonlight. I thought about Isa leaning her head on my shoulder like she'd been doing ever since we were little. Those memories seemed so long ago, but they weren't. I could still taste the food. I could still smell the bonfire and s'mores. I could still feel Isa's thick hair tickling my shoulder. But none of them were there. It was just me.

God, I miss you so much, Mom and Dad and Isa.

I wished Isa could hear me. I wished I could tell her for real.

The last bite of protein bar formed a lump in my throat. A humongous lump. I snapped my eyes shut, a crazy delusion fizzing in my head. Maybe if I wished hard enough, I'd open my eyes and be back on Pebble Island. My parents were alive and well, and none of this had ever happened. Isa was cracking one of her stupid jokes while making me a cappuccino to go with my croissant. But when I opened my eyes, nothing had changed. Absolutely nothing. I blinked, feeling hollow and numb. The hairs on my arms and legs stood on end as if I'd been shocked with an electric current. It may not have been literal, but I was shocked.

Everything that had happened. All of it was still so unreal. Yet here I was on an island in the middle of nowhere.

I shuffled into the cave and opened another water box, taking only two small sips before putting it away. The pile of debris by the cave entrance caught my eye. *Wait. Hmmm.*

An idea was brewing in my mind. I ripped open the poncho, the plastic crinkling as I scooped the entire pile into it. I managed to trudge the load all the way to the beach while huffing and wheezing. Somewhere in the middle of the shoreline, I dumped everything onto the sand. The pile looked suddenly small, so I started hoarding anything I could find around me: shells, rocks, corals, driftwood, and coconut husks. I paced up and down the beach, tracing my foot on the sand to form letters. Drenched in sweat, I began arranging the pieces of debris. My body screamed at me with every movement. My muscles, my bones, my skin, even my hair seemed to ache. Was that even possible? The sunlight was so strong my eyes squinted into slits. But still, I persisted.

I arranged the debris along the lines, until my work was complete. It took me an hour, maybe longer. I was drained, exhausted. But it was done. A giant *SOS* smiled up at the sky. If an airplane or a helicopter flew past, surely they would see it, right?

I'm going to be rescued. Of course I am.

Until I did, the only thing I could do was survive.

TEN
Isa

WHEN I GOT HOME, I SNEAKED INSIDE, AVOIDING the creaky spots on the staircase so Mom and Dad wouldn't hear me. I was exhausted, mentally and physically. All I wanted was to lock myself in my bedroom, because if I was alone, if I didn't have to hear them talking about what had happened, then maybe I just imagined the whole thing. It wasn't real. None of it. I pulled my blanket over my head and closed my eyes so tight it hurt.

Knock-knock.

"Anak, I know you're in there," said Mom from the other side of the door.

"No! Leave me alone!"

Knock-knock.

"Isabel . . ." Mom only ever used my full name when she wanted to have a serious mother-daughter talk. But talking to Mom, especially Mom, wasn't something I could handle. Not at that moment. Because she had this way of seeing the bright side in every situation, no matter how bad. She was like a human air freshener—*Spring*

Cheer or *Forest Fantasy* or *Lavender Dreams*. Every time she waltzed into a room, she spritzed her cheer and optimism all over until it reeked. And there wasn't any possible way she could have made this situation better. I mean, you could spray a bathroom after someone took a big dump with an entire bottle of *Vanilla Fields*, and after a minute it would just smell as if someone had crapped out a dozen vanilla-frosted cupcakes. So, no. I was not about to open the door and let her in.

Knock-knock-knock.

I just ignored her. Silence. And then her footsteps echoed down the hallway. I exhaled and pulled the blanket off my face. The moonlight was almost too bright, its incandescence shining into my bedroom. I blinked and squinted. But after a couple of seconds, my eyes adjusted to the light. A breeze swirled through the open window, making the curtains float and flutter like dancing ghosts. Outside, I saw the starry sky, the streaky white clouds, the full moon making the sea glimmer.

Somewhere, halfway across the world, Coral was standing under the same sky. I was sure of it. I could feel it in my bones. And nothing, I mean, not one word anyone said to me, would make me believe otherwise.

ELEVEN
Coral

SUNLIGHT CREPT INTO THE DARK CAVE. THE LEAVES
under my poncho bed crunched like corn flakes. Cereal.
Fresh blueberries. Cold milk. Just the thought of it made
my mouth water.

I dragged my achy body out of bed and chugged
some water, taking several sips until the box was empty.
My gaze landed on the pile of protein bars. Their shiny
wrappers winked at me, as if taunting me. *Eat us, Coral.
C'mon, you know you want to*. But I had to resist. Instead,
I reached for a pack of berry-flavored energy gel, sucking
the pink goop out until it was gone.

If only I could have one of Mom's fruity yogurt
smoothie bowls—a purple-pink superfood blend, topped
with fresh berries, muesli, chia seeds, and toasted coconut flakes. *Ooohhh*, or better yet, one of Tita Sunshine's
epic Filipino breakfasts—a glorious mound of garlic rice,
sunny-side up eggs with crispy edges, and fried bangus
with lots of vinegar. My mouth watered so much that

saliva leaked from the corner of my lips. I wiped it away with the back of my hand and groaned.

Get up, Coral.

I willed myself to stand, closing my eyes and picturing Dad's radiant smile, his dimple always there to greet me. My heart squeezed and throbbed in my chest. It hurt really bad, but I stood anyway. Outside, the waves were crashing on the rocks, splashing me with a fine mist of seawater. It was like one giant conspiracy, the sky full of promises, the sun tempting me with its mellow rays. The world was telling me that everything was going to be all right if I just opened my eyes and did something about it.

"*Anak, kaya mo iyan,*" I heard Mom's voice speaking to me. "*My child, you can do it.*" It was what she said to me every time I doubted my strength, my abilities. She was my biggest cheerleader. "Thanks, Mom," I whispered. Somehow it felt as if maybe she really was there, listening to me as I spoke to her. In a way, it hurt, trying to imagine what she would look like, what she would say in this scenario. But despite the pain, it was comforting, too. I needed her, I needed Dad, I needed Isa. I needed them, period, to be able to survive.

I gazed at the golden-orange sky, flecked with swirls of blue. From where the sun was positioned, I guessed it wasn't even six in the morning. "*Too early for anything civilized,*" Dad would have said with a haughty British accent. It was his favorite joke because he preferred the wilderness over the city. Well, he sure would have loved this place, because there was nothing civilized about it.

My bare feet stepped out onto the warm, rocky ledge. For a moment, I thought, *Maybe today will be better*. But then I saw something that made my heart drop. The *SOS* sign was gone, decimated by high tide.

Nothing, not even Mom and Dad, could have prepared me for that feeling of utter hopelessness spreading inside me like a vile, exotic virus. Surviving the wilderness was supposed to be fun—a game—something we could reminisce about while roasting marshmallows by the campfire. Before any of this happened, I thought I was invincible. God, I was so wrong. I stared out at the lonely expanse in front of me and repeated my new mantra. *This is not a game.*

Today was day two. Barely forty-eight hours had passed. Yet there was already this weight at the back of my mind, pulling me down, as if a brick had been tied to the ends of my long hair.

What if they never find me?

My temples throbbed, and sweat dribbled down my arms and legs. I was so dizzy I had to sit. My heart was beating too fast. My feet and hands were ice cold. Everything in my body was out of whack. Was I having a panic attack? *Breathe. Breathe. Breathe.* I took deep, even breaths, focusing on anything to make the spinning stop: Mom's neatly braided hair, silky and soft as I held it in my hands, braiding and unbraiding it. I inhaled a whiff of her coconut milk soap, the scent reminding me of the palitaw she sometimes made for merienda.

My hands gripped the ledge for support. Slowly, the spinning stopped. I opened my eyes, zeroing in on a dried-out sea urchin nearby. With my fingers, I traced the contours of its smooth, round shape.

I smiled. It reminded me of better days. Of another epic journey, when things hadn't gone so horribly wrong. At the time, I was ten years old. It was the year we had sailed the Mediterranean, cruising from one picturesque Greek island to another. Dad had anchored close to shore so we could relax and admire the view of Navagio beach. He sat with his legs dangling off the side of the boat with a cold glass of Prosecco in his hand. Mom was down in the galley arranging a platter of cheeses, olives, and crackers.

I watched Dad as he stared at the sky, lost in his daydreams. When I was sure he wouldn't notice, I leaned in and drew a heart on the frost of his glass. As soon as he took another sip, he saw it. His eyes went all sparkly. And then he grabbed me and kissed me on the cheek as I giggled.

"*So, honey, you up for something fun today?*" he asked with a grin.

Being my dad's most dependable companion, I nodded eagerly.

He pushed himself up and grabbed the bag with our snorkel gear before shouting down to Mom, "*Alma! We'll be back in a bit. Just going to show Coral something.*"

Mom never, ever bothered to question Dad's hare-brained ideas. I skipped behind him as we made our way to the dinghy. Even from the other side of the boat, we heard Mom shout at us, "*The two of you better be back soon; otherwise, this cold lunch won't be very cold!*"

We cruised along the shoreline, the deep sapphire water transforming to a vibrant shade of turquoise. When Dad spotted a white buoy, he turned off the motor and secured the dinghy. He handed me my flippers and mask, instructing me to put them on. Then he said, "*I'm going to show you how to harvest one of the most prized delicacies in the world!*"

Dad grabbed an empty bucket and rope, his jaw tensed, brow creasing while he worked. It was the very same expression I made whenever I was intensely focused—or at least that's what Mom always said to tease me. I studied him as he tied the bucket to the rope and then threw it into the water so half of it was submerged. Then he checked my snorkel gear and counted to three.

He held my hand as we jumped in. I immediately felt at home. The current of the water seemed to expect us. Dad motioned for me to follow, his strokes strong and deliberate as he led me to a shallow spot where we could see through to the bottom. We took deep breaths before diving down to the seafloor—a breathtaking shelf of rocks and corals, fish darting in between. Dad pointed out some sea urchins nestled on the rocks nearby. They looked dangerous, like spiky grenades waiting to explode. He pulled gloves onto his hands and grabbed the diving knife from his utility belt. His jaw tensed again as he nudged the urchins off the rock and into a mesh pouch around his neck. By the time he had collected half a dozen or so, we were running out of air, so we ascended, hitting the surface gasping.

When we finally arrived back on the boat, Mom was waiting for us, barefoot, with a tall glass of calamansi juice in her hands. She beamed when she saw us hauling the bucket full of sea urchins.

"*Is the cold lunch still cold?*" Dad asked jokingly.

"*Luckily for you, it is.*"

She placed a large ceramic platter on the table, handing Dad a sharp knife and some lemons. I watched him place a few of the urchins on the platter, and one by one, he cut them in half, revealing the bright orange flesh inside. He squeezed a bit of lemon juice on top and looked me straight in the eye. "*You see, Coral, anywhere you go in this world, you can find food in nature. Sure, supermarkets and restaurants are convenient, but before any of that stuff ever existed,* this *is how people survived.*"

He scooped up a piece of the glistening orange flesh and handed it to me.

"*You sure?*" I asked, examining the glob on my fork.

Dad nodded. "*I promise you won't regret it.*"

I sniffed it, curious how this creature that dwelled at the bottom of the sea would taste. When I placed it in my mouth, the flesh melted on my tongue, releasing a sea-flavored butter that was almost indescribable.

Dad scooped up another piece, and as it dangled on his fork, every inch of his face beamed, freckles hopping triumphantly. "*With ingenuity and an open mind, a person will never starve out there,*" he said, pointing at the open sea.

The memory faded, then disappeared. I gulped, trying to get the lump down my dry-as-chalk throat. The dried-out urchin sat by the palm of my hand. I studied the bumps on its surface, searching for answers before flinging it into the sea. Dad's words spun around and around me, sparking as if they were charged with magical ions. The hairs on my arms stood on end.

If I'm going to survive this, I have to try harder.

TWELVE
Isa

I DIDN'T WANT TO DRINK. I DIDN'T WANT TO EAT. ALL I wanted was to wallow in my sadness. After hours and hours of Mom knocking on my door, it was finally Dad who managed to coax me out in the morning.

"*Honey, open up . . . Your old man needs a hug,*" he'd said through the door.

At first, I thought it was just a ploy. But when I allowed what he was saying to sink in, it dawned on me that I wasn't the only one hurting. I wasn't the only one scared. Tita Alma, Uncle Jack, and Coral weren't just my family. They were Mom and Dad's family, too.

I went downstairs and found them in the kitchen. Mom was shredding some leftover adobo, presumably to make adobo flakes, and Dad was smashing and peeling garlic on a wooden chopping board. He looked up at me, his greenish-blue eyes soft and faded like a worn-out piece of sea glass. Without saying a word, he wiped his hands on a kitchen towel and spread his arms wide. I wandered into his embrace, leaning my cheek over his heart.

"I-I'm sorry, Dad . . . ," I whispered.

He wrapped both of his arms around me. "It's okay, honey. I know you're in shock. We all are."

For a long moment, all I wanted to do was soak up his warmth, breathe in his comforting scent—salt water, strong black coffee, and Irish Spring soap. Everything around me, the butter-yellow walls, the weathered white cabinets, the pale blue lacy curtains, the potted herbs on the windowsill, was sort of a blur. It wasn't until I lifted my cheek that I noticed the patch of wetness on Dad's gray T-shirt. Tears. It had been a long time since I last cried. Maybe even years. When I was younger, I would cry when I skinned my knees or fell off my bike or some bully at school would call me names like Shorty or Smurf or Oompa Loompa. It all seemed so silly now.

I gazed up at Dad. There were also tears in his eyes, snaking past the maze of freckles and the stubbly beard on his face. Dad may have been a big, strong fisherman dude, but he'd always been a softie. He would get emotional whenever Mom forced him to watch her cheesy Hallmark movies, or whenever he looked at old photo albums, or whenever there was a wedding or graduation or funeral.

Mom was the tougher one. Her cheer and resilience may as well have been made of steel or maybe titanium. I watched her get up from the kitchen table, grab a pan from the rack, and place it on the stove. She turned the burner on and reached for a bottle of cooking oil with trembling hands.

"Mom?" I said, taking a step toward her.

Her hand paused midair, and after a second, she tightened it into a fist and turned around to face me. "Whatever happens, we'll get through this. Together," she said with a shaky voice.

I sucked in my breath and held it. Because the woman standing in front of me didn't look at all like my mother. It was as if she'd shrunk, as if the color had been erased from her complexion, as if the cheer had been sucked out of her.

Slowly, I trudged over to her and took her hand in mine. It felt weird at first, as if I were trying to force two puzzle pieces together that didn't fit. But after a moment, our palms cupped together, our fingers curled into one another.

"Don't worry, Mom. They're going to find them. I know they will," I said so loud my words echoed.

THIRTEEN
Coral

I GRABBED THE SURVIVAL KIT KNIFE FROM INSIDE the cave and set out, traversing the rock face toward the beach. Somehow it felt as if I'd stepped back in time, way before I was even supposed to exist—a Neolithic girl—and I had no choice but to survive out in the wilderness.

At the beach, I collected more debris and began the painstaking task of redoing the *SOS* sign. This time I arranged the letters more inland, in the hopes that doing so would help avoid another high-tide obliteration. By the time I was done, I was covered in sweat. It even oozed from between my toes.

I inhaled and exhaled. My eyes scanned the beach and the sea. It was still really early. The mostly orange sky reflected on the water, making it look like a rippling sheet of lava. Even the sand on the beach was tinged orange, so it was a shade of peach instead of white. In a few hours the sand would be too hot to walk on, but for now, it was cool on my feet. It was a good time to walk around and search for . . . I gulped hard. The lump was in my throat again. Mom and Dad. What if they'd washed up on the island, too? I knew it was highly unlikely. I mean, what were the chances? But I'd never know unless I looked for them. I had to at least try.

So I walked up and down the beach, searching the shoreline, searching the sea, going behind smooth boulders in various shapes and sizes, and fallen trees studded with shells and hermit crabs. Keeping my eyes peeled for any sign of Mom and Dad. But there was nothing.

By the time I was done, my throat was completely dry. I was so thirsty I could have chugged an entire ocean's worth of water if it weren't so salty. It was obvious that my remaining water boxes wouldn't cut it. Dying from thirst—delirious, immobile, cramped, and feverish until every system in my body eventually collapsed—was not the way I imagined spending my last days on earth. I had to find an alternative. Fast.

A gust of wind whirled by. The coconut trees swayed as if they were whispering, *Hey, Coral. Here we are. Come and get us!* Suddenly, it was so clear to me. Coconuts. I slapped myself on the forehead and yelled at the coconut trees, "Now you tell me!" I leaped and did a ridiculous happy dance. "Whoo-hoo!"

I gawked at the abundance of green and yellow coconuts right smack in front of my face, on the trees and scattered all over the beach. Coconut water was like five dollars a carton back on Pebble Island, but here it was all over the place for free.

I sprinted, kicking up sand with every stride. I felt like a little kid again, lifting the coconuts as if they were Christmas gifts, shaking them one by one to guess what was inside. Though a few seemed kind of empty, the majority swished from the liquid trapped inside them. I made a pile of bright green ones and then sat with my legs crossed. *Now what?* I thought and thought, until my brain exploded like a pulsating star, swelling and shrinking as ideas burst and died. I held the knife up, wishing it would mutate into a giant machete.

I exhaled in frustration. It seemed my only option was brute force. *Okay, I'm going to have to break this sucker open.*

Nearby, a handful of sharp rocks sprouted from the shoreline. I plucked a coconut off the pile and went over to the closest rock, climbing it until I was about ten feet up—high enough that if I fell, I might actually crack my skull open. I raised the coconut above my head and grunted hard before throwing it. I held my breath. Waiting. Watching. Hoping. The coconut landed hard, thudding and bouncing off to one side. I jumped off, leaping from boulder to boulder until I reached it.

My hopes, my faith, whatever optimism I had left, shriveled up as I examined the barely bruised coconut shell. I tensed my jaw and pulled my shoulders back, climbing the rock to repeat the process. This time, I tossed the coconut even harder. The grunt escaping my mouth sounded more like a frustrated bear's. When it landed,

I heard a slight cracking sound. I pranced back down, confident it had worked. But when I got to the battered coconut, it had split just a bit. There wasn't a dribble of liquid in sight.

"Gahhh!" I yelled as loud as I could, feeling helpless and betrayed. Why did Dad always make it seem so easy? So effortless? If he were here, he probably would have had at least twenty coconuts opened with DIY straws and cocktail umbrellas made out of leaves.

My heart felt tight in my chest. It was childish to blame him. None of this was his fault. But I just couldn't help it. I closed my eyes to calm myself, picturing Dad, his jaw tensed, brows creased with focus.

Okay, Dad. I'm not going to give up.

I climbed two more times, but the stubborn coconut managed to survive every single attempt. Its shell was as hardheaded as mine. On the fifth try, I hurled the coconut with less force, exhaustion making my limbs feel like soggy breadsticks. I sucked in my breath and held it. Waiting. Watching. Hoping. As soon as it landed, there was a loud crack before it finally split in two.

I jumped off the rock, shrieking in victory. But soon I realized that my celebratory wails were premature. The precious coconut water had all spilled out, pooling on the sand for a quick moment before being completely absorbed.

I collapsed on my knees and wept, scooping up the coconut-soaked sand as if I could squeeze the liquid back out of it. But then my gaze wandered, landing on one of the coconut shell halves. It sat there on the sand like a giant cereal bowl. Inside was a glistening milky white color. My cheeks stung. Really, really stung. As if some invisible person had slapped me on the face. How could have I forgotten? The coconut meat was the best part!

Maybe there was a silver lining after all.

The slippery flesh of the coconut was intact—silky and shiny. I plucked it from the sand, rinsing it in the ocean before scraping off a ribbon of coconut meat and devouring it. *Yummm* . . .

Who knew that failure could taste so delicious, so sweet, so unbelievably good?

I stomped over to the pile of coconuts, more determined than ever. If one kind of brute force didn't work, maybe it was time to try another. I whipped the knife out, its edge almost nicking my finger. It was a good knife—razor-sharp, tough, and durable. Dad was never chintzy when it came to buying supplies.

With the coconut gripped with one hand, I hacked away on one side until it lay flat on the ground. Then I jabbed the knife in. Surprisingly, it went through easily. But as soon as I tried to carve a hole, the knife refused to budge. I pulled it out with a sigh.

What would Dad do? My mind searched and searched for something—memories, clues, tidbits of information. Then, suddenly, I remembered. Autumn, fallen leaves whirling in the breeze, while Dad, Isa, and I carved pumpkins out on the front porch. The pumpkin man's triangular eyes glared as if to tell me something.

I stuck the knife back in, stabbing the coconut repeatedly, each time a little farther down until a V shape appeared. Then I yanked the knife out and made one last cut. There was my triangle. I followed the lines with the tip of the knife, slicing, hacking, until it loosened. The nervous anticipation made my heart pound.

Pop! It was the most glorious sound in the universe. The triangle dropped into the coconut, leaving a crudely shaped hole behind. I leaped into the air, whooping, arms and legs swinging like a hyperactive clown. Eventually, all the shrieking took its toll.

I knelt on the sand, cupped the coconut with both hands, and tilted it to my chapped lips. The cool, refreshing water gushed into my mouth. I drank until it was all gone. My thirst finally quenched, I collapsed with the hollowed-out husk on my lap.

FOURTEEN
Isa

WE WERE ALL TOO SHOCKED AND SAD TO ENJOY Mom's famous adobo flakes with garlic-fried rice and tomato, onion, and salted-egg salad. It was one of my favorite breakfasts, but I found myself pushing the food from side to side while staring at the rim of my plate. Every once in a while, I'd look up and catch Mom eating tiny bird bites, mumbling small talk, her eyes sort of staring off into nothing. Dad, on the other hand, was scooping forkfuls of food as if he were a human trash compactor. When he was done with one plate, he served himself another. I was pretty sure he wasn't even tasting the food.

I guess we were all coping in our own ways—me not eating or talking, Mom pretending to eat and be fine, and Dad shoving his emotions down his throat. It was painful and awkward. I so wanted to escape, but for whatever reason, my butt stayed put.

Ten minutes passed—ten minutes that felt like ten hours.

And then a fork clattered loudly on a plate. I flinched and glanced over at Mom and Dad. Dad's face was blank, and then after a few seconds, it collapsed like one of Mom's experimental soufflés. His forehead creased, his eyes pooled with tears, his lip twitched, his jaw shook. I just stared, because I didn't know what else to do.

"Oh, honey." Mom reached out and squeezed his hand. "We'll get through this . . ." She was trying to comfort him. But I could tell she was also on the brink of tears.

I held my breath. One second, two seconds, three. And then, there they were, tears—big, fat tears pushing out of her tear ducts. She leaned over, and so did Dad, her head landing on the crook of his shoulder. They both cried and cried and cried while I just sat there and watched like a robot. My eyes stung; the back of my throat swelled. But I didn't want to cry. Not at that moment. Not with Mom and Dad falling apart right in front of me.

So I pushed my chair back, and without saying a word, I made my escape. I ran out of the kitchen and out of the house, not knowing exactly where I was going.

I hopped on my bike and pedaled as hard and fast as I could, leaving a trail of crunchy gravel behind. It was already hot, but thankfully, it was breezy. I rode past the neighboring houses, all of them with faded wooden clapboards, large porches facing the ocean and bedecked with colorful pots of herbs and flowers. Finally, I reached the main road going into town, except I didn't want to go into town. Because that meant crowds, and I didn't want to have to deal with too many eyes and too many questions. Instead, I went the opposite direction toward the other side of the island, where the bigger houses were, the mansions of residents whom we only saw but never really got to know all that well. They wouldn't care about me one bit. I was just some random kid.

I passed the pale butter-yellow house with multiple chimneys and a lawn that went on forever. I passed the white modern minimalist house with its giant windows and superlong lap pool. I passed the gingerbread-colored house with green shutters and a tennis court. House after house after house, I kept going until I couldn't go anymore. It was as if my breath had run out. I pulled over to the side, hyperventilating. It felt like I was having a coronary, my chest tight and uncomfortable.

"Hey there. How you doing this fine day?"

I knew who it was even before I looked up—Captain Charlie. He was the owner and sole employee of Captain Charlie's Clam Shack. The shack had been there way before any of the fancy houses had been built. It was the only reason weekenders ventured to that side of the island. His snack shack was basically fifteen feet wide with four picnic tables under a giant willow tree. As usual, he had on his navy blue captain's hat, white T-shirt, overalls, and a denim apron with a red lobster on it.

"Hey, Captain Charlie," I said, trying to be polite.

"You look like you could use an ice-cold lemonade," he said with a smile.

I glanced down at my bottle holder. It was empty. "Yeah. I forgot my water bottle."

"Sit," he said, gesturing at the nearest picnic table. He went inside the shack and came back with a mason jar filled with ice and lemonade. "Here." Captain Charlie smiled, handing it to me.

I leaned my bike against the tree, sat down, and chugged half the lemonade before taking a breath. "Thank you."

Captain Charlie chuckled. "You should know better than to leave your house in the middle of the summer without something to drink. You looked like you were darned near about to faint!"

"Yeah. I kind of left the house in a rush."

He sat across from me, his face suddenly serious. "I heard. I'm so sorry, Isa. I was going to stop by later to see if your folks needed anything . . ."

"Thanks." I said, fiddling with my fingers instead of looking him in the eye.

It was quiet for a moment. And then Captain Charlie pushed himself up off the bench with a grunt. "Well, I better get started with the lunch prep. It's going to be busy today. I can feel it," he said, marching off toward the shack. With every step he took, my insides became tighter. It felt as if I had a billion ants crawling all over my skin. For whatever reason, I was feeling panicked at the prospect of being alone at that picnic table.

"Wait!" I called after him.

He halted and turned around, his dark skin covered

with a light sheen of sweat. "You need something else, Isa?" he asked.

I did, but I didn't know quite what it was I needed. Somehow, though, my body did. My bones and muscles acted on their own until I was standing. Then, moving forward, one step, two steps, three steps, four. "I—I was wondering if I could, um, stay . . . ," I stammered.

I expected Captain Charlie to look confused. But not at all. He grinned a toothy white grin and waved me over. "Sure. As long as you don't mind helpin' out during the lunch rush. Now, I can't pay you or anything, but I can sure feed you a good lunch . . . What was it now?" He held his chin and looked up at the sky, thinking. "Fried clam strips, fries, and coleslaw with a wedge of lemon and a side of mayo and cocktail sauce, am I right?"

I nodded, feeling better all of a sudden. Because helping out at the Clam Shack was precisely what I needed. If my mind and hands and feet were busy, then I probably wouldn't think about everything that was happening and everything that could go wrong.

FIFTEEN
Coral

A WEEK HAD PASSED, AND THERE WAS NO SIGN THAT help was on the way. Not one boat or helicopter, not a single plane flying across the never-ending blue sky.

Every day, I gazed out at the horizon, hoping to spot something, anything, that was man-made. Every day, I searched the shoreline and surrounding waters for Mom and Dad. Every day, I made sure the SOS was still intact. But every day came and went, and still there was nothing.

I wanted to scream a whole bunch of curse words, but I knew Mom wouldn't approve. She would glare at me with raised eyebrows and say, "*Curse words are a lazy form of expression, Coral. You can do better . . .*"

If I didn't get rescued soon, I was going to run out of food and water. I shook my head. I didn't want to think about the inevitable. Even though I'd been rationing my food supplies, I was down to a few measly protein bars and energy gels. The last time I stripped down to rinse my clothes in the ocean, I gasped at the sight of my body. My legs were bony, my ribs shadowy under the harsh sunlight.

Back home, I never really gave my appearance much thought. Whenever I'd say I didn't get the fuss about makeup, or cute clothes, or how my hair looked, Isa would always give me this pained expression while saying something snarky like, "*Only pretty girls can get away with saying stuff like that.*"

Well, I didn't really care about being pretty or being skinny or being tall. For me, what really mattered was what my body could do. How fast it could run, how high it could climb, whether it could handle the physical challenges thrown its way.

I never expected to feel so devastated seeing my body change, even just a little bit. My muscles were shrinking, my long hair was dry and knotted and bleached by the sun and salt water, my skin was peeling and patched with sunburn. I looked like what the cat dragged in. Or actually, what the cat dragged in, ate, and puked up. If I was going to survive much longer, I had to find a real food source—forage, hunt, fish, whatever it took to prevent me from losing more weight.

So I marched to the tide pools, determined to find something to eat, no matter how disgusting. Today, I would eat something besides a packet of neon-colored energy gel. Armed with my knife and a hollowed-out coconut shell, I searched the shoreline. By then, it was low tide; the natural craters of the rocks had trapped a whole gang of sea creatures. At first, most of the animals I came across were smart enough to escape. Dodgy little fish slipped through my fingers; crabs scuttled away too fast. But then I stumbled on easier prey—sea snails and shellfish too slow and stubborn to move. I collected some of the fatter-looking ones, cringing as I plopped them into my coconut bowl.

On the beach, I found tender fronds of seaweed with grapelike clusters. *Hmmm* . . . Salad. I tossed a bunch into the bowl and then headed away from the shoreline, searching for the perfect clearing to build a fire. It had been way too long. Dad's lessons on picking just the right kinds of twigs and the perfect tufts of dry matter for building an old-fashioned campfire were just a hazy memory. So for the time being, I decided to forget about the harder method. *Sorry, Dad.*

It felt like a cop-out. But I was overwhelmed. Every aspect of survival was fraying my nerves. My patience was running out. Fast. Stressing about food, water, shelter, and being rescued plagued my mind constantly.

"Okay. Let's get this show on the road," I said out loud. Even if it was only me saying it to myself, I needed all the encouragement I could get.

I pulled out the precious waterproof matches from the survival kit and stared at the label. Forty matches. I breathed a little easier. Forty days didn't seem like such a long time, but at that moment, right then, they were forty days that I wouldn't have to worry about starting a fire, forty days that I could cook and keep warm at night as I gazed up at the constellations.

I arranged a pile of twigs, leaves, and small branches in a wide-open area. Once I had the makings of a good foundation, *good bones*, as Dad would call them, I knelt down on the sand. Then I struck a match, cupping it with my hand so the flame would hold. At first, it flickered, but eventually it steadied. I leaned in, held my breath, and placed it below the layer of leaves and twigs. I did it a couple more times around the pile, working fast as the match dwindled to a nub. Finally, the fire began to breathe. The crackle of flames was like a sudden burst of conversation.

"Well, hello there," I said.

Knowing the fire would keep me company for at least a couple of hours made me a bit giddy and relieved. I put the coconut bowl with the ingredients for my meal in front of me. And then I searched for a thin but sturdy-looking stick on the beach. It may as well have been rocket science. Cooking was always Mom and Tita Sunshine's department. Anytime they asked for my help, I'd skip outside and pretend I already had some adventure planned. I wished just once or twice, I'd allowed their culinary wisdom to infiltrate my mind, even if they weren't quite as exciting as Dad's wilderness lessons.

Too late for regrets, now.

I picked a snail from the bowl, eyeing it for a moment before hanging it from the stick. "I'm sorry, little guy," I whispered, holding it over the flames until the smell of cooked flesh wafted in the air. I dumped the roasted snail into an empty bowl and waited for it to cool before pulling the flesh out with my knife. The steaming-hot snail dangled in a not-so-appetizing way. *Here goes. One, two, three . . .* I closed my eyes and stuck it into my mouth before I could change my mind.

It wasn't quite as bad as I'd imagined, the texture like a wad of flavorless bubble gum that had been chewed for too long. I gulped it down and roasted the rest of my meal—the mussel-like shellfish the clear winner, with sweet, juicy flesh that reminded me of Mom's ginataang tahong—a Filipino stew made with mussels, tons of garlic and ginger, and coconut milk.

When I was done eating, I leaned back on a fallen coconut tree and tried my best to pretend I was full. I pushed my stomach out and slumped as if I'd just eaten a dinosaur-size steak, a baked potato loaded with bacon and sour cream, and heaps of creamed spinach. As if that wasn't enough, I imagined devouring a giant slab of dense, dark chocolate cake with layers of salted caramel inside. It almost worked. But then my stomach grumbled. I never imagined that this was what being hungry actually felt like. All the hunger I'd experienced before seemed weak in comparison.

The sun turned into a bright orange fireball, mellowing as it began to disappear. I sat by the fire and stared at the sky as it transformed into shades of blue, pink, violet, crimson, and yellow. In the past, watching the sun dip into the horizon would have been something I enjoyed, but at that moment, it only made me feel lonelier.

I yawned. The warmth from the fire, combined with the little bit of food in my stomach, made me sleepy. My eyelids sagged, and my vision got hazier and hazier. For a moment, I must have dozed off. But then an unexpected feeling startled me awake. I pushed myself up from the sand. The fire was almost dead, just a pile of glowing embers. Dry leaves and twigs crunched a distance away, as if someone or something was in the darkness behind me.

My heart was racing. Even though I was pretty sure I was alone, the noises spooked me. I snatched my knife. Chills prickled my skin as I turned around and around, scanning the shadows.

Again, the leaves crunched. "He-hello?" I cried out with a shaky voice.

Crunch. Crunch. Snap! It didn't sound like that cinnamon-colored bird from the other day. The sound was louder, like a twig breaking under a foot. So I ran down the beach as fast as I could until I reached my cave. All I could do was hide in a corner, heart still racing, breath too shallow, as I gripped the knife in front of me.

SIXTEEN
Isa

I STAYED AT THE CLAM SHACK UNTIL WAY AFTER dinner. At some point in the afternoon, Mom and Dad wouldn't stop calling my cell phone. So I let them talk to Captain Charlie, who reassured them in his oh-so-charming way that I wasn't dead in a ditch somewhere.

Besides serving customers their food, I'd also done my fair share of eating, managing to stuff two orders of fried clams and french fries, several pieces of corn bread and butter, and a slice of key lime pie into my stomach.

So after the dinner rush, all I wanted was to be alone. But my messy, stuffy, cluttered bedroom wouldn't cut it. What I needed was fresh air, the wind blowing on my face, somewhere that would comfort me.

The dunes. It was one of our favorite places. Coral and I would go to chill, to talk, to stare up at the night sky and count the stars. After all, we *were* the Star Sisters.

I left the Clam Shack on my bike, cruising at a leisurely pace until I reached our spot—where the sand was high enough to see over the wooden picket fence, where there was a nice, flat clearing in between two tufts of feathery grass.

At first, all I did was gaze out at the shimmering sea and watch the moon paint the waves with a silvery-white light. I went over to a patch of grass and sat with my legs straight out in front of me. The night sky was a dark, velvety blue with so many stars it looked as if sequins were embroidered on it. Except one star was the brightest— Sirius, the dog star. Even though I knew almost nothing about astronomy, it was one of the stars I recognized. Because over the years, Coral had drilled it into my brain. *"It's supereasy to remember, Isa! Repeat after me: Sirius the dog star equals the brightest star in the sky."*

And every single time, we would both chant out loud, *"Sirius the dog star equals the brightest star in the sky."*

Eventually, one of us would cough or mess up or blurt out some ridiculous joke. *"Coral! Wait! Hold on, I have a good one . . . ,"* I'd say, interrupting our chant.

Coral would lean her head to the side, rolling her eyes as if she knew what was coming. *"What now?"*

"Where should a dog never go shopping?"

"I dunno. Where?"

I snorted and then chuckled and said, *"A flea market!"*

"OMG. You're so corny, Isa," she would say after every single bad joke I came up with.

And then I would roll my eyes back and reply, *"Well, news flash, you're just as corny as I am!"*

There would be a moment of silence before we

inevitably cracked up and screamed in unison, *"The Corn Sisters! The Corn Sisters!"* until we collapsed, hyperventilating.

With my hand, I traced the spot where she used to sit, flattening the mound of sand to look as if someone had just sat there. For a second, I could see her so clearly, her long legs pulled up against her chest, her bare feet buried under the sand, her eyes as bright as the stars up above.

I sighed. Suddenly, the moon decided to hide behind a streaky black cloud. Everything became dimmer, almost completely dark, but not quite. Tiny dots of green light flickered. Fireflies. They seemed to appear out of nowhere, floating over me, around me, as if they were trying to get me to remember. How could I forget? The night we discovered our spot.

I was maybe seven or eight. Dad had burst into the kitchen with a huge grin on his face. *"Isa! Coral! Wait till you see what I got for you girls!"* He showed us a net with a handle. *"I'm going to teach you how to catch fireflies . . . Meet me out front in a few minutes!"* he had said, already halfway out the door.

Coral and I had stared at each other and cheered, *"Whoo-hoo!"*

When we got outside, Dad was standing next to a row of glass jars, holding a flashlight. *"You ready?"* he asked us.

"Yes! Yes!" we both shouted.

"Good," he said, handing Coral the net. *"Coral. Your*

job will be to catch the fireflies with this net and coax them into the jar that Isa will be holding."

We nodded and followed him down the dark road, with only the narrow beam of the flashlight to guide us. As soon as we arrived at the dunes, Dad turned the flashlight off. We stood still, waiting for any trace of the fireflies. We waited. And waited some more.

Then, suddenly, hundreds of glowing dots and flashes appeared.

Coral shrieked and kicked off her flip-flops to race after them, her hair slapping her back with each leap. Nothing could have stopped her. She chased every green spark, completely unaware that she was going farther and farther into the darkness. She disappeared, and so did the fireflies.

"*Dad!*" I called out to get his attention. When the beam of his flashlight landed on my chest, I said, "*Coral. She's gone . . .*"

"*C'mon, follow me. We'll find her,*" he replied with a calm voice.

My heart skipped a beat. Usually, I was brave. Things like that never scared me. But for whatever reason, I was panicked. Fear crawled through my insides.

"*Coral! Where are you?*" I shouted as loud as I could.

"*Coral! Coral!*" Dad said from somewhere ahead of me.

Then I heard something.

"*Hello? Isa? Uncle Henry?*" It was Coral.

"*We're here! We're here!*" I ran and spun around looking for her.

"*I'm here! I'm here!*" her voice echoed nearby.

Cutting through the shadows, like a hopeful ray of sunlight, Dad's flashlight landed right smack on Coral's forehead.

A split second passed, and then a floral-clad apparition whirled into my arms. Coral hugged me so tight I could barely speak.

"*I thought we'd lost you,*" I whispered in her ear.

"*I wasn't lost, silly. I just wanted to see if you could find me,*" she whispered back.

That spot was precisely the spot where I was seated. I gazed out at the horizon, the memory making my heart shrivel and twist and throb in my chest. It ached so bad, but I tried to ignore it. Instead, I stood and took a deep breath.

"Coral! I'm here! I'm here! I'm here!" I screamed into the wind.

SEVENTEEN
Coral

I OPENED MY EYES. THE KNIFE WAS STILL IN MY hand. It was resting on my neck, the razor-sharp blade close to my jugular. Just one accidental slice and I'd be dead. Like dead, dead.

Then my stomach grumbled. And I knew I couldn't ignore it anymore.

I stepped out of the cave to survey the horizon and nearly fell flat on my face. "Crap . . . Ffff . . ." A curse word almost slipped out of my mouth. "Sorry, Mom," I mumbled under my breath, and then turned around to see what had caused me to trip. Just outside my cave, nestled on the ledge, was a large black bird. *Corvus enca*? *Corvus unicolor*? I smiled because I could almost hear Isa calling me a "*bird nerd*." Well, maybe it was true, because Mom, Dad, and me were a family of birders.

Anyway, whatever kind of crow it was, it looked peaceful, as if it were just taking a short nap or something. But I knew it was dead. I crouched down in front of it and poked it with my finger. It was still warm. Not stiff or anything. *Huh. Weird.* It was dead. And it was fresh, really fresh. I could eat it. Right?

The crow's beady black eyes stared back at me. Just the thought of scavenging like a hyena and ripping meat off a carcass seemed wrong and gross and totally unnecessary. But the pain in my stomach. The constant hunger alternating with waves of dizziness. It was the worst kind of torture. I exhaled and stared at my knees. Bony. Not an ounce of fat in sight.

I surrender. I have no choice.

I took the bird to the beach and crouched down on the sand. Pluck. Pluck. Pluck. Black feathers floated in the air around me, swirling into the clear blue ocean before being consumed by the waves. At first, I had no clue what I was doing. But desperate times called for desperate measures. *Just do what you have to do, Coral. Figure it out along the way.*

After a while, the plucking started to feel sort of normal. Like pulling lint off a cozy, old sweater. Once I'd gotten most of the feathers off, I glared at the naked bird. Its ashy-colored skin was repulsive. *Beyond* repulsive.

But then something caught my eye. There were holes in its chest. I stretched the skin tight. Bite marks. I shuddered. A tingle traveled up my spine. The crunching sounds from the night before echoed in my head. I stared off into the jungle behind me. The morning sun cut through the bright green foliage, allowing beams of light to shine into the clearing. It was tranquil. Beautiful. Not at all scary like it was last night. But was there something out there I should be afraid of?

Try not to think about it, Coral. So that's what I did. I tried to erase the fear from my mind, concentrating on the task at hand. I walked away from the water, my battered feet caked with sand. The dead bird's feet in my grasp as it dangled.

When I reached my bonfire, I busied myself adding more kindling and stoking the coals before arranging pieces of wood on top. I struck another precious match and lit the fire again, tending to it until it was revived. It was time to cook. My mouth salivated at the thought of a perfectly roasted piece of meat.

I searched for a thin yet sturdy piece of bamboo. Then I stabbed the bird's flesh, jamming it into the carcass until it was all the way through. For a moment, I stood there, kind of proud of what I'd accomplished. An image of Mom flashed in my mind. It was Thanksgiving, and she was grasping a ginormous, pink turkey. In front of her was a bucket of salted water with herbs and spices floating on top. "*Coral, the secret to a perfectly juicy roast turkey is to brine the meat the night before,*" she explained.

I glanced at the ocean. There was salt water. Lots of it. So I took the bamboo-skewered bird and dipped it into the sea, washing the skin for several minutes until it kind of plumped up. Then I returned to the fire and roasted the meat over the coals, watching it carefully so it wouldn't burn. It smelled a bit gamy, like the quail or venison Uncle Henry sometimes brought home from his hunting trips. But I was too hungry to care. The smokiness of the fire and the salty tinge in the air, mixed with the aroma of cooking meat, were intoxicating. When the skin sizzled, I placed a large, waxy leaf on a rock and waited for the roast to cool.

The anticipation was killing me. I had to keep my mouth closed to prevent the drool from leaking out. Finally, when the meat was no longer steaming, I sat on a fallen coconut tree to devour my meal—roasted crow, seaweed salad, and a coconut water cocktail. It was far from elegant. In between bites, I licked my fingers one by one. My hands and face were smeared with juices. I was like a baby in a high chair making a huge mess with my first ever meal.

The bird was chewy and tough, but to me, it tasted like heaven. I gnawed away all the flesh, even attacking the tastier-looking innards, sucking and pulling at all the bones and pieces of cartilage until all that was left was a skeleton. For the first time since washing up on that island, my hunger was actually satisfied. And I could sit on the beach and look out at the peaceful ocean without my stomach complaining. *Whoosh. Whoosh.* The waves were rocking me to sleep. *Whoosh.* I dozed off. But the peace and quiet didn't last long.

Crunch. Crunch. Snap!

My eyes flew open. Sweat gushed down my face and body as if someone had dumped a bucket of water over me. From the corner of my eye, something brown and furry scurried into the jungle.

Holy crap. My body stiffened. I pushed myself up and scanned the perimeter. Where did it go? When my gaze landed on my waxy leaf plate, I realized the leftover carcass was gone, only bone fragments, cartilage, and smears of grease were left.

Could it be a wildcat or monkey? Had it seen humans before? Maybe it hadn't? It was probably just scared of me—a tall, gangly, two-legged creature with a mess of knotted hair. Yeah, that was it. It was more scared of me than I of it. Surely it was harmless. Right?

By then, the fire was dwindling. I looked out to the sea; the sky had turned gray all of a sudden. I knew from years of sailing with Mom and Dad that a sky that gray usually meant something ominous was up ahead. A storm. Within seconds, angry, dark clouds formed swirly patterns on the horizon. The sea went from a gentle sway to an angry swell, swallowing more and more of the shoreline with every crashing wave.

I grabbed my knife and made a panicked dash toward my cave, certain that within minutes a rainstorm would hit the island.

Run!

Just as I reached the base of the ridge, curtains of wind whacked me, and water began falling in sheets, as though someone had opened up the heavens and poured out a year's worth of rain all at once.

I climbed the now-slippery rock face as rainwater pummeled me from all directions. Finally, I lifted myself over the ledge and hurried into the safety of my cave. I crouched down on my bed and trembled. My head throbbed. Blood gushed through my veins too fast. The constant flow of fear made me unsteady, disoriented. To make matters worse, my cold, wet clothes clung to me. I shivered, feeling like a vibrating ice block. There was only one thing I could do—remove all my wet things and sit there on my poncho bed, naked. Who cared? Nobody else was around anyway.

Drip, drip, drip. I looked up. Rainwater was dribbling from a small crevice in the cave's ceiling. Great, a leak. That was all I needed. The rainwater landed on my forehead and trailed down my face onto my lips. I stuck my tongue out to wipe it away.

Wait. Hold on.

Rain was water. And I needed water to drink. To survive. *Oh my god!* I was such a fool. Not because I was hunched on the ground, naked and cold, but because fresh water was actually falling from the sky. Water I could drink! And I wasn't doing anything about it.

I didn't think it was possible to feel embarrassed, all alone, without anyone else to laugh at me. But there I was. My cheeks burned. I didn't know what to feel more stupid about—not realizing I should have been collecting drinking water or being flustered about it.

I yanked the rubber poncho off the ground and wrapped it around myself. When I neared the cave's entrance, the force of the wind pushed me back inside. I gathered all my strength and pushed, until I was outside in the thick of it. Then I climbed back down the slippery rock wall, cursing my absentmindedness the entire way down.

Eventually I made it to the pile of empty coconut shells on the beach. I lined up dozens of bowls hollow-face-up so they could catch the rain as it fell. When I was done, I faced the sea and let the storm whip my hair and poncho into the air. I held my arms out and stared at the sky, opening my mouth so that the water could quench my thirst.

I spent the rest of the day inside my cave while the storm continued to thrash the island. The last protein bar sat on my lap. It felt heavy. Really heavy. But my hunger wouldn't back down. It was like a particularly tenacious rat eating away at my insides, at my soul, breaking down any rationality I had left.

I ripped off the wrapper and took a big bite, the regret in my throat making it hard to swallow. So I nibbled on it in between sips of coconut water. As soon as dusk fell, my eyelids got droopy. The wind still howled outside. But I was too exhausted to care.

Finally, the last bite of protein bar lay on the palm of my hand. I took a deep breath and stuffed it into my mouth, savoring the last bite of chocolaty goodness.

Now it's real. I have no food left.

✳ ✳ ✳

At long last, morning came. Beams of sunlight streamed into the cave. The storm had passed.

I stood and positioned my body in the path of the light, allowing the warmth to wash over me. As soon as I stepped out, I felt the full force of the sun over me. The island was magnificent. The beach was smooth and white. The turquoise waters bubbled on the shoreline. The sky was the most intense blue.

I had this sudden desire to run into the sea and go for a morning swim. But before I could, something stopped me.

A black bird lay by my feet, almost on the same exact spot as the first bird. *What the heck?* Yet I wasn't scared. Instead, I was surprised. Even curious.

Because it seemed that somewhere out there, I'd made a friend.

EIGHTEEN
Isa

A WEEK PASSED, AND NOTHING. NOT A SINGLE word. Not one update from the authorities, from the coast guard, from the US Embassy. Dad spent every night with his ear glued to the telephone, calling everyone and their mothers for answers. But nobody seemed to know anything. They'd tell him things like:

"*We'll update you soon . . .*"

"*We will contact you when we know more . . .*"

"*We're doing our best, Mr. Rousseau . . .*"

It was all a bunch of excuses.

There were times I was tempted to yank the phone from his hand and give those supposed authorities a piece of my mind. But I was just a kid. Why would they even bother listening to lil' ole me? Dad was the adult. A kind and patient one. Maybe *too* kind and patient. And yet, they didn't bother listening to him, either.

So I just bit my tongue and kept my two cents all to myself, because my anger, my frustration, wouldn't do anyone any good. Especially Dad, who seemed sadder and more hopeless with every day that passed.

"Dad?"

I found him seated out on the porch after his nightly long-distance phone calls. He was facing the beach, slumped forward with his hands covering most of his face. When he heard my voice, he flinched and looked at me over his shoulder.

"Hey, hon. Wanna join me?" he said, patting the chair beside him.

Part of me wanted to retreat to my room. But the other part wanted to stay and keep him company. *Stay. Go. Stay. Stay it is.* I went over to the chair and plopped myself down next to him even though my feet were heavy and my legs were numb. For a second, we sort of stared off at the blue-black ocean, at the moon peeking behind the streaky clouds, at the stars just starting to twinkle over the horizon. But when the second passed, I glanced over at him and said, "Are you okay, Dad?"

His thick, hairy arm poked out of his sweatshirt sleeve as he reached out for my hand to squeeze it. "Oh, honey. You don't need to worry about me. I'm just tired and frustrated, that's all . . ."

That's all?

His only brother, his sister-in-law, and his niece were missing, yet he still insisted on downplaying the situation. Of course, I knew it was for my sake. His words were saying one thing, but his expression, his posture, was saying another thing altogether.

He pulled my hand toward his chest and embraced it as if it were a tiny kitten or something. "Honey, how are you holding up?"

"I'm fine . . . ," I said, staring at my lap.

No. I'm not.

"You sure?"

I nodded.

Dad leaned down, searching my eyes. "It's better if you don't bottle up your emotions, Isa. I'm here any time you want to talk. Okay?"

Again. I wanted to believe him, but everything about him looked broken. As soon as I met his gaze, it was like staring into an ice-covered pond slowly cracking. I wasn't about to pour my heart out and drain whatever ounce of strength he had left in him.

"They're going to find them, Dad. I know they will," I said.

He exhaled and opened his mouth to reply but couldn't. There was this sound, kind of like a gurgle and cough combined, that slipped out. And then all hell broke loose. His chest started shaking, his shoulders slumped, his forehead and cheeks and chin turned red and wrinkly and jiggly.

"*Ahhhhh . . . ,*" he wailed, covering his face with his hands.

I was stunned. I mean, I'd seen my dad cry lots of

times before. But this . . . was different. It was the kind of bawling that was soul-wrenching. Tears you could drown in, cries that could shatter glass, heaving that could move mountains.

I stood and backed away.

Mom appeared through the sliding doors. She took one look at Dad and rushed over to him, embracing his large frame with her teensy-tiny one. She comforted him. He comforted her. They comforted each other.

And me, I did nothing. I was useless. I may as well have been invisible. So I ran off before they could say anything, down the stairs, across the beach into the darkness, into the unknown, because I didn't know what else to do.

My bare feet sank into the cool, damp sand. The summer breeze transformed into a sudden gust, whirling around me as I made my way toward the shoreline. On the horizon several bolts of lightning shattered the blacker-than-black sky. It was almost as if the sky were broken. Except I didn't know how to put it back together again. Coral was the one who knew about astronomy. She knew where the constellations belonged. Not me. Her. If we could somehow switch places, she would know what to do, how to save me. She wouldn't waste time doing nothing. Like me.

Pebbles and shells dug into my soles. And then the seawater touched my toes. I went deeper. It was cold. With every second that passed, my feet, my calves got more and more numb. I just stood there waiting and hoping for the numbness to spread, to take over my entire being. Because then maybe all the pain would go away.

The wind, though, had other ideas. *Thwack!* It slapped my face until my cheeks stung. It pulled my hair out of its bun. It whipped my T-shirt up my torso as if to expose me.

You can't run away from the pain, Isa.

"Fine! I won't!" I screamed.

So I faced the sea and the sky and the wind, and then I lifted my arms up and allowed the storm of emotions to overcome me.

NINETEEN
Coral

FOR WEEKS, I FOUND GIFTS AT THE ENTRANCE OF my cave. There were all kinds of birds; a few rodent-like creatures, perhaps shrews or water rats or cloud rats; a variety of lizards; and even a huge snake, all freshly killed and ready for butchering.

I was thankful. More than thankful, really. I mean, I owed my life to this new friend of mine. If they hadn't shown up when they did, I would have probably starved to death already. That intense gratitude made me even more determined to meet my benefactor face-to-face. Somehow I had to pay them back for their kindness.

So, every second, every minute, every hour of the day, I was on high alert. When a shadow flashed, my pulse quickened. The tiniest of noises made me whip my head around. But not once did I catch a glimpse of this furry brown phantom. At least, not yet.

I was pretty sure my new BFF was out there, somewhere on this godforsaken island.

I really want to meet you, friend . . .

In the meantime, I left offerings, usually the carcass of whatever it was I cooked that day. The exchange made it feel like we were somehow connected. Like we were slowly getting to know each other.

By my calculations, about two months had passed since I washed up on the island. Every day, I checked the *SOS* sign, realigning the debris to make sure it was still legible. Every day, I searched the beach for traces of Mom and Dad. But with every day that passed, my hope was running out.

Maybe no one was even looking for me anymore.

Maybe Mom and Dad were dead.

Maybe . . .

No. I shook my head.

I have to stay hopeful.

Even though I tried to make do with my thoughts and memories to keep me from going crazy, it started to feel like I was losing touch with myself, forgetting the sound of my own voice, forgetting what it was like to care about anything besides staying alive.

Having another being to interact with, to sit next to while watching the sun go down, would make a world of difference. I needed it. I wanted it so badly. I'd always had my family, most especially Isa—my cousin, my sister, my best friend. Being all by my lonesome, like, really, truly alone, was something I didn't think I'd ever have to deal with. Yet here I was, dealing with it as best as I could.

It became clear to me that people didn't just need food

and water and oxygen to survive. People needed love and companionship. People needed laughter.

To keep myself relatively sane, I resorted to pretend games. I closed my eyes and imagined someone was there. *"Dad? Where are you?"* Sometimes it worked, and he answered back, *"Right here next to you, Coral."*

But there were also bad days. My words would float out of my mouth, twirling in the air to find their intended audience. But nobody was there. Crickets. My words fell flat.

On those days, I would breathe deep and try to remember their scents.

Dad's hugs = a whiff of salt air and soap.

Mom's hands = herbs and coconut oil.

Isa's shoulder = a strange combination of slept-on bedsheets sprinkled with cinnamon.

Sometimes it almost felt as if I could reach out and touch them, as if they really were there. Even for just a split second. Then, *poof!* They would disappear, and I'd be all alone again.

Today was just another one of those bad days. I peeked outside my cave to see what was on the menu. *Hmmm . . .* It was a rodent the size of a small cat, maybe a giant tree rat or something like it. "I'm sorry," I said out loud, as if the dead creature could hear me. Why was I even talking to it? It was dead. *Obviously.* Even though I felt kind of bad for it, the reality was that seeing it there made me happy. If I rationed the meat, I might have enough food for breakfast, lunch, and dinner. I reached for the box of matches, each day its contents getting lighter and lighter. But I couldn't bring myself to count them.

Maybe tomorrow, or the next day, or the next day after that.

When I finally did open the box, my stomach dropped. Only three lonely matches remained inside. Technically, I should have already run out since I was nearing the fifty-day mark. I'd been good about keeping the fire alive when I could, though. So I was able to conserve them. But there wasn't any beating around the bush now. After this next meal, I had to suck it up and learn to make fire the old-fashioned way.

When I got to the beach, matches, knife, and rodent in tow, the first thing I did was light the fire, and then stoke it until the flames were strong. Once that was out of the way, I proceeded with the disgusting task of skinning my meal. *Ugh*. What I would have given for a bowl of Cheerios or some Eggos or even a Pop-Tart.

"*Coral, Pop-Tarts aren't real food, you know,*" Mom would say every time she caught me eating one.

I'd always grin and then take a big bite before saying, "*They taste real to me, Mom . . . Real good!*"

Mom would roll her eyes, and I would giggle, spraying Pop-Tart crumbs everywhere. The memory made me smile, made me happy for a moment. But it also made me sad. *Real* sad. The back of my throat ached. And my heart was tight in my chest. I swallowed, trying to imagine I'd just chomped down on a brown sugar cinnamon Pop-Tart. The taste was there for a second. And then it was gone. Just like the memory.

Get on with it, Coral.

I walked down to the shoreline, kneeling in the shallows so that every time a wave rolled in, the water kissed my knees. If only I was just going there for a leisurely swim. But no, I had an animal to skin; otherwise, there would be nothing to eat. And I couldn't afford to get weak or lose any more weight. So I laid the rodent on the wet sand and cut along its skin while scraping off as little meat as possible. I gagged, nearly puking from the bloody smell. It was gross. Like, supergross. The dirty, rotten, coppery smell wafted into my nose and stayed there. I tried to breathe through my mouth instead. But it didn't work. It *never* worked. The stench of bile and innards lingered. I gagged again and caught a whiff. *No. Don't do it* . . . I leaned to the side and vomited strings of clear greenish saliva.

It was all so humiliating. So degrading. The entire process made me feel like a failure and a fraud. My cheeks burned hot at the thought of Dad's seeing me like this. The fact was, I had to eat to survive, and I couldn't eat unless I cleaned this. I had to suck it up and do what I had to do.

I gripped the rodent's skin and peeled it from its body like a wet glove. I flung it into the sea as far as I could. *See you later, alligator.* Then I rinsed the carcass with salt water before carrying it back to the fire for roasting.

When the meat was golden brown and sizzling, I placed it on a leaf platter.

On the menu: Stringy bits of cooked rodent with a side of seaweed and a lukewarm cup of coconut water. I ate, pulling the meat off the bones until half of it was gone. The rest was for later. It wasn't a brown sugar cinnamon Pop-Tart, but it was something. And something was better than nothing.

Breakfast: done.

Time for a bath. I took off my shorts, underwear, and T-shirt, which by then looked as if moths had munched on them. I jumped into the cool water and scrubbed all over. *Scrub-a-dub-dub!* Sometimes I pretended to be in my bathtub at home. But the fantasy would fizzle away as soon as I felt my dried, damaged hair, which before had always been silky and wavy. The only thing I could do was run my fingers through the tangles, losing clumps of it. By the end of my bath, my sunburned skin and scalp hurt like hell. I was covered in pink and tanned layers of flaky, peeling skin.

But at least I was clean. Sort of. I put my clothes back on and went over to my favorite coconut tree—one that grew at an angle so I could comfortably lean on it and daydream, which is pretty much all I did in between chores. I would daydream about being rescued. I would daydream about Mom and Dad being alive. I would daydream about all the food I missed. I would daydream about gossiping and laughing with Isa. By the time I was done daydreaming, it would be afternoon and I'd be thirsty and hungry all over again. Time for another meal.

In between bites of leftover meat, I sipped on some more coconut water. When I placed the coconut back down on the sand, I noticed it had what resembled eyes, a nose, and a crooked smile. "This isn't so bad . . . Right?" I said, staring at it. And for a split second, it looked as if it were laughing at me. Of course it was laughing at me. Because what I'd said was ridiculous. The situation was bad. Of course it was.

But for the sake of my sanity, I had to try to be positive—it could have been worse. Way worse. I mean, as far as deserted islands went, this one wasn't the absolute worst. I had somewhere to sleep. There was shelter from bad weather. There was some food and coconut water.

Still, all I felt was emptiness. No joy, nothing to make my existence bearable. How many postcard-worthy sunsets could someone enjoy before they became inconsequential? How many days could someone swim in crystal clear waters before the novelty wore off?

Early on, I tried to muster up the courage to explore the island, but the fear of what lay beyond my semicozy existence kept me grounded. The adventurous spirit that used to consume me seemed to have died, replaced with an anxiety I couldn't comprehend. I found myself gazing at the jungle and the foreboding cliffs behind it, my muscles twitching as if they were nagging me.

"It's time to explore. Go on and see what's out there."

That's what Dad would have told me. There must have been something beyond the periphery, something worth risking my security for. It was a battle I fought every single day, but so far, fear had won every single time.

The person sitting on the sand, relaxing on the coconut tree, felt like someone else. I clasped my hands to the side of my head. *Coral, where are you?* I tried my hardest to remember her—the old Coral. The Coral from before any of this had happened. The Coral who dared to do anything at least once.

But I couldn't find her.

TWENTY
Isa

MONTHS PASSED.

How was I supposed to just pretend everything was all good?

"*Anak, I think the best we can do right now is to stay hopeful, and to go on with our normal day-to-day lives . . .*" I knew Mom meant well, but her thoughtless comments rubbed me the wrong way.

There was nothing normal about this situation. The only thing worse than pretending everything was normal was having Mom lecture me about it daily. So I had to suck it up and get with the program—the summer program, which was basically a job at Sunshine Deli and Bakery.

I crawled out of bed and took a long, hot shower, doing my best to look like a normal person, whatever that was.

Normal-person T-shirt. *Check!*

Normal-person ripped jeans. *Check!*

Normal-person black-and-white Converse sneakers. *Check!*

Normal-person messy bun. *Check!*

I arrived five minutes early. The only people at the bakery were Mom and Emmet, the resident baker. They were busy with their morning duties, so I went ahead and started mine without a peep, because frankly, I wasn't in the mood for small talk. I wiped down the espresso machines and stainless steel counters. I cleaned the floor, sweeping carefully under the tables and the chairs and in between the floorboards. I refilled the take-out cups and stirrers and sugar packets. I sprayed some glass cleaner on the bakery and deli displays, making sure I didn't miss any spots, because god forbid I leave a streak or two. Mom had this superannoying habit of not saying anything whenever she disapproved, instead standing there with her lips pursed judgmentally.

Whatever.

Finally, I finished setting up. All that was left to do was slouch on the counter and wait for our early-bird customers. I passed the time watching the marina action through the large bay windows. It was almost like TV. There were the wealthy yacht owners dressed in white, schmoozing and laughing, and the marina workers in their navy blue uniforms, dashing from one dock to another. The boats bobbed up and down as if they were showing off their newly cleaned hulls.

Cring, cring. The bell over the door rang. *Here come the customers . . .* I sprung off the counter and plastered a service-with-a-smile look on my face. A woman with wavy black hair streaked with electric-blue highlights walked in. From the neck up, she looked like a superhero from a Marvel movie, but from the shoulders down, she looked more like a housepainter in her oversize overalls and boots.

"Good morning. Can I help you with some coffee or something?" I asked.

She approached the counter with smiling eyes and smiling mauve-colored lips. "Mmm . . . coffee does smell good. But first, I need to talk to the owner, Sunshine?"

At the sound of her name, Mom emerged from the back with a squeal. "Ayyy! Ate Jo! You're here. Welcome, welcome!" she said, giving the rando woman a hug.

"Ate Sunshine, it's been too long!" the superhero-painter woman replied.

I frowned and ogled them. Who the heck was this lady?

Finally, Mom's gaze found mine. "Anak, this is my cousin Josefina from New Jersey."

I furrowed my brows. "Cousin?"

"Yes, my father and Jo's father were second cousins. You know, Isa, we have family all over the country. Many that you haven't even met yet," explained Mom.

Huh. "Oh. Um. Hi . . . ," I stammered.

There was this awkward moment of silence. I shuffled my feet and stood there like a big dork. Jo leaned toward me as if to kiss my cheek. "Isa . . . I'm so glad to finally meet you in person! I've seen so many of your photos over the years on Facebook."

I stepped back. My cheeks might as well have been Flamin' Hot Cheetos, because not only did I hate seeing myself in photos, but I hated the idea of complete strangers looking at them.

Jo backed off, pretending not to notice my snubbing her. "Anyway, we're so excited to help out with the store and whatever else," she said, looking at Mom.

"We?" I meant to say it in my head, but it ended up coming out of my mouth.

Mom glared daggers at me, but thankfully, she didn't attempt to lecture me in front of Jo. Again, Jo ignored my bad manners. Instead, she stepped aside, revealing a kid lurking behind her.

"This is mi única hija, Ada," she said.

The girl rolled her eyes. "Ugh. Mom!"

"Ugh. Mom. What? Say hello to your cousin Isa and your Tita Sunshine," scolded Jo.

The girl stared at me, and I stared back.

She must have been around my age. Maybe a bit older. She was short and skinny and dressed like one of those kids who liked to cosplay their favorite anime characters. Her jet-black hair was in pigtails, and she had on this outfit that was like a sailor-themed cheerleading uniform with white tights and red knee-high boots. Basically, she stood out like a sore thumb. Well, maybe not a sore thumb. More like someone wearing a Halloween costume, except it wasn't Halloween.

"Hey," I said with a stiff wave.

"Hey," she said back.

Cue the awkward silence.

Mom cleared her throat. "Come, why don't I show you the apartment upstairs where you'll be staying," she said, gesturing for them to follow her. "It's a bit dusty and sparse, but I'm sure you'll make yourself at home in no time."

I watched them exit the front door and head over to the stairway at the side of the building. Once they were gone, like, gone, gone, I scowled.

Help out with the store? Why does Mom need more help if I'm *here? Who the hell are these people?* I was suddenly annoyed. Maybe a bit angry, too. Because this was not the right time.

I wasn't interested in meeting my long-lost family members when my family, my *real* family, was lost at sea. That's all I cared about. Not some rando cousin and her rando kid showing up out of the blue.

I didn't need another cousin.

I didn't need another friend.

I needed Coral and Tita Alma and Uncle Jack back.

TWENTY-ONE
Coral

IT WAS TIME TO PLAY WITH FIRE.

Most parents would warn their kids about the dangers of anything arson-related. But not my dad. When I was little, he taught me how to build a campfire, the safest way to extinguish it, and even how to make one from materials out in nature. At the time, I didn't really think it was that important. Sometimes his lectures would go in one ear and out the other. But now I hoped that deep down in my brain, I'd absorbed enough information to do it for real.

Okay, Dad . . . I'm ready to give it a shot.

I stood tall with my shoulders pulled back. If I was going to get this done, I would need to look confident, as if I knew exactly what I was doing. *Right?* But for some reason, I was stuck in place, my feet partially buried in the sand. Maybe I just needed a moment. I stared at my bonfire site, at my makeshift kitchen with its coconut bowls, stick utensils, and rocks in various shapes and sizes for pounding and scraping. And when I was done staring at all those things, my eyes scanned the beach, which was almost blindingly white. I glanced at the *SOS*, slowly tracing the letters with my eyes one by one. The waves were practically nonexistent that day, the turquoise water so calm it was like staring at a beautiful, clear sheet of blue glass.

Obviously, I was killing time. Procrastinating.

But I had to get my butt in gear. There was work to do. I began by sorting pieces of wood, forming neat piles of thick branches, thinner ones, twigs, and dry fibers from coconut husks. From the first pile, I plucked a straight stick, trimming it with my knife until it was as smooth as possible. Then I took a short but chunky piece of wood and began to carve a semicircular groove on the edge, just as Dad would have done—he called this the *stabilizing board*. That step alone took me hours and hours. I kept at it, chipping and scraping until the groove was about the diameter of a penny.

By the time I was satisfied, I was covered in sweat and wood shavings. My arms and shoulders were so sore that every time I moved it felt as if they were going to fall off. *Ouch. Argh. Gah.* All I wanted was to collapse on the sand and do nothing. But I couldn't waste any more time. I had to make it work.

The breeze stopped as if it knew that whatever I was up to was of the utmost importance. I rubbed the end of the straight stick against the groove, using my palms to rotate it in place. Back and forth, back and forth. No matter how hard I tried, though, I couldn't seem to make the fire come alive. I spent hours waiting for the delicate wisps of smoke to appear. Even when I added the fibrous strands of coconut husk to the mix, nothing happened.

Zilch. Zero. Big fail. Crap.

I kept at it all afternoon until I was convinced that my arms actually had fallen off. I stared down at the sand, searching for my bloody appendages. *God, I'm losing it . . .*

When the sun started to set, I finally gave up. I felt like the biggest loser in the universe. What was the point of being a nerd if I couldn't even hack something that Dad had taught me like a million times before? What was wrong with me?

I screamed at the wind, at the sky, at the darkness. My disappointment turned to anger. Unlike the fire, my mind was roaring, burning, blazing.

Only two matches left! Ugh. Think positive thoughts, think positive thoughts . . .

I visualized brown, gooey marshmallows. But in reality, all I had were a few morsels of rodent meat and a handful of mollusks to go with my seaweed. So I ate, prolonging the barely there meal, hoping that the more I chewed, the fuller I'd feel. But it didn't work. By then, the beach was pitch-black except for the glow of the moon, which was even brighter than usual from the ring of light around it. A lunar halo. Dad had once explained to me that the halo was caused by a refraction, reflection, dispersion of light through particles of ice that were stuck in clouds. Sort of like a rainbow appearing through sunlight and rain. According to weather folklore, a lunar halo was a sign of an impending storm. But from what I could see, there were no traces of rain or dark clouds or lightning. I mean, the sea did seem awfully calm. It was probably just one of those superstitions that ancient mariners believed in. Instead of worrying about it, I lay on the sand and stargazed. As if somehow the twinkling lights could fill the gaping hole in my stomach.

Almost immediately, I spotted Scorpius, one of the brightest constellations in the Southern Hemisphere. Its curved tail looked as if it were about to strike. The Greek astronomer Ptolemy had named it after the scorpion that Artemis sent to kill Orion, the hunter.

Yup, still a nerd. I grinned. Because, somehow, looking at the stars made me feel like my old self again. The Coral who could do everything and accomplish anything.

I'm going to build that fire.

I'm going to survive.

I'm going to get off this island.

There. I said it. I pushed myself off the sand because I had this sudden urge to do something. *Hmmm* . . . The creature. My new friend. Somewhere out there it was curled up sleeping. Or maybe it was busy hunting for tomorrow's meal. *Our* meal. We were connected somehow, and our fates had collided for a reason. And I was determined to find out why.

For a while, I knelt on the sand and thought about my options. I needed a plan. But as I thought and thought and thought some more, the only one that seemed fool-proof was hiding and waiting for it to appear at the entrance of my cave. Then we'd finally meet. Face-to-face.

I strolled back to my cave, maneuvering up the incline with ease. My hands and feet had memorized the cracks and grooves. Darkness didn't faze me anymore. But when I got to the ledge, my visibility got hazier. The moonlight waned as a cloud passed over it. It wasn't bright enough to scope out a proper hiding place. I scanned my surroundings, but it was no good.

I needed more light. I retrieved the squeeze flashlight from the survival kit, cranking it several times. Luckily, it seemed to be working okay. I shined the beam of light all over, doing a grid search for places that might camouflage me. About seven feet up to one side was an oval-shaped ledge that seemed large enough. The only problem was that the wall directly below it looked kind of steep. But I was sure that sheer determination would get me up there. The back of my neck tingled with anticipation. *This is going to work. Of course it is . . .*

I went back inside and hydrated because I would need every ounce of strength I could muster. Then I went ahead and placed my daily offerings in a coconut bowl by the entrance—a rodent carcass and a few cooked mollusks. That would be the bait. When I was done setting it up, I tucked the flashlight into the waistband of my shorts and stared at the wall. My biggest obstacle yet.

I tucked my foot into a groove and grabbed a piece of rock jutting out above me. My arms were still super-sore, heavy like concrete blocks hanging from my shoulders. But I ignored the pain. My foot slipped into the next groove. For a second, I held the position, steadying myself while I caught my breath. Again, I reached for another rock, stretching because it was almost out of reach. I inhaled and stretched and stretched, pushing my arm and shoulder out so far I could almost hear the socket pop. *Ouch! Almost there.* One final hurdle before I reached the ledge. My limbs were trembling. I keep on going, though. With all my strength, I pushed and pulled and grabbed on to anything that would hold my weight.

My waist was finally level with the ledge—high enough for me to kick my leg up and roll over. I was flat on my back, hyperventilating as if I'd just finished a bunch of sprints. It seemed to take forever, but eventually my leg and arm spasms went away. The sensation of burning, aching muscles returned. I flipped onto my stomach and leaned on my elbows so I could spy on the cave entrance.

There it was. The coconut bowl. From my vantage point, everything was crystal clear. The ledge was the perfect lookout.

I turned off the flashlight and waited. The twinkling stars kept me company. So did Isa. Well, just the memories of her. I imaged her on the porch with her ratty sneakers perched on the table, wondering if I was still alive, wondering if somewhere out there I was staring up at the same night sky as she was. She hadn't given up on me. I could feel it deep inside, in my gut, in my bones, from the top of my head to the tips of my fingers and toes.

Sigh. How long is this going to take?

To pass the time, I searched the sky for more constellations—Pegasus, the flying horse; Delphinus, the dolphin; Cygnus, the swan, one after the other like familiar faces among a crowd. The hours went by, and even though I tried my hardest not to fall asleep, I couldn't help but nod off. My head jerked every time I snapped awake.

The sky was still black, but in the distant horizon the color began mutating into shades of gray. I flipped over and peered down again, hoping that my friend would show up soon.

Scrape. Scratch. Thump.

Suddenly, noises were coming from the shadows. At first, I saw nothing. But after one second, two seconds, three seconds, four—a slight movement. I flattened my body even more, keeping only the top half of my head out. Inching forward, I craned my neck, eager for a glimpse of the creature. *Where are you?* It seemed like it was taking its sweet time. Maybe it could see me or smell me or hear me. Maybe I'd already spooked it or something.

Then I saw it. A silhouette darting up the incline, hiding in the shadows. *Oh my god. There it is.* My palms were sweaty. My thighs were numb from pressing them down so flat. I shifted the flashlight so that I gripped it with my right hand, ready to point it the moment the creature was front and center.

Slowly, really slowly, the silhouette crept in, inching across the rock floor. I counted silently, *one . . . two . . . three . . . four . . . five . . . six . . .* I whipped out the flashlight, shining it over the scene.

The creature froze. Its scared eyes glowed green.

For a moment, all we did was stare at each other. Nothing registered. But after a minute or so, it finally clicked. What I was seeing, what was right in front of me, wasn't some exotic jungle creature. It was a dog. Just an ordinary-looking mutt—medium-size and lean. The dog had the reddish-brown fur and upright ears of a deer. Even its startled, wide-eyed look reminded me of a Disney character, Bambi.

All of a sudden, the flashlight conked out.

It was dark again. I cursed at myself and rapidly cranked the flashlight to get the power back on. But when the beam of light returned, it was too late. The dog was gone. The contents of the bowl were gobbled up, and next to it was the corpse of a large black bird.

TWENTY-TWO
Isa

I IGNORED MOM THE REST OF THE DAY. EVERY TIME she'd say something to me, I'd nod or shake my head and mumble an "uh-huh" just to get her to go away. But inside, I was still seething. In fact, the more I thought about Jo and Ada and Mom inviting them to Pebble Island like some cloned replacement family, the angrier I got. And not saying anything just made it worse. So much so that, by the time Mom got home for dinner, I was ready to explode—like, nuclear-level explode.

I stomped downstairs and found her in the kitchen, unpacking a bag of groceries. "So that's it? A few months go by and you replace them just like that?" I snapped.

Mom placed a carton of eggs down on the table, gently, as if she were worried that my rage would break them. Then she looked at me with her head tilted to the side. "Isabel, calm down."

"Calm down? Really? Is that all you can say, Mom? Calm down?"

She straightened her head, her gaze becoming sharper.

"You know I can't talk to you when you're like this . . . So when you calm down, then we can have a discussion. All right?"

Discussion-schmiscussion. I fast-walked to the chair across from her and plopped myself onto it with a huff. "Okay. I'm calm."

"Okay." She sat with a stiff back and tense shoulders. "Anak, I'm not replacing anyone."

I crossed my arms. "Well, it sure feels like it."

"Do you remember when Tita Marilen came out from Queens to help with the bakery when we first opened up?" she asked.

I nodded.

"Well, this isn't all that different. Except that Jo really does need a job. Her husband died last year, and she's been having a hard time making ends meet. We always need extra hands during the summer season. So I thought it would be a good way for us to help each other . . . You know, she needs work, and we need more staff." Mom reached out and squeezed my hand. "That's what families do for one another, anak. We lift each other up in times of need."

I jerked my hand back. "What about Coral, Uncle Jack, Tita Alma? They need our help, too!"

Mom sighed. "Just because we're helping one person doesn't mean we're forgetting about everyone else. But we do have to be realistic, anak. We have to start accepting the possibility that they might actually be gone."

"NO!" I pushed my chair back and stood.

"Isabel."

"NO!"

"I'm sorry, Isa. I know it's hard . . ."

I backed out of the kitchen, shaking my head. "NO! NO! NO!"

"Anak. Please . . ." Mom's face crumpled with worry.

But I didn't care. I kept on backing out, my cheeks, neck, and hands tingling hot. "They're not gone! They're not!" I screamed one more time before sprinting back up the stairs and slamming my door shut.

✳ ✳ ✳

Knock. Knock. Knock.

"Honey, Tita Jo and Ada are here for dinner. Can you come down and join us?" said Dad through my bedroom door.

Of course Mom sent Dad to do her dirty work. But whatever. I wasn't falling for it even though I had a much tougher time being mad at him, because Dad was Dad. He was a softie, kind of like one of those life-size teddy bears.

"Leave me alone," I replied.

"Honey . . ."

"Dad. Please . . ."

I heard him inhale and exhale. "Fine. But if you change your mind, if you get hungry, just come on down. Okay?"

"Okay," I mumbled back.

He went away, his footsteps making the floor vibrate as he lumbered off. I could hear chatter and laughter downstairs. It sounded like a dinner party at someone's happy, carefree home. Not at my house, where tragedy had decided to move in and stay a while.

How the heck could Mom and Dad act like nothing was the matter? Like there was actually something to be cheery about? I mean, I just couldn't deal.

And to make matters worse, I actually was pretty hungry. The smell of food wafted through the space under the door, and through my window, which was open to let the summer breeze in. I sniffed the air. *Mmm* . . . Mom's special lumpiang togue, some sort of grilled fish, pinakbet, and maybe some fried pork belly? The drool was pooling in my mouth. I gulped it down and smashed a pillow over my head.

As the minutes passed, I heard the clinking of glasses and the clattering of silverware and plates. Laughter, *ha ha ha.*

What could possibly be so funny?

Oh, our brother and sister and niece are lost at sea.

They might even be dead!

Ha ha ha ha!

Yeah. Real funny.

An hour or so went by, and there was another knock on my door.

"Go away!" I yelled.

There was a long pause. And then a voice, sort of soft and squeaky like a little mouse, spoke up. "Ummm. We brought some buko pie. My mom, she, uh . . . asked me to bring you a piece."

Great. It was that girl, Ada. What kind of name was that anyway? It sounded like laundry detergent.

Knock, knock, knock.

"Hello?" This time her voice was a bit louder.

"I'm not hungry," I grumbled through my pillow.

"Oh." Her shoes shuffled from side to side as if she was trying to decide what to do. "Okay . . . uh. I'll just leave it here, then."

There was a sound of a plate thudding on the floor, a fork or a spoon clinking on ceramic. And then, just like Dad, her footsteps vibrated down the hallway.

At least she got the message. I turned over onto my stomach, hoping that the weight of me would shut up the grumbling and groaning so I could go to sleep and erase everything from my mind. But it only made my insides seem emptier.

After what seemed like forever, I finally caved and sat up with my legs dangling over the edge of the bed. From outside, the metallic noises of a car door opening and closing echoed. More voices and laughter. I stood and tiptoed to the window, hiding behind the curtain as I peeked out as inconspicuously as possible. There was a beat-up sedan with dents and scratches galore and a black trash bag taped up on one of the back windows. Mom and Dad took turns hugging and kissing Tita Jo, who'd changed out of her overalls into a flowery, long skirt and blue tank top that matched the highlights in her hair. Over on the side by Mom's planter box filled with lavender Ada slouched in another costume-like outfit—an aviator hat and goggles on her head, some sort of belted beige uniform, a blue scarf tied at her neck, and brown work boots. The wind must have blown right by her, because she stuck her nose up and inhaled the air, bending down to sniff the lavender flowers when she realized what she was smelling. It was the sort of thing Coral would have done.

My heart twisted and squeezed itself so much it hurt.

Then, suddenly, as if she could sense me looking at her, Ada gazed up at my window. She smiled and waved at me. I pulled the curtains shut and backed all the way to my bedroom door. I waited to hear the car's engine. *Vroom. Sputter. Vroom. Vroom.* Its tires crunched on the gravel driveway, farther and farther until I could no longer hear it.

Phew . . . they're gone.

I opened my door a crack and peered down at the floor. There it was. The plate and the fork and the magnificent slice of buko pie.

Well, it would be a shame to let it go to waste.

TWENTY-THREE
Coral

I SAT ON THE BEACH, WONDERING HOW THE HECK I was going to eat my next meal without wasting the remaining matches. The plucked bird seemed to stare—its eyes glaring at me while I weighed my options.

I gripped my knife and started cutting away at the flesh, slicing thin, little pieces and placing them into an empty bowl. It was horrible, gross, disgusting. It ended up taking forever to get every bit of meat off the teensy-tiny bones and tendons. Sweat dripped down my face, neck, and back. After what seemed like hours, I finally had a bowl of stringy bird meat. I stared at it and stared at it and stared at it some more. Could I really eat it raw? What if it made me sick?

I shuddered. The thought of eating the foul-smelling flesh made me gag. But I had no choice. No fire meant that from then on, my meals would have to be raw. If I didn't eat, I'd die. Plain and simple.

I took a quick bite and began to chew. But the sliminess made me gag. I spat the meat out. The barely chewed mouthful resembled a slug crawling along the sand, my frothy saliva oozing on its surface. My eyes watered because the stench traveling through my sinuses smelled as if ammonia had just been squirted up my nose.

I chugged some coconut water and swished it around my mouth, but the disgusting taste lingered. The bowl of pinkish-gray meat sat there, taunting me.

God, I was so hungry. But I just couldn't stomach another bite. How on earth could I make it more appetizing? *Think, Coral. Think* . . . My nearby stash of coconuts caught my eye. I grabbed one that I'd cracked open earlier. The milky-white flesh was intact.

I browsed my small collection of utensils and picked out an elongated rock that was like a pestle. Totally improvising, I placed a few of the meat slices into the coconut and tossed in several seaweed fronds on top. With my rock pestle and coconut shell mortar, I slowly ground the contents into a paste. It ended up looking like a quivering pink glob of snot with flecks of mold. I gaped at it, daring myself to take a bite.

Do it! It can't be that bad . . . I scooped some out with my fingers, closing my eyes. Then I went ahead and stuffed the mixture into my mouth before I could change my mind. As soon as it hit my tongue, I wanted to gag again. But I resisted, allowing the slimy mouthful to settle before forcing myself to swallow.

It was far from delicious. But it also wasn't as gross as I thought it would be. The saltiness of the seaweed cut down on some of the gaminess, and the slightly sweet coconut gave it a milder aftertaste. I continued eating until half the paste was gone.

Even though the small meal quieted down my grumbling stomach, I knew that eating raw meat was a crappy idea. Not only was it gross, but worms and all sorts of parasites were in wild animals. It might keep me from starving, but it also might poison me or something.

I had to figure out how to make a fire without matches. I shut my eyes and blocked out everything around me. "Dad, help me. Tell me what I'm supposed to do. Please, don't let me down. I need you," I whispered.

But no one replied. Crickets. Nobody was there to help me. I leaned back on a coconut tree and sulked. But a few seconds passed, and I had this urge to kick something or throw something in frustration. As soon as I got up, though, a cramp pulled at the side of my stomach. I was dizzy and clammy all of a sudden.

Maybe I should go lie down . . .

Miraculously, I was able to stagger my way back to the cave without falling and cracking open my skull. I collapsed on my poncho bed and closed my eyes. Without warning, another cramp pummeled the side of my abdomen. It almost felt as if someone were pinching my insides with pliers. I doubled over and cradled my stomach. The cramps continued in short bursts all over my gut, with the occasional searing whopper. I was hot all over. But my skin was cold.

And then the vomiting started. Pink and white slime dribbled down my chest and thighs. It wouldn't stop. More vomit gushed from my mouth. Every time I hurled, it sucked more and more energy from my body. Pretty soon I was weak and dehydrated.

Why is this happening? Can't I just get a break? For once?

I reached for a coconut I'd opened earlier in the day and took small sips. When the water was all gone, I crawled out of the cave and somehow made it to the sea, letting the waves pull me in several inches deep. I rinsed my face and body, trying to wash the vomit off. Sopping wet and feverish, I struggled to get back up, my limbs still wobbly. I crawled back to my cave and collapsed onto the floor, the poncho making squishy sounds as I tried to find a position that would soothe me. But nothing worked.

My head pulsated. My body trembled. One minute, I was burning hot, the next ice cold. I lay there in my cave, going in and out of consciousness. When the cramps and puking ended, the diarrhea started. I was so weak the only thing I could manage was dragging my sorry butt out of the cave and emptying my bowels onto the rock ledge.

And as the day progressed, it got even worse.

I scrambled for the survival kit, shaking as I ripped it open. Its contents tumbled onto the ground. Advil. Yes! I shoved two capsules into my mouth and swallowed them dry.

Eventually, I managed to sleep—a shallow, restless

slumber. At times, my dreams were so vivid I thought maybe I was somewhere else. But when I jolted awake, nothing had changed.

I was still sick, still on this godforsaken island.

That was when the hallucinations took over, making me see things I knew weren't there. Mom and Dad were drinking tea from the ceramic set we bought in Japan, laughing and smiling as if the cave were our cozy sitting room at home. Isa was playing hopscotch, her pigtails bouncing. Uncle Henry was gutting a bucket of fish on the deck of his fishing boat. Tita Sunshine was squeezing a bazillion little calamansi fruit into a glass pitcher.

Eventually, after what seemed like hours, the cramping and diarrhea subsided. But my fever was back with a vengeance.

I couldn't take it anymore. Despite the cool breeze blowing into the cave, I felt as if I were in a sauna. Through the sweat in my eyes and the tendrils of hair plastered to my face, Mom and Dad appeared again, smiling. They reached their hands out and whispered, "*Coral, come . . . We want to show you something.*"

As if some celestial force were pulling me off the ground, my body floated toward them. I stretched out my arm until my fingertips touched theirs.

And then, *zap!* The cave was gone. The island was gone.

I was in Montana, Mom and Dad's favorite place to go camping. The sky was a bright blue dome, plopped over a landscape so vast it felt never-ending. It was mountains, lakes, forests, and prairies as far as the eye could see.

Dad would fish for trout while Mom foraged for mushrooms, huckleberries, and wild cereals, cooking the meals over the fire the old-fashioned way. Days were spent together, hiking, swimming, and learning. It was like one giant classroom where Mom and Dad taught me about animals, plants, rocks, minerals, even basic survival skills.

I walked over the prairie grass with my bare feet until I saw someone. Dad. I knew by the way he was standing that he was preparing for his daily fire-making ritual. He started off the way he always did, by organizing neat piles in a row: first a pile of dry mosses and grass, then sticks of all thicknesses, from spaghettilike kindling to pieces the size of my wrist. Once the piles were done, he cleared a spot on the ground, sweeping the leaves and debris to reveal the flat, solid earth below.

There was something magical about watching him create flames out of thin air. Sometimes I would picture him wearing a cape and a top hat like a hokey magician. The flair and drama made it seem as if he were standing onstage with an audience. Of course, it was usually just me, kneeling somewhere nearby with fascination etched all over my face.

"*Dad*," I said, trying to get his attention.

He turned around and grinned at me. "*Oh good, you're*

here. Pay attention, Coral. You might need to know how to do this one day."

He positioned the ash collector down and the baseboard on top, bending his knee to the side so he could hold it in place. With his drill stick nestled in the groove, he rubbed the stick back and forth so efficiently he didn't even break a sweat.

As time passed, little wisps of smoke materialized, floating out of the groove as the friction intensified. Dad stopped and nudged the smoldering ashes out of the groove with a twig. *"The grasses, Coral,"* he said, pointing at one of the piles.

I plucked the straw-like fibers and handed them to him. My breath was trapped in my throat as I watched. Dad proceeded to dump the acorn-size pile of ashes into the grass, wrapping it with even more grass before gently blowing on it. He swung the burning grass up and down until flames grew stronger.

"It's working!" I cheered.

The finale was short and sweet. Dad placed the burning pile down on the ground, layering the sticks on top, from thinner to thicker. And then we stood back and watched the fire blaze.

He looked up and gazed at me. *"You want to know the secret, Coral?"*

"The secret to what?" I replied.

"The secret to the fire," he said, gesturing at the

bright orange flames in front of us. "*You have to speak to it, make it believe that it wants to live.*"

For a minute, I thought he was joking. But the reflection in his eyes revealed a depth, which to me confirmed he was dead serious. The corner of his lip curled like he knew something I didn't. Then, as if some invisible father-daughter string connected us, I giggled at the exact moment that he chuckled. I ran around the fire screaming, "*Live, fire! Live!*" until the fire screamed with me.

Zap! The cave was back. The island was back. And Dad was gone.

I blinked. The corners of my eyes were caked with dried sweat and tears. I was so exhausted that even moving my eyelids seemed impossible. It was pitch-black, but this eerie glow from the moon crept into the cave.

Awww . . . Awww . . . Awww . . .

I froze. My eyes were still adjusting to the darkness, so all I could see were shadows. I blinked again. Shapes. I could see shapes.

Awww . . . Awww . . . Awww . . .

It was whimpering.

My heart pounded against my chest. I pushed myself up onto my elbows. A shadow appeared by my feet. I traced its shape with my eyes—a set of pointy ears, skinny legs, a long tail, the silhouette of a bird dangling from its mouth.

This sudden warmth was inside me. I stared into the darkness at my guardian angel's shadow and whispered, "Hey, Bambi."

TWENTY-FOUR
Isa

IT WAS TEMPTING TO PLAY HOOKY FROM WORK THE next day. Except, well, being annoyed and mad wasn't really a good excuse to stay home. I was pretty sure Mom wouldn't let me hear the end of it. She never did. One of her favorite subjects to lecture me about was having a good work ethic. *Work ethic-schmethick.* I could grumble about it all day, every day. But if I wanted to avoid one of her lectures, I would have to suck it up and go to work.

That didn't mean I couldn't slack off by taking a gazillion breaks. It was the only way I could deal. If I was inside for too long, I'd get this suffocating feeling as if I might pass out or something. It was probably the tension, so thick and heavy that it made it hard to breathe. Especially when Mom would hover, pretending to tidy up shelves when she was really coming to check up on me.

So there I was, on my second midmorning break, sitting on the dock, my legs dangling from the edge as a flurry of croissant flakes fell onto the water below. Seagulls swooped in and pecked at the floating crumbs.

On summer days like this, I always took my breaks at the marina with a snack and a cold drink. Being around customers all day annoyed me. So whenever I had the chance, I'd sneak outside for some alone time, with the sunlight shining on my skin, the waves making the boats bob up and down, the breeze teasing the flyaway strands of hair off my face.

The croissant crumbs disappeared, and the seagulls flew away to look for food elsewhere. Opportunistic jerks.

I reached for the bottle of pink lemonade between my legs and took another sip. The wooden plank below my butt vibrated with a set of heavy footsteps that could only belong to Steve—one of the marina workers who was quite possibly the most dude-bro-iest guy I'd ever met. I braced myself.

"*Pffft* . . . Pink lemonade is pointless, you know."

I looked over my shoulder, from his scuffed-up work boots all the way up to the tips of his curly blond hair. He was like a cherub on steroids. "And I care because?" I said with a dramatic eye roll.

"Because it's lame," said Steve, flexing his bicep muscles as if to make a point.

I scowled at him. "Oh, let me guess. *Hmmm* . . . Is it because pink is gay?"

"You said it. Not me." He shrugged.

I widened my eyes and ogled the sliver of pink sock peeking over his work boot. Steve frowned, confusion stamped all over his face as he bent over to inspect his feet. As soon as he spotted the offensive pink sock, his cheeks turned a matching color. "What? It's not my fault my mom can't sort the laundry properly."

A high-pitched giggle, sort of like a cross between a pig squealing and a hyena laughing, echoed from behind us. Steve and I whipped our heads around.

"Dude. You're, like, how old and your mom *still* does your laundry?" said Ada with a raised eyebrow.

Steve clenched his jaw. I could tell he wanted to give Ada a piece of his tiny brain, but for all he knew she was a kid of one of his customers, so he just stomped off without saying a word.

"Geez. Guys like that just get on my nerves," said Ada, shaking her head.

"Yeah, I'd say something more, except my mom might come out here and chew me out for cursing," I replied.

"I hear you . . ." Ada shuffled her brown leather ankle boots, which were oddly old-fashioned. In fact, her entire outfit was strange—a calf-length green dress with puffy sleeves and buttons at the neck, a straw hat with a maroon-colored band over her braided hair, and black tights.

Who the heck wore tights in the middle of summer?

"Sit," I said, gesturing at the empty space beside me with my chin.

For a split second, her eyebrows shot up. But then she grinned and plopped down like it was no biggie, as if all along we'd had a date to hang out or something. "Hey,

I'm sorry about bugging you last night. Your mom and my mom are kinda pushy, if you know what I mean," she whispered, peering over her shoulder to make sure nobody was eavesdropping.

"I do know exactly what you mean." I sighed. "It must be a Bituin family thing. Fair warning, I'm kinda pushy, too."

Ada snort-laughed. "Me too!"

And then, it was silent. We both kicked our dangling legs, and for a moment, it felt as if we were on a playground on swings, our kicks in sync one moment, out of sync the next. I turned my head toward her and gawked at her outfit again. "Um. So what's with all the costumes, anyway?" I blurted out.

She glared at me with this look on her face that screamed, *Duh*. But then she shrugged and lifted her boots up as if I was supposed to admire them. "Have you not seen any Studio Ghibli films? They are *ah*-mazing! Like amazing, amazing. I have a closet full of Ghibli-inspired clothes . . . This one"—she lifted the hem of her green dress—"is a character named Sophie from *Howl's Moving Castle*."

"Oh." I tried to pretend I knew what she was talking about even though I didn't.

"I know you must think it's weird. Most people do. But it makes me feel good, you know? Like I can sort of escape my boring life for something more exciting."

I nodded. "Yeah. I get it . . ."

Ada dropped her boots and swung them back and forth again. "Hey . . . I'm really sorry about your cousin . . . and your aunt and uncle. I can imagine how worried you must be."

My chest got all tight, because for a second, I'd allowed myself to forget, to live in the moment, to feel something other than worry, anger, and sadness. I stared at my lap, not wanting Ada to see the guilt in my eyes. "Coral. That's her name. And I guess, in a way, she's your cousin, too."

Ada stared off into the horizon and said nothing. I stole glances, studying her heart-shaped face and button nose, her thick eyebrows and round cheeks, and her bottom lip, which was thicker than the top. If I stared hard enough, I could see the resemblance—the Bituin features that the women in our family had inherited. Yet there was also something pretty different about her. Maybe it was something from her dad's side of the family. Except, well, I would never really know because he was dead.

"Hey, I-I'm sorry about your dad," I said.

Ada clenched her fists, her knuckles white. "Thanks. I really miss him."

"Yeah," I mumbled.

We went back to swinging our legs. Our own thoughts, our own memories, our own hopes and dreams shattered by the gaping holes in our chests.

TWENTY-FIVE
Coral

EVEN THOUGH I WAS STILL A BIT WEAK AND FEVER-ish, I managed to force myself out of my poncho bed the next morning. Surprisingly, Bambi was still there. She was curled up by the entrance of the cave, watching me. When I approached her, she flinched and crawled backward a couple of inches.

Skittish—that was the word I would use to describe her.

It was obvious I'd have to earn her trust. Big-time. So when I moved, I moved slowly. When I spoke, I spoke with a soft and gentle tone.

"Hey, you want to go for a walk, Bambi?"

She lifted her head off the ground, her ears darting up into alert mode. When I exited the cave, her eyes were glued to me. For a couple of minutes, I just stood there, stretching my sore muscles without looking at her. After a while, she propped herself up on one limb at a time and then sneaked over to the far end of the rock ledge. She could have run off. But she didn't.

I decided that the best game plan was to ignore her.

Well, not ignore, *ignore*. More like, act indifferent to her presence. If I just went ahead with my day-to-day routine without minding her, then maybe she would begin trusting me. *Fingers crossed.*

"Okay, here I go," I said casually. "You coming?" I peeked at her from the corner of my eye. She watched me with caution. So I ignored her again. Instead, I focused on climbing down the ledge with my wobbly arms and legs. *Tap. Tap. Tap.* I heard her doggy nails hitting the rocks as she followed. From the sound of it, she was a good eight or ten feet behind me.

Rather than taking a right toward the beach, I decided to head left, where the tide pools were. It was still early enough, so the sky was a molten orange. The light reflected onto the tide pools, making it appear as if there were pools of lava among the jagged rocks.

Bambi climbed onto a rock formation. When she reached the top, she stood still with her tail tucked between her legs. The only part of her that moved were her amber-colored eyes. She studied me, trying to figure me out, as if I were some complex math equation.

This wasn't the time for any sudden moves. I didn't want to spook her. So I went over to the nearest tide pool and sat down on its rocky edge. I stuck my bare feet into the water and relaxed. In the pool were electric-blue starfish, green and purple sea anemones, and tiny silver fish that were almost see-through. I watched all the creatures doing their thing—inching, darting, swaying, swimming. It was the closest thing to a TV that I had. I was so captivated that I'd completely forgotten about Bambi.

Grrr. Suddenly, she was about four feet away, standing on her hind legs so she could gaze into the same tide pool as me. *Grrr*, she growled again. Though she didn't seem to be growling at me. She was growling at something in the water. I opened my mouth to say something to her, but I stopped myself. Bambi seemed so focused. It would be a shame to frighten her. So I continued watching my island TV, keeping an eye on her with my peripheral vision. The growling stopped. She was frozen, only her tail would wag once in a while, as if she was seeing something exciting. Then *splash!* She dunked her muzzle into the water and emerged with one of the see-through fish between her teeth. I almost yelped in excitement but stopped myself. Bambi wasn't just a hunter, she was clearly a fisherman, too.

By then, her tail was in full wag mode. She somehow reminded me of those photos of fisherman holding up their supersize catches after a long day of fishing. Except her catch was teensy-tiny—so small that she could swallow it in one gulp. But she didn't. Instead, she did this weird doggy tiptoe toward me, and when she was about two feet away, she flung the fish as close to me as possible. It landed on the ground and flopped around.

"For me?" I said.

Bambi stared at the fish and then at me and then at the fish again.

I bent over and plucked the fish off the ground. Part of me wanted to toss it back into the sea. But the other part knew that I had to eat it. I didn't want to hurt her feelings. So I dipped it in the water to rinse it off and then counted to three—without even thinking about it, I tossed it into my mouth and swallowed. I almost gagged, feeling the fish wriggle as it went down my throat.

Woof! Woof! Was that a doggy seal of approval? I could have sworn there was a smile on Bambi's face, teeth, gums, and all. It was progress. She was beginning to trust me. But still, I acted like it was no biggie.

"Thanks, Bambi," I said before sticking my feet back into the tide pool.

She went off to her side again, and I went back to watching my island TV. We were doing our own thing. Together. And for the first time since washing up on the island, I didn't feel so alone. And, somehow, that made me feel stronger, more energized, as if I could accomplish anything.

I pushed myself off the tide pool, as if I'd just chugged a shot of espresso. "C'mon, Bambi! It's time . . ."

The fire, I could hear it calling out, waiting for me to speak to it. To breathe life into it. The fever dream was still fresh in my mind. Suddenly, I felt Dad's presence. He whispered in my ear, *"Pay attention, Coral. You might need to know how to do this one day."*

Determined, I marched to the bonfire with Bambi trotting a distance behind. Remembering what Dad told me that day made me want to persevere. I needed to stop fixating on the motions. Instead, I had to concentrate on being in the moment. I had to nurture the fire, coax it to life with my heart instead of my head.

Just as I had done before, I collected all the materials I would need. I arranged all the pieces of wood just as Dad had done. And then I took a deep breath, silently pleading, *Dad, help me bring it to life. Please.*

My hands gripped the stick, and my foot held the base steady. I rotated it with my palms, faster and faster, all the while keeping an eye on the hole at the base for signs of smoke. *Dad, help me bring it to life. Please.* Even though I was rubbing like crazy, the skin on my palms sloughing off, nothing happened. Absolutely nothing. But I wouldn't give up that easily.

So I rested for a few minutes, gathering my patience and strength, before giving it another shot. *Okay, it's going to work this time, Dad. I just know it.*

I picked a thicker stick, whittling the tip just a tad so it fit snugly in the groove. I rubbed with all my might. "*You can do it, Coral! Keep at it! Harder! Stronger!*" With every rotation, I pictured Dad's face. "*You have to speak to it, make it believe that it wants to live.*"

I rubbed and rubbed and rubbed, shouting, "Live fire! Live!" My palms were raw, bleeding, but still I persisted. "Please live! I need you, fire. Breathe! Breathe! Breathe!"

By then, I was sweating so much that I almost missed the beginnings of smoke. But after wiping the sweat from my eyes, I saw it. At the base, a solitary wisp of dark gray smoke appeared. *Breathe, breathe, breathe*, my mind commanded.

For a moment, the smoke looked indecisive, but then I bent down and blew on it softly. *Whew . . . whew . . . whew . . .* Then I stopped, held my breath, and stared at the wisp, hoping, pleading, crossing every single finger and toe.

Suddenly the wisp of smoke billowed. *Yes!* Quickly, I tapped the smoking clump into the nest of fibers I had arranged nearby. Almost instantaneously the dry strands caught fire, smoldering as I swished them up and down. The chain reaction was lightning fast, layers of sticks consumed within minutes.

I stood and listened to the crackling fire speak to me. Its flames kicked and screamed like a newborn baby.

The fire was alive.

It's alive! Whoo-hoo!

TWENTY-SIX
Isa

EVER SINCE CORAL DISAPPEARED, I'D KEPT THE BALI postcard with me at all times. If it wasn't in my back pocket, it was folded in my wallet for safekeeping. When I was bored or had nothing to do, I'd take it out and stare at it, reading her words over and over again. Maybe it was just my imagination, but lately I'd noticed the ink fading a bit, especially where I'd rubbed the letters with my finger.

Wish you were here!

I sighed and felt the sting in my eyes. The tears were there, waiting for the right moment to come out. I pushed them back. Because the last thing I wanted was to cry into some poor customer's cappuccino. I swallowed the pain away and tried my best to distract myself, reading labels and fidgeting and dusting objects that had been dusted, like, a million times before.

I tucked the postcard back into my pocket. Out of sight, out of mind. Right? *Cring. Cring.* The front door opened, and in walked a handful of weekenders, dressed in their crisp white linen and pastels and their perfectly high-lighted hair. They perused the shop, *oohing* and *ahhing* at all the homemade gourmet goodies and quaint offerings.

I rolled my eyes and glanced at the giant wall clock behind me. 1:55 PM. Five whole minutes until my shift was over. *Cring. Cring.* Great. More customers. I glanced at the door. It was Ada, except she looked different. Instead of her usual costumes, she wore a one-piece strawberry-colored swimsuit, denim shorts, flip-flops, and, on her shoulder, a blue batik canvas bag.

"Hey," she said, approaching the counter with a lop-sided grin.

"Uh, hey," I replied.

She scanned the shelf of cookies and muffins, and then she gazed over her shoulder at the refrigerated case with cold drinks. "So my mom kicked me out of the house because, apparently, I'm in need of some fresh air . . . I figured I'd get some snacks and head on over to the beach. Word is, it's a fifteen-minute walk from here," she said.

"Yeah, Crescent Beach is that way. You'll see a blue sign and then take a left onto the dirt road. You can't miss it," I explained, just as I'd done for every clueless tourist over the years.

Ada nodded. "Cool."

My eyes wandered over to the wall clock. 1:59 PM.

"Well, fresh air it is then . . . ," she said with a scowl that made it seem as if she were headed to a funeral or something. Ada turned around and headed toward the chip display.

"Wait!" I blurted out.

She halted, waiting for me to say whatever I was going to say. What *was* I going to say?

"That beach is packed with tourists and annoying little brats . . . You're better off heading to Sea Glass Point. But it's kinda hard to find." I peeked at the wall clock again. 2:00 PM.

And then I retrieved my backpack from under the counter. "Um. Well. My shift is actually over. If you want, I can take you there."

"Oh. Sure. I'd like that," Ada said with a toothy grin.

✳ ✳ ✳

We rode my bike—me steering and pedaling, and Ada standing behind with her hands on my shoulders. Even though she was literally breathing down my neck, it was my back pocket that bugged me. The Bali postcard was like a hot brick against my butt cheek. Somehow it was weighing me down. Every time I remembered it was there, it burned, as if I were being punished. *Don't ignore me! Read me!* the postcard seemed to be shouting. I tried my best to brush off the guilt gnawing at my insides. But it was hard because I was supposed to be angry and sad. Not gallivanting with some distant cousin. It didn't feel right to be heading to the beach for sun and fun. Especially without Coral.

*Okay. I'm just going to bring her there . . . then make
an excuse to bail.*

"Here we are," I announced as soon as I pulled into
the unofficial dirt parking lot, which was basically a flattened area with patches of weeds and gravel.

"This is it?" said Ada, hopping off.

I leaned my bike against a tree and gestured for her to
follow. "C'mon. You'll see."

I led the way toward the edge of Sea Glass Point. Most
tourists didn't know about this place because, driving by,
it looked like a cliff with a lookout area, an abandoned
lighthouse, and not much else. But a set of crudely made
stairs led down to a small beach in between the two inlets.

When we reached the bottom, Ada gasped. "Wow.
You're right. This *is* nice."

"Yeah . . ." For a second, I stood there shuffling my
sneakers on the sand. I was supposed to come up with
some dumb excuse to leave, but my mind went blank.

Ada scanned the entire length of the beach, placing
her hand over her brow to shield her eyes from the sunlight. "So how come this place is deserted?"

I shrugged. "It's mostly locals coming here early in
the morning or late afternoon to walk their dogs . . . At
night, older kids like to party here," I said, pointing at
the circle of logs and tree stumps with the remains of a
bonfire nearby. "That's why we call it Sea Glass Point.
Because all the broken beer bottles would end up as sea
glass . . . But I haven't seen a broken beer bottle on the

beach in a while. I guess cans and kegs are more popular now."

"Ah." Ada went over to a log, kicked off her flip-flops, and sat on it with her legs crossed.

I gazed up at the stairs leading to my bike and then at Ada sitting there all by herself. My back pocket felt heavy again. When I thought about the Bali postcard, my stomach churned with worry and guilt. Like maybe it would disintegrate in my pocket if I neglected it for too long.

But Mom would chew me out if she found out I abandoned Ada. And that was the last thing I needed. I shuffled over to the log and plopped down beside her.

"You seem preoccupied," said Ada.

I glared at her. "Really?"

"Uh-huh. I can tell. My mom says I'm an empath."

"An empath?" I asked, squinting suspiciously.

Ada straightened her back and curled her hands on her cross-legged knees as if she were doing a yoga pose. "Yeah. I can always sense what other people are feeling . . . Sometimes it's almost as if I absorb their emotions, like they become my own."

"*Oh*-kay," I said, emphasizing the "Oh," because I wasn't quite sure I believed her. *But whatever.* If she wanted so badly to know what was on my mind, I'd tell her. I pulled the Bali postcard out, flattening it before handing it to her. "This was the last postcard I got from Coral . . . before . . . you know."

She took it without saying anything. I watched her

as she read it. By the time she got to the bottom, her eyes were glossy with emotion. "I'm sorry. It must be so hard not knowing," she said, handing the postcard back to me.

"It *is* hard." I hugged the rectangular piece of paper against my chest. "But I do know. She's alive. I know it sounds crazy, but I can feel her presence inside me, in my bones, in my gut, in my heart."

Ada nodded. "I believe you."

"Thanks," I said, unzipping my backpack so I could tuck away the postcard for safekeeping. "*Anyway*, so that's that."

For a moment, I just stared at my lap, at my backpack, at my sneakers covered with sand. And then the log we were sitting on started to roll back and forth a bit as Ada scooted closer. "Why don't you write Coral back?"

I peered at her and frowned. "Write Coral back?"

"Yes. After my dad died, I wrote him a letter every week for months. It helped me feel closer to him, somehow. Like he was still there, listening to my stories."

Huh. It hadn't occurred to me. "But—but what would I do with all the letters?"

She bumped her shoulder with mine. I flinched, because bumping my shoulder was something Coral used to do. "Keep them in a box. And *when* she comes home, you can give them to her," she said with sparkling eyes.

When not *if.*

Maybe Ada wasn't so bad after all.

TWENTY-SEVEN
Coral

BAMBI AND I HAD AN ARRANGEMENT. I ACCEPTED that I wasn't allowed to touch or go too near her, and she, in turn, understood that my speaking to her as if she were another person was totally normal. *"So, Bambi, when we get off this island, we should order pizza, huh? Or maybe cheeseburgers, fries, and strawberry milkshakes? What do you think?"*

She trailed me wherever I went—my shadow of sorts. Which was fine by me. Life on the island had improved, like, one billion percent since Bambi miraculously appeared in my life. I yearned to be near her, to run my fingers through her coppery fur. It was the kind of intimacy I'd been missing—another living being, another heart, another soul besides my own. We were creating our own rhythm. Together.

I never thought friendship would be possible in such a hellish situation. Yet there we were, sort of, kind of almost friends?

Even though I was sure she didn't fully understand

what I said to her half the time, it was clear that sometimes she did, or at least made an effort to. There was this slight head tilt she did whenever I spoke to her, her ears and eyes perking up with curiosity.

"You know, Bambi, sometimes you remind me of Isa," I said with a chuckle. "She's just as moody as you when she hasn't had enough sleep."

Bambi grumbled, opening one eye before slumping forward on the sand. She tucked her face between her front paws, peering at me as if I were an alien or something. I giggled. Then I exhaled and leaned back, taking full advantage of the last few minutes of relaxation before the day got started.

Because it was a big day. It was time to explore the rest of the island.

When Bambi finally woke from her nap, she trotted over to the tree line and looked back at me with her doe-like eyes. *Hey, c'mon, lazy butt. It's time to go,* I imagined her saying to me.

As soon as she saw me following behind, her tail sprung from between her legs—*wag, wag, wag.* It was like watching a little kid bounce up and down with a balloon in their grasp.

"Where are we going, girl?" My steps were slow and deliberate.

Bambi responded with more tail wags. *C'mon! Hurry!* She leaped into the foliage, disappearing into a tangle of trees and vines and giant ferns.

I inhaled and exhaled. With only the ratty clothes on my back and zero shoes to speak of, I wasn't really dressed for a trek. But whatever, I chased after her anyway. "Bambi! Wait up!"

It was a lot dimmer under the canopy of dense jungle, with only the occasional ray of sunlight breaking through. Several feet ahead, I spotted Bambi waiting for me.

Woof! she barked as if to encourage me.

"This better be good!" I said, catching my breath.

Bambi pranced toward a semisteep incline, maneuvering through rocks and a maze of trees with ease. Clearly, she'd done it, like, thousands of times before. Her paws took exact steps. Meanwhile, I was falling behind, my efforts a hopeless mess. Every step I took was filled with so much doubt that it felt as if my ankles were made of Jell-O.

Ouch. I was seriously beginning to doubt I could make it much farther. My bare feet took a beating on sharp rocks, thorny vines, and other nasty bits of nature strewn along the way. But eventually, we made it to the top of a hill. Bambi waited for me a few feet away, watching as I agonized over my battered feet.

She whined. It almost sounded like she felt sorry for me. As much as I wanted to chicken out and go back to more familiar surroundings, my determination to keep going was like a Mack truck at full speed.

Suck it up, Coral. I ignored the pain. Surely, a couple of cuts and scrapes wouldn't kill me, right?

I glanced at Bambi with my hands on my hips. "Okay, girl . . . now what?"

Woof! Bambi darted through the trees, tail wagging at warp speed. This time she headed downhill, toward a part of the jungle that was so dense I was doubtful I could get through without a giant machete. By then, my feet were numb, caked with so much dirt, debris, and blood it almost looked as if I were wearing muddy slippers.

Eventually, we hit a barrier of monstrous-looking trees. Green canopies and curtains made of vines and orchids with polka-dotted petals hanging from the massive trunks of tropical trees.

"Wow." I gawked at the scenery.

Bambi was even more animated. Like, the most animated I'd ever seen her. She bounced in place, doing a wiggle dance, while staring past the wall of green foliage.

"What's the matter, girl?" I asked.

Bambi whined and squatted on the ground. Her hindquarters flat against the mossy carpet below. She stared straight ahead, releasing short bursts of barking.

Why was she acting so weird? I got down on all fours, thankful for the cushion of moss under my bony knees. As soon as I saw what she was looking at, it became crystal clear as to why she was so worked up.

Beyond a tangle of fallen branches was a tunnel of sorts. *Huh*. It must have been Bambi's secret spot—over time, plants had given way, allowing her access to whatever it was on the other side.

I crawled forward, my blood pumping, my muscles taut with anticipation. As I inched my way through, I cleared the fallen branches one by one. The minute the pathway was clear, Bambi's ears popped up. She darted past me like a rabbit speed-hopping through the forest.

"Wait up!" I shouted after her.

But I could do nothing to slow her down. So I just followed her. This time, my hands took a beating—rocks, thorns, sharp sticks, and splinters cut and scraped my blistered palms and fingers.

I reached the clearing on the other side, hands bleeding but pride intact. "Holy moly," I mumbled as I got off my hands and knees. It was as if I'd stepped into a Jurassic Park movie. I blinked and blinked again, to assure myself that it wasn't a hallucination. As my vision cleared, it was all still there—a majestic waterfall with a turquoise blue pool, rock formations that resembled petrified giants, ancient blooming trees, and a bunch of plants and flowers that looked as if they could swallow a human whole.

It *was* all real . . .

TWENTY-EIGHT
Coral

BAMBI'S BARK ECHOED STRAIGHT INTO MY EAR. I snapped out of it. I whipped my head around and then, *boom!* The magnitude of the situation hit me.

Oh my god . . . water!

Bambi knelt by the pool, drinking to her heart's content. I rushed to her side, bending down to scoop some into my mouth. *Ahhh . . .*

As soon as I swallowed, I tasted nothing but clean water. I'd forgotten how something so basic, so tasteless, could be so refreshing. I frantically scooped up some more, drinking until my stomach made that audible *glug, glug* sound.

I couldn't believe it. All those days spent worrying about dying of thirst, wishing I'd had something else to drink besides coconut water, and here this was the whole time. I mentally kicked myself. Had it not been for Bambi, I would have never discovered this.

"Thanks, girl," I said.

Her tail wagged, and then she bounded off chasing

after a butterfly. I leaned back against a mossy boulder, listening to the rush of the waterfall, the distant chorus of birds, the stillness and beauty of the jungle surrounding me. Mom and Dad would have *really* loved this place. I could feel tears pushing out of my eyes. Because, despite the amazingness of this place, despite the discovery of precious water, I couldn't help being sad and bitter and heartbroken. I could picture Dad jumping into the lagoon fully clothed, screaming "*Whoo-hoo!*" as he floated on his back. I could picture Mom gazing up at the treetops with wide eyes, searching for birds and fruit and rare insects. Except they weren't here to do any of those things. It was just me and Bambi.

I wiped the tears away with the backs of my hands. *Focus on the positives, Coral. Focus on the here and now.*

Bambi lost the butterfly and moved on to chasing iridescent dragonflies and jumping on piles of fallen leaves. Eventually, she settled down and curled up for a snooze under a canopy of hanging flowers. She looked like an angel or a fairy. Yup, my guardian angel, my fairy godmother.

Even though I didn't really believe in god, I gazed up at the sky and whispered, "Thank you."

I was grateful. So, *so* grateful. I just needed to say it out loud to whoever was out there.

My gaze fell on the pool of water, so clear I could almost see all the way to the bottom. It had been too long since I'd felt clean. Seawater baths weren't good enough. Layers of dried salt caked on my skin, from my scalp to my toes, making me feel like I was always dirty. So I took off my clothes and slipped into the pool, dunking my head underwater until I couldn't hold my breath any longer. I rinsed and scrubbed every part of me, massaging my scalp and hair to get as much of the gunk off as possible. When I was done, I simply floated where the water would take me, my worries temporarily forgotten.

I gazed at the trees up above, a tangle of branches competing for the small patches of sunlight that somehow managed to seep through. The cawing of birds echoed from every direction. Parrots. Their green feathers so perfectly camouflaged that I almost didn't see them. Dozens of them in a low-lying tree with a pale trunk, its branches covered with clusters of bright red fruit.

Fruit! Never in a million years did I think the sight of fresh fruit would bring out the same reaction as a moist and gooey brownie. But the lack of produce in my diet had me drooling. I gulped the saliva down and scrambled to the edge of the pool to get out. The birds were cawing at one another, pulling at the red globes greedily. One by one the discarded peels fell to the ground below. I put my clothes back on, which, strangely, felt stiffer than they had before. Then I tiptoed over to the spot underneath the tree. When I found the scattered peels, I picked one up and examined it. Weird. It was like nothing I'd ever seen before—bloodred and hairy, with a tough, almost leathery texture.

Bambi woke from her nap with a snort. She trotted

over and watched me with a curious side-tilted stare. From up close, the tree was smaller than I'd originally thought. Its low-lying branches were weighed down by the heavy clusters of fruit. *Hmmm* . . . From experience, I was pretty sure the tree wouldn't hold my weight, even though I was now practically a pile of skin and bones. But the tree next to it—a massive, ancient-looking specimen, might be sturdy enough.

Okay. Here goes nothing. I climbed the base of the trunk, sticking my bare feet into the notches and grooves. Bambi watched me and whined. Clearly, she thought it was a very bad idea.

I gazed down at her. The way her eyes slickened with worry somehow reminded me of Isa. Because Isa always thought my ideas were terrible. Every time I attempted to do something adventurous or even dangerous, she would scowl and say something like, "*For real? If my mom finds out, she's going to kill us.*" And then I'd wink at her and say, "*She's going to kill you, not me.*"

I gave Bambi the most reassuring look I could muster. "It's okay, Bambi, I've done this lots of times. It'll be a piece of cake."

She whined back at me. I guess my look wasn't as reassuring as I'd hoped. I continued my climb, grabbing branches as I went higher and higher. When I reached the spot where the branches were intertwined with those of the fruit-bearing tree, I moved horizontally, balancing as if I were a tightrope walker in the circus. *Steady, Coral* . . .

Unfortunately, though, once I was close enough to the fruit, the branches sort of tapered off—too thin and weak for me to stand on. I leaned over and stretched with the tips of my fingers, reaching and reaching and reaching until I felt the base of a cluster. I curled my index and middle fingers around it, gathering enough momentum to pull. *Snap!* Leaves and birds flew into the air as the cluster popped off. A dozen or so fruits tumbled to the ground.

Bambi bent down to sniff the alien-looking orbs. *Yummm.* I could almost taste their sweetness in my mouth. But there was one more cluster nearby. Unfortunately, it was a few inches too far. My fingers grazed air. *Dang it!* I scooted over, inching my torso forward until I could just touch the fruit. *Push, Coral! Push!* I stretched and stretched. *Almost there!* Suddenly, a loud cracking sound spooked me. For a split second, I thought I'd broken the branch of fruit off. But instead, it was my body that dropped. Fast.

I screamed. Then *thud*. I hit the ground and passed out.

The searing pain brought me back. My eyelids fluttered. Flashes of white light momentarily blinded me as the pain radiated from my ankle up to my ribs.

I groaned and shifted so I was flat on my back. *Awww, awww, awww.* Bambi circled me as she whined.

"I—I think I'm okay." I pushed myself up onto my elbows and winced. "Ugh. No, I'm not . . ."

The throbbing pain felt as if someone had just kicked me in the ribs. I wanted to cry, to break down in hysterics. But I didn't want to freak Bambi out. I found her amber eyes and tried to reassure her. "It's all right, girl; I'm just a bit bruised, nothing broken. I *think*," I said with a calm voice.

My words seemed to appease her. But I sensed she was still worried. Her ears stood upright in full-alert mode. I took deep breaths and lifted my body off the ground, ignoring the pain even though it was almost unbearable. I was pretty sure my ankle was sprained, not broken, since I could still rotate my foot. *Thank god.*

When I pulled my T-shirt up and tilted my eyes downward, angry red bruises glared back at me. "Shoot," I mumbled under my breath.

I felt stupid and reckless. I could have died. And for what? Some fruit? The flush of anger crept into my cheeks and down my neck. I limped over to the fruit and gathered them into my shirt, tying the slack material at my waist to create a sort of DIY pouch. I must have gathered around twenty or so of the golf-ball-sized fruit in there. "Geez . . . I almost killed myself for this stuff. It better be good."

Bambi barked as if she were agreeing with me.

Since my limp was slowing me down, I searched for a long stick to use as a cane. *Aha!* Several feet away, I found it—straight and solid, with a gnarly top to hold on to. I leaned on it and whistled to get Bambi's attention. She bounced up and down a couple of times and then led the way with a gallop.

I hobbled along, taking my time so I wouldn't stress my already swollen ankle. The inner me wanted to sprint, to leap, to climb my way back to the beach. But the reality was downright depressing. My movements were more like those of an old lady walking down the street with a cane.

God, what I wouldn't give for one of those walkers, or an electric scooter, or one of those all-terrain wheelchairs.

Finally, after what seemed like an eternity, we made it to the other side of the jungle tunnel. I collapsed on a fuzzy mound of moss and ferns, a sweaty, exhausted mess. Could I really make it all the way back? I stared at the incline up ahead, silently cheering myself on.

You can do it, Coral. I pulled my body up with the help of my makeshift cane, knowing that the longer I rested, the more discouraged I'd get. With my gaze, I carefully studied the route, memorizing my path so that I'd have small trees and branches to help me on my way. The first step was excruciating. But I continued with sluggish steps until I made some progress.

In a matter of minutes, Bambi reached the top. She turned back and watched me like a mama bear eyeing her cubs. "Don't worry, Bambi. I'm all right," I called out to her.

She didn't look convinced.

I wrapped my hand around the next branch, struggling to make that final push to the top. My body desperately wanted to give in to the physical and emotional exhaustion, but I held on to the cane for dear life, resting only for seconds before continuing.

You can do it! You're almost there! On and on and on and on . . .

And when I was just about ready to collapse, we reached the final barrier of foliage separating us from the beach.

"Gahhh!" I screamed with relief, suddenly emotional, overwhelmed by the multitude of highs and lows.

I took a deep breath and then limped toward the beach with Bambi's fur brushing up against my shins. The sand and the sea appeared—a panorama of white, ripples of blue dancing across the shoreline.

Phew. We made it.

TWENTY-NINE
Isa

AFTER HANGING OUT AT SEA GLASS POINT, I TOOK Ada home, because I was not about to let her walk all the way back and get heat exhaustion or something. Of course it would be my fault, and I would never hear the end of it from Mom.

When we pulled up to the side of Sunshine Deli and Bakery, we both hopped off my bike, me breathless, Ada sweating buckets and a bit sunburned. Her nose and cheeks were pink, and I spotted angry tan lines on her shoulders.

"Hey, you wanna come up for a while? I have snacks and movies," said Ada, wiping the sweat off her forehead.

I glanced at my watch. It was a couple of hours before dinner. Then I glanced into the side window of the bakery. Mom was still in there, trying to upsell a bunch of gourmet food items to some clueless tourists. Thank god I wasn't at work anymore. Listening to her trying to persuade customers to buy stuff they didn't really want was megacringey.

"Uh. Yeah. Sure. I can come up, I guess."

"Awesome."

I leaned the bike against the side of the building and followed Ada up the narrow metal staircase. It had been a while since I'd been up there. My parents used to rent the unit out, but it ended up being more of a hassle than anything else since the tenants always complained about the noise below. So it was transformed into a storage unit of sorts.

Ada unlocked the door. "C'mon."

I followed her inside, expecting a huge mess, but it was already surprisingly homey. The apartment had the same antique wooden floorboards as the bakery, the same high ceilings with exposed pipes, the same giant bay windows overlooking the marina. The living and dining areas were in one large room along with the kitchen, which had an L-shaped counter and a large farmhouse table instead of an island. Ada's mom had spruced it up with a couple of black-and-white throw pillows for the mustard-yellow sofa, a circular rainbow-colored throw rug that looked like it was some sort of Filipino-native weave, and a bunch of potted plants.

"Nice," I commented.

Ada smiled. "Yeah, we're used to moving. So we've pretty much got decorating down to a science." She headed to the smaller of the two bedrooms and motioned for me to follow. "Let's hang in my room."

I thought her room would be a mess of costumes,

walls covered with anime posters. But instead it was neat and kind of minimalist. There were clean blue sheets on the white wrought iron bed, an old-fashioned quilt, and a smaller version of the throw rug in the living room. By the window was a white desk next to a small white bookshelf filled with books. And the only sign of her costumes, I mean clothing, was a metal garment rack with wheels by the bathroom door.

"I like your room," I said, plopping onto the bed.

Ada tossed her bag on a chair and plopped down next to me. "Yeah. It's much nicer than our last place, which smelled like mold and stale Doritos," she said, scrunching her nose.

I chuckled. "Stale Doritos doesn't sound so bad . . ."

"You had to be there to fully experience it. Believe me, eau de stale Doritos is not a pleasant aroma." She reached for the drawer of her bedside table and pulled out a laptop. "You wanna watch a movie?"

"Sure. What do you have?" I said, leaning back on a pillow.

She opened the laptop and clicked open a folder. "How about *My Neighbor Totoro*? Have you seen it?"

"No." I grinned lopsidedly. "Is it embarrassing to admit I've never watched an anime movie?"

Ada stared at me wide-eyed, as if she'd morphed into a spooked owl or something. "*No.* For real?"

"Sorry," I said, feeling my cheeks get a bit hot.

"Well, it's time to remedy that . . . *My Neighbor Totoro*

it is. You'll like it; it has a happy ending." She clicked on a file and pressed PLAY. "I'll go get us a snack."

She hopped off the bed and went to the kitchen. The movie started, and as much as I wanted to focus on it, I could hear Ada scrounging around for stuff in the other room. After a few minutes, she returned with a bowl of potato chips, onion dip, a bag of Choc Nut, and two glasses of calamansi juice.

It was kind of noisy with our munching and slurping. But after a few minutes, I got sucked into the story of two girls, Satsuki and Mei, who move to an old house with their dad so they can be closer to the hospital where their seriously ill mom is recuperating. One day, Mei befriends a giant nature spirit named Totoro, who looks like a cross between an overstuffed teddy bear, a koala, and a cat.

"Isn't Totoro the cutest?" said Ada. "Ohhh. This is one of my fave scenes . . ."

We watched as Mei and Satsuki wait for their dad's bus to arrive. Mei falls asleep, and Totoro suddenly appears. It starts to rain, and Totoro uses a giant leaf as an umbrella. And then the weirdest thing happens; a bus pulls up, except it's not any ordinary bus—it's a cat bus. I mean, a real live giant cat that's also a bus. It has a toothy smile like the Cheshire Cat in *Alice's Adventures in Wonderland*.

"A *cat* that's a bus?" I said, glancing at Ada dramatically.

"Yeah, can you imagine how they must have come up with that idea?" she said with a yawn.

I frowned. "Hey, if you're tired, we can finish the movie some other time."

"No, it's okay. I think I just had too much sun."

So we continued watching Satsuki and Mei's adventures. An hour or so must have passed. I was so mesmerized by the movie that I didn't even notice how quiet it was. Ada's breathing was shallow. I looked over at her. She was conked out with a Choc Nut in her grasp, her head almost falling off her pillow. Something about her was peaceful, as if she were a little kid who'd fallen asleep after a super-long day.

Anyway, I guess she'd probably seen the movie a gazillion times. I didn't have the heart to wake her up, and besides, I kind of wanted to finish the movie and see what happened. Five minutes. Ten minutes. Twenty minutes went by. All the chips were gone, and I was about to scarf down the last Choc Nut, except tears were dribbling down my cheeks.

I *never* cried in movies. Like, *never ever*.

Except seeing Mei and Satsuki's mom finally come home, and seeing them reunited as a family, made my heart ache, but it also made me hopeful. Ada was right; it was a happy ending. And as great as that was, it made me yearn for my family to be reunited, too. It made me wonder why this tragedy had to happen. Why us? What did we do to deserve this?

THIRTY
Coral

MY HAND GRIPPED THE BALL-SHAPED SEEDPOD behind my back. Bambi was crouched a few feet away. Frozen. Even her usually hyperactive tail stood still. I waited for the waves to recede before gathering momentum to push forward. Her nose twitched as if she'd already guessed my next move. The waves crashed. I flung the seedpod. It was barely out of my grasp, but Bambi was already midair. It was as if she were floating, mouth open, amber-colored eyes fixed on the prize. *Thud.* She landed gracefully and caught the seedpod. Again and again.

"Yes, Bambi! Good job!" I shouted and clapped.

It had taken weeks for my injuries to heal. But today, I felt pretty confident that I'd finally made a full recovery. Our game of catch on the beach made me feel a million times better.

While preparing our breakfast, a pleasant breeze swayed the trees, and cotton candy clouds drifted across the sky, mellowing the morning sunlight. It was a perfect day—perfect for an excursion to the other side of the island.

Chomp. Munch. Crack. Bambi was chewing on a carcass, the crunch of bones and tendons made for an eerie sound effect.

"Should we explore? What do you think, girl?" I asked her.

Bambi stopped gobbling her meal long enough to yip once. I took it as a *yes* and drank the rest of my coconut water while plotting out our route. From my guesstimation, the island wasn't all that big, but from where I was standing, it felt as vast and unknown as another universe. The jungle was dark and foreboding, filled with all sorts of dangers. With my lack of footwear, the terrain would be a huge challenge even with my calloused soles.

I gathered a couple of the water boxes, which I'd refilled; some cooked meat; seaweed; and a handful of red fruit, which, thankfully, turned out to be delicious, like a cross between a grape and a lychee. Bambi saw me packing the survival kit and did a frenzied dance on the beach, leaping and twirling like she was in a bouncy carnival ride.

"You ready?" I said with a chuckle.

Woof! she barked back.

Sometimes her barks sounded like words—a series of muffled *yeses, nos, okays, whys.* We'd developed this sort of weird way of communicating that included speaking, shouting, barking, laughing, yipping, growling, and tons of body language.

Bambi sprinted toward the tree line as if she already

knew exactly where we were going. Now that we were making daily trips to the waterfall, I wasn't quite as intimidated. The fragrant orchids popped from the shadows; the lifelike vines twisted and tangled, forming curtains of greenery; the moss-covered boulders and rocks were smooth and slippery. Everything was so beautiful, but there were also unknown dangers. One false move and I could hurt myself again. Or worse, get myself killed.

As time passed, I learned to listen, to *really* listen to the sounds around me. When I first got to the island, all I heard was silence, interrupted by the occasional cawing of birds and the whooshing of waves. But now that my senses were more acute, I could hear it all—the humming of a swarm of insects, the breeze fluttering the coconut tree fronds, even drops of condensation pitter-pattering on leaves. Sometimes it made me feel like a superhero. Wishful thinking. Because if I really were a superhero, I wouldn't have been stuck on this island.

"C'mon, Bambi! Let's go!"

We walked for hours, stopping only to drink a few sips of water. After a while, the jungle transitioned into rockier terrain—huge limestone formations sliced through the greenery. The easiest path seemed to zigzag between the formations, going higher and higher until, finally, we reached some sort of summit. On it was a clearing all the way to the edge of a cliff, as if someone had created a lookout for tourists. If I squinted, I could almost visualize the spots where the railings would be, where the kids would jump up and down, pointing at the incredible sights as their parents looked on. It reminded me of Sea Glass Point back home on Pebble Island.

The view was breathtaking—an endless ocean, waves like the glinting scales of a fish, faraway islands sprinkled in various shapes and sizes. I wondered if any of them had names or places on a map. Nothing was artificial, no boats, no planes, no houses, nothing to indicate civilization.

Zip. Zilch. Nada. I really am all alone.

A disorienting sensation overtook me. One part of me was calm, like everything I was looking at was how it was supposed to be—me and Bambi standing side by side, gazing out at this place that had become our home. But this other part wouldn't let me be—a yearning for the familiar, the rustling of clean sheets, crisp unopened books, chaotic breakfasts, chatter popping in my ears like cooking popcorn. I was torn between acceptance and hope.

I sat with my legs hanging off a rock and pulled out the lunch I'd packed. Bambi waited by my side, her long pink tongue hanging out.

"You hungry, girl?"

Woof! Woof!

I ripped a waxy leaf in half and placed her share on the floor between us. While I took my sweet time chewing the cold meat and seaweed, Bambi gobbled hers up in five seconds flat, taking care to lick the leaf afterward in case any extra juices were left behind.

When we were done, I patted her on the head and stood. A fleeting image barged into my head. I could see it so clearly. Bambi and Isa and me, running and leaping on the beach back home. *Not now. Stop daydreaming, Coral.* I closed my eyes and made the image vanish. The last thing I needed was to distract myself with fantasies. "Bambi, let's go," I said, whistling as I slapped my leg.

Bambi dashed down the side of the mountain. As we made our descent, she became even more sure-footed, her four legs balancing on the rocks like a fearless mountain goat. About an hour in, my legs started to burn. I took a break on a shelf rock and massaged them until the burning turned to numbness.

Awww . . . Awww . . . Awww . . . , Bambi whined, and paced from side to side. She kept staring downhill as if something was preoccupying her. She obviously knew something I didn't.

"What's the matter, girl?" I said with a frown.

Awww . . . Awww . . .

The moment I got up, she hopped from rock to rock with excitement.

"Okay, okay. C'mon."

Bambi zoomed toward a cluster of trees growing on one side of the mountain. I chased after her, the anticipation of what was up ahead making the blood rush to my head.

When we reached the spot, the first thing I noticed was how odd the trees looked. Instead of growing toward the sky, they veered to the side, almost horizontally, as if drawn to some weird magnetic force. There was a mixture of rock and soil on the ground, the tree roots gripping both earth and stone to prevent from slipping down the mountainside. The landscape was so bizarre that I wouldn't have been all that surprised if a fuzzy-haired Pixar film character popped out of the shadows.

When I finally passed the barrier of tree trunks, rays of sunlight momentarily blinded me. I squinted until my eyes adjusted to the brightness. And then, *pow!* Something astonishing appeared in front of me. A huge black rock the size of a surfboard jutted from the ground. It was covered with carvings. There were swirls and symbols and grooves with abstract shapes, some recognizable—a lifelike fish swam on one corner, a circle that resembled the sun moved from one side to the other, or maybe it was the moon? And a series of waves that got bigger and bigger.

Hmmm. I peeked past the slab of rock. Behind it was the top of some crudely made steps. I wobbled. My body begged me to sit. But I just couldn't.

Wow. Civilization! People! What if they're still here?

"Bambi, hold up!" I yelled after her.

But she was already halfway down. I inhaled and exhaled.

Here goes nothing.

THIRTY-ONE
Isa

SECONDS, MINUTES, DAYS, WEEKS WHIRLED BY TOO fast. Usually, I didn't mind it when time passed me by. But when all I had to cling to was hope, time was my worst enemy. Sometimes it would get so overwhelming that I had to escape to somewhere, anywhere, that didn't remind me of Coral, Uncle Jack, and Tita Alma.

That place ended up being the abandoned house down the beach from us. It had been empty since before I was born, so I never knew the people who owned it. The house was damaged during a hurricane, half its roof flew off, and the place was severely flooded. So the owners left and never came back. A FOR SALE sign had been up there forever, but nobody was interested in the place. More and more shingles fell off every year, more and more paint would peel and fade, more and more weeds would grow in its cracks and holes and crevices.

I got the idea to go over there one night after tossing and turning and barely sleeping. It was four in the morning. Mom was already at work supervising the early baking.

Dad was out on his fishing boat. I climbed out of bed with this weird feeling that I had to go somewhere. It was as if ants were crawling all over my body, forcing me to move, to free myself from the confines of my bedroom.

I put on an old hoodie over my T-shirt and shorts and went downstairs to make some coffee. I poured some into a thermos and went outside, slipping on the pair of flip-flops I always kept by the front door.

Outside, it was cool. I mean, relatively cool for summer. It was still dark, but a hint of grayish-blue light was peeking from the horizon. I took the dozen or so stairs down to the beach and then strolled while sipping my piping hot coffee. I walked past the pale blue house owned by the Johnsons, the modern gray bungalow owned by the Robinsons, the bright white cottage owned by the Castellanos. Five, maybe ten, minutes passed. The horizon had brightened in that short time. Enough for me to see the abandoned house pretty clearly.

For a moment, I stared at it. I had no memories of it. None at all, other than seeing it in passing. It was just a derelict house that had belonged to other people. While I stared at it, I wondered what they were like. Were they a happy family? Did they play board games every night? Was there a grill on the patio where they'd cook up juicy burgers on hot summer nights? Just thinking about all those questions and scenarios immediately made me feel better somehow. Like I could obsess over this family, their lives, instead of thinking about my own family.

I looked around to make sure nobody was nearby. Then I approached the house, still peering nervously over my shoulder. Yeah, it was kind of paranoid of me. But Mom had this knack of turning up when I least expected. As if she had eyes planted everywhere, watching, waiting to catch me doing something I wasn't supposed to do.

When I reached the house, I climbed up the porch steps, careful to avoid the broken ones. There were too many creaks for my liking. And the patio sort of shifted when I put my weight on it. *Uh. Maybe this isn't such a great idea . . .*

But then I took a peek inside the sliding glass doors. There was a kitchen table with built-in seating. On it were a couple of broken teacups and a dusty and moldy package of cookies. There were still curtains, except they were stained by water damage and covered in cobwebs. Strewn all over the tile floor were branches and dried up leaves and clumps of bird poop.

I reached out and pushed the sliding glass door open. It squeaked and kind of stuck. But I pushed harder, and it gave way. A musty smell immediately traveled up my nose. I sneezed because, *hello*, allergies. But I went inside anyway. The living room was an even bigger mess. It was where the ceiling had been ripped away, so roofing and plaster and bits of concrete were everywhere. There was even a sofa set, coffee table, rug, and TV beneath all the debris. I stayed in the kitchen area since it seemed safer. I went over and opened a couple of cabinets. They were mostly empty, but there were some rusted cans, packs of unrecognizable food, dusty spice jars, and a whole lot of dead bugs and dirt.

I stood still for a moment, getting a feel for the room. Were the owners inside when the hurricane hit? Was anyone injured? How come they never came back? I had so many questions. It was weird having my mind filled with scenarios about people I didn't know. Complete strangers. But it was a relief not having to worry about anyone close to me. Even if it was just for a short while.

Through the sliding glass door, I could see the beginnings of dawn, a pale orange light emerging from the horizon. Soon I'd have to go back home and get ready for work. But I wanted a few more minutes to bask in someone else's tragedy. So I sat down facing the window and the sea and the rising sun and sipped my coffee, taking my sweet time. Maybe I'd even be late for work. I didn't care, though.

As the sky changed to a tangerine orange tinged with blue, I imagined the family who'd lived here waking up. Maybe the dad would come down first and make coffee or tea. Then the mom would follow and start whipping up some pancakes and bacon while the kids slept in for a bit longer. And when they were all awake, they'd have breakfast where I was seated, chatting about their plans for the day.

I took another sip from my thermos. The last sip. And the morning sunlight was out in full force. It was time to go. I stood and went over to the sliding glass door. But before leaving, I gazed around the room one more time.

"Have a nice day," I said out loud to no one. My voice echoed. Nobody was there to reply to me. It didn't matter, though. I knew I'd be back. And back and back again. Because it was a lot easier to worry about other people and their problems.

Not mine. Not Coral's or Uncle Jack's or Tita Alma's.

"See you later," I said, glancing at the kitchen table as if the family were there to see me off.

THIRTY-TWO
Coral

I COULDN'T QUITE FIGURE OUT WHETHER I SHOULD be happy or afraid at the possibility of human life on this island. What if they were hostile? What if they decided to hurt me instead of help me? When I reached the bottom of the crudely built stairway, my feet landed on sand.

Whooooooshhh . . . There it was. The sea and a beach, one I'd never seen before. For a second, I lost sight of Bambi. I panicked. "Bambi! Bambi!" I yelled at the top of my lungs.

I slapped my hand over my mouth. *Crap. What if someone heard me?*

I stumbled back, suddenly unsure of what could be ahead of me. But then I heard Bambi's barks through a maze of trees. She sounded normal. Not alarmed or anything. I followed the sound until I came upon a large clearing surrounded by several thatched structures. It felt the way it had in Montana with Mom and Dad, driving through the desolate old West towns, not the tourist traps filled with souvenir shops and cheesy saloons, but the ones that were truly dead—layers of dust-covered structures with not a footprint in sight.

This place was dead. I could feel it. But unlike the old western towns, I could somehow tell this island village hadn't been abandoned that long ago. I could sense a presence. There were still gaps in the slightly overgrown plants that had been walked through. There were spots in the dry and brittle thatching that were relatively clear of dust and cobwebs. There were pieces of wood that hadn't yet rotted and crumbled.

Bambi leaped out of a hut, jumping on me and licking my fingers with her sandpapery tongue. "Here you are," I said, rubbing her furry head and neck.

I scanned my surroundings more carefully. Could this have been Bambi's home? She certainly seemed comfortable and at ease.

As we strolled through the ghost of a village, Bambi barked and ran circles around me as if she was telling me an animated story. Even from the outside, I could see signs of what life used to be like. Old fishing nets hung from a nearby tree branch. Woven baskets were piled on top of one another, slowly disintegrating. There was even a wooden canoe that had seen better days, its hull split and cracked, rendering it useless. Maybe a storm had damaged it? I stared at it and gritted my teeth, pondering the *what-ifs*.

What if I could fix it?

What if I could use it to get off the island?

What if? What if? What if?

Sigh. I approached one of the huts, pausing in the open doorway. A section of the thatched ceiling was gone, inviting the light to stream in. I couldn't quite tell how it had been damaged. But upon closer inspection, it seemed as if a strong wind had blown it away. *Yup. A storm.* Inside, the floor was made of bamboo cut lengthwise so that it lay flat in elongated slats, creaking and groaning with every step. The walls were woven out of a similar material as the roofing, framed with thick pieces of bamboo. Everything was sturdy, considering it wasn't made of stone, brick, or concrete. But time and the elements had taken their toll—fraying, tearing, fading the structure—turning it into a fragile skeleton of a house. There wasn't much left behind, only a brittle mat, a broom made from long twigs, a pile of ripped fabric, and in the corner, a ball of dried fibers, maybe a child's toy.

I inspected every single hut, searching for clues as to what might have happened to the people who'd lived here. But I came up with no answers, as if I'd just read a book only to find out the last chapter had been ripped out. My only guess was maybe they'd moved somewhere else. To some other island that was better protected from storms and tsunamis. But where exactly had they gone? And how? The lack of information left me feeling hollow.

Seeing and touching all those objects created by human hands reminded me of death. Without people, the village was nothing, a lifeless habitat that only made me lonelier.

I exhaled, suddenly exhausted. The sky had darkened. The sun was a mellow yellow. The midafternoon haze crept past me, and soon night would fall.

"It's time to go back home," I mumbled at Bambi, who was resting by my feet.

Woof! she replied as if in agreement.

Before leaving, I gathered a few odds and ends that I could carry with me and might come in handy—a woven mat, a couple of cracked but usable wooden cooking utensils, an old plastic bottle, and one solitary flip-flop, a faded blue one, just a tad too big. I piled everything into one of the old fishing nets and made a bundle that I could tie around my shoulders.

"Let's go, girl. It's getting late." I looked back at the abandoned village, feeling somewhat disappointed. Finding it had been exciting. Thrilling. Yet leaving it left me with no real answers other than the possibility that it had once been Bambi's home. It wasn't truly a *real* mystery. There was no plot twist. All it was was an abandoned village. That was it.

Bambi sprang into action, running up and down the beach. I looked out at the ocean and scanned the shoreline. It occurred to me that maybe we could follow the coastline instead of hiking back the way we'd come. My muscles were already too sore. It was almost low tide, so with a bit of walking, and wading, and maybe some swimming, we could likely make it back to our beach in half the time.

"This way, girl!"

Woof! Woof!

We began at a relaxed pace, passing over a stretch of tide pools. Bambi pranced along, sniffing a shell here and there, steering clear of the crabs that snapped at her nose when she got too close.

"Yeah, you better stay away from those critters, Bambi. Remember what happened the last time?" I said, chuckling as she peered at me with one ear propped up.

In the pools of clear, calm water, fish in every shade of the rainbow darted around, hermit crabs peeked from the crannies, mingling among brown, red, and blue starfish. I used to be fascinated by curious little creatures and their habitats, always eager to learn from Mom and Dad. But now I saw them differently—no longer curiosities, but potential sources of food. Every time I came across something wriggling, swimming, or crawling, my first thought was whether it was edible and how easily I could catch it. The fascination was gone, replaced with a matter-of-fact approach that, for some reason, disturbed me.

Well, you gotta do what you gotta do . . .

Finally, we neared the other side of the cove. There were black rock formations rising up in the distance. But first, we'd have to wade through a shallow pool. Suddenly, without warning, a stinging pain whipped around my ankle, radiating up my leg within seconds.

"Owww!" I leaped from the pool as if it were electrified, landing on the sharp rocks with my knees. "Owww!" I screamed again. The skin on my knees was scraped raw and bleeding, pink welts appeared around my calf and ankle, making it simultaneously numb and burn.

"What the hell was that?" I leaned over the pool to look for whatever had hurt me. Floating along, as if it didn't have a care in the world, was a small, translucent jellyfish. I exhaled with relief, remembering Dad's somewhat unscientific jellyfish advice, "*Violet, violent. Brown, frown. Blue, feeling blue. Clear, in the clear.*"

Bambi whined, her eyes slick and droopy with worry.

"It's okay, girl. It's just a stupid jellyfish," I reassured her.

I hopped on one leg, leaning on Bambi's back to balance myself. Just a short distance ahead, the tide pool ended. The only way to get past was to swim through deeper water and dive under a rock archway to get to the other side. But with the waves pushing and pulling in wide swells, the passage through the archway had to be timed just right. The risk of hitting our heads was real.

What now? It's too late to turn back. I hesitated because it wasn't only my safety I had to worry about. It was Bambi's, too. *Crap.* Swimming was definitely the better option, though. My leg was in no shape for a tedious hike.

Bambi sat poised at my feet, waiting for my decision. I closed my eyes and filled my mind with positive thoughts.

It's going to be okay. It'll be fine. Nothing bad is going to happen.

"Come, Bambi, let's go for a swim," I said, splashing the water with my hand.

We pushed off together. At first, the current was barely there, allowing us to make our way toward the archway—me doing a lopsided breaststroke, and Bambi dog-paddling. As we got closer and closer, something in the water shifted. A force pulled us the wrong way, sending chilly undercurrents below. The swells rolled higher, causing Bambi to drift farther away from me. "Bambi!" I kicked my legs hard and grabbed hold of her with the tips of my fingers. When I had a good grip, I positioned her body in front of my chest, between my arms.

Paddle, paddle. Push, push. Paddle. Push. I always kept the target in sight, compensating with my strokes when the swell pushed us back. About an arm's length away from the archway, I halted and gazed off to the side, trying to gauge the strength of the next wave.

Careful. Hold on. Wait. Go! I made one final push, hoping that we'd clear the archway before the next wave. But suddenly, a wall of water pummeled us from behind, propelling us toward the top of the archway. There was no time to think. I wrapped my arms around Bambi.

Duck!

Both of our bodies went underwater seconds before our heads smashed into the rock. Bambi struggled, but

I held on tight, counting to keep myself from freaking out. *One, two, three, four, five . . .*

Finally, a wave pushed us back to the surface. I sucked in air as we tumbled onto the beach. Bambi and I collapsed onto the wet sand, stunned and disoriented, spitting up salt water. I placed my arm around her and hugged her sideways.

"We made it," I whispered.

She panted and coughed up more seawater but managed to reply with a soggy wag. After a couple of minutes, I pushed myself off the sand and gazed up and down the beach. I spotted a familiar rock face on the other side of the expansive shoreline.

Thank god. From there, it was only a short walk back to camp.

THIRTY-THREE
Isa

MY ENTIRE WORK SHIFT AT THE BAKERY WAS A DAZE. When someone ordered a cappuccino, I handed them a flat white. When someone asked for soy milk in their coffee, I gave them a pitcher of regular skim milk. Whenever a customer tried to get my attention, it took a good couple of minutes for me to notice.

"Isabel! Gising ka na," Mom would say to me every time she noticed me zoning out. *Wake up!* Except I wasn't asleep. I was just pretending to be somewhere else in my mind. In the abandoned house with the imaginary family. On some far-flung tropical island with Coral, Uncle Jack, and Tita Alma. In Ada's room, watching another movie with a giant bowl of buttered popcorn.

So when my shift finally ended, I hightailed it out of there. But before heading back home, I needed to make one stop. I'd been meaning to do something for a while but kept forgetting.

I crossed the busy street and headed toward Main Street Stationery, which was pretty much an island institution. It was on the corner next to the town's ice-cream shop, Island Scoops. Weekenders and tourists loved going there and browsing for hours. To be honest, it was kind of a tourist trap, because you couldn't go there and buy just one thing. If you went in for a map, you'd end up with a bunch of magnets, T-shirts, books, and maybe even a bag of candy by the pound. The owner, Myrtle, who was probably in her nineties, had this knack for charming money out of people's wallets. For real. It was, like, a legit talent of hers.

Ding-dong! A couple of years back, Myrtle had an electric doorbell with a flashing light installed because she'd started to lose her hearing.

"Hey, Myrtle," I said as soon as I spotted her rearranging the magazine racks.

At first, she didn't hear or see me, but when she did, her freckles seemed to bounce off her wrinkly face. "Well, what a nice surprise seeing you in here, Isa! It's been too long," she said, reaching out to squeeze my hand.

My cheeks got all hot. It had been a while since I'd dropped in to see her. I mean, I'd meant to, but with everything that was happening with Coral, Uncle Jack, and Tita Alma, my to-do list sort of just fell through the cracks.

"I'm sorry. I've been busy . . . ," I mumbled.

"I know. I know. You kids, these days," she said with a shrug and a smile. "Speaking of kids. Where is that Star Sister of yours? I haven't seen her in ages!"

For a second, all I could do was stare at her silver

hair, at the bright blue veins at her temples, at the liver spots on her chest. I gasped, and then I coughed. I didn't want Myrtle to be embarrassed. Recently, she'd started to get kind of forgetful. Dad said it was her old age finally catching up with her. But I didn't want to make her feel bad. So I just grinned and pretended nothing was wrong.

"Um. She's out sailing, you know, with Uncle Jack."

"That's nice, dear." Myrtle nodded. "Oh, and speaking of nice, I just got a new shipment of those sour watermelon ropes you like," she said, nudging me toward the clear plastic candy bins. With a pair of metal tongs, she pulled out a piece of sugar-encrusted gummy rope and handed it to me.

"Thanks. But I'm actually here for some postcards." I took the candy from her because I wasn't about to waste a freebie, and then I scanned the jam-packed store, searching for the postcard stand.

For a moment, Myrtle seemed puzzled. "Postcards, you say?"

"Uh, yeah. I sort of have a pen pal. Like, you know, someone I'm writing to far away from here," I muttered, hoping she wouldn't interrogate me about my supposed "pen pal."

"Well, it's lovely that you kids still do some things the old-fashioned way. There's something so nice about opening your mailbox and getting a handwritten letter." She led me to the postcard stand in the corner of the store and whirled it around and around. "Take your pick!"

There were postcards with sunny beaches, sunsets at the marina, the ferry with seagulls hovering above, Main Street with its charming storefronts, the old lighthouse, and sailboats, lots and lots of sailboats. None of them were all that interesting. Pebble Island was small and boring and predictable. But it was home. And I had a feeling Coral was somewhere out there really missing home.

I took one of each postcard and handed the pile to Myrtle. "I'll take all of these."

"That must be some pen pal you've got there," said Myrtle, heading to the cash register. I guess twenty-five postcards was a lot. But it might be a while before Coral was rescued, and I didn't want her to miss out on anything.

I handed Myrtle the money, and then she handed me back my change. "Thanks, Myrtle."

"You are most welcome, my dear. And make sure you tell Coral to drop by sometime. I've got those chocolate-covered blueberries she likes so much," she said with a smile.

I froze. An image of Coral and me sitting out by the docks, tossing chocolate-covered blueberries into each other's mouths, flashed in my head, clear as day, as if she were there. I could even smell her favorite lavender soap.

"Uh. Um. It was nice seeing you, Myrtle," I mumbled, hurrying out of the store before I completely lost it.

When I got outside, I inhaled and exhaled several times. *In. Out. In. Out. Phew* . . . A group of people came out of Island Scoops, holding cones with pastel-colored ice cream and sprinkles. They were smiling and laughing as if they were having the best day ever. By the looks of it, they were family—the whole lot of them with coppery red hair, freckles, and pasty white skin. The two daughters, one around my age, the other a few years younger, were cracking up, licking their cones around and around to prevent them from dripping. After a minute, they switched cones so they could try the other one's flavor.

It was the kind of thing we used to do. Coral and me. The Star Sisters.

I felt the tears stinging my eyes.

The two girls glanced at me. When they saw I was crying, they quickly looked away as if my sadness could somehow infect them. I wiped away the wetness with the back of my hand. And then I shoved the brown paper bag with the postcards into my pocket before getting on my bike.

Don't look back, Isa.

But I couldn't help myself. I looked over my shoulder at the girls one more time. So carefree. So happy. So loved. I envied them.

I pushed off, pedaled, and kept on pedaling, even though my eyes had filled with tears again.

THIRTY-FOUR
Coral

MY TOES BURROWED IN THE SAND AS I LAZED UNDER the shade of a coconut tree. Nearby, Bambi was sprawled on her back with her legs jutting out. Her eyes studied me, watching my every move—the batting of my eyelashes, the wandering wisps of my hair, the shooing away of obnoxious flies with my hand. The only thing that could make the moment any better was if she could speak to me. Because I had a ton of nagging questions that needed answering.

Ever since our trek to the other side of the island, I couldn't stop thinking about the abandoned village. When I was bored, I would make up all sorts of scenarios in my head, some plausible, some bordering on ridiculous.

Did the villagers drop dead because of some mysterious tropical disease?

Did they move away to another place with more people on it?

Did they escape after a storm ravaged the island?

Hmmm . . . My guess was a storm. Small islands like this one were vulnerable to typhoons, tsunamis, and whatnot. Still, I couldn't help but wonder if that was the real reason. And how had they all gotten off? Did they have a bunch of canoes? A bigger boat? The constant barrage of thoughts was exhausting. Sometimes I wished I could just turn off that vivid part of my imagination. But overanalyzing was part of my nature. I would just have to deal with it.

Sigh. Why don't I just take a nap? My eyes fluttered. My thoughts became hazier. As my vision blurred, I caught a glimpse of Bambi. Her fur seemed to meld into the sand moments before I dozed off.

Then I was startled awake, my brow crumpled, sweat dripping down my temples, neck, and chest. This voice was whispering in my ear . . . *What if they come back?* My breath quickened. If someone did return, would I run into the jungle to hide? Would I fall to my knees with relief? But what if they weren't friendly? What if they saw me as some kind of threat?

I lifted my head off the sand, trying to think of something else. Anything to calm the chaos in my mind. The sunlight was beginning to mellow. All of a sudden, Bambi flipped over, tucking her tongue back into her mouth. She wagged her tail. Her eyes wandered to the nearby fishing net hanging from a tree.

"Is it time to fish?" I asked her, even though I knew that was what she was telling me.

Woof! Bambi led the way. I pulled the net from the tree branches, careful not to snag it. Then I bunched it around my shoulders while Bambi pranced round and round. Through trial and error, I'd figured out that the best time to fish was late in the afternoon—the golden hour, as Dad used to call it. As usual, he was right. It really was golden. The sun dipped lower on the horizon, creating a subtle orange shimmer on the sea.

We took the short walk to the spot on the shoreline where the sand turned into wet sludge. As soon as my feet touched the cool water, my footprints disappeared. With every step, the temperature turned just a bit cooler.

"Okay, wish me luck," I said to Bambi, who was pacing up and down the shoreline, watching me.

I reached over my shoulder, looping the line around my left wrist first and then gripping it. My arms flung wide. *Swish!* The net spread open in one fluid movement. I let it sink and settle. Hopefully, the fish would wander into my trap. I waited. My breath was on pause. A tingle radiated from the tips of my fingers up my arms. It was the tingle of anticipation. I felt a tug on the line. *Jackpot!* Before any of the fish had a chance to escape, I quickly dragged it back to the beach. But god, the resistance was strong. There must have been four, five, maybe even six fish.

As I got closer to shore, Bambi's pacing became even more frenzied. She had a knack for always knowing when the catch was a good one.

Woof! Woof!

Finally, my feet emerged from the water. I reeled the

rest of the net in. "C'mon . . . ," I muttered under my breath.

The trapped fish jerked and bounced, desperate for an escape. That was the moment that always killed me. When I slackened the net and caught sight of the bulging fish eyes pleading for their lives, I just couldn't help feeling bad for them.

"I'm sorry." What else could I say?

I let Bambi inspect our haul. She seemed pleased, sniffing the air like a fancy wine connoisseur. Once again, I gathered the net and flung it over my shoulder. Except, this time, fish bodies were wiggling and slapping my back as I walked.

"Come, girl, let's go make some dinner."

Back at my kitchen, I started with the messy task of cleaning the fish. There really was no way to sugarcoat it—the job stank. But I'd become an expert at dealing with all this crap. I was pretty sure I'd managed to earn a college degree in "crapola." Every new horrible experience thrown my way was just another aspect of survival.

"*Pfft. Survival-schmurvival*," were the precise words Isa would have uttered in such a situation.

So that's what I had to do: Deal with it and survive.

I scraped off as many of the fish scales as possible before piercing my knife into their guts and removing all the organs. Bambi always went zippy at the sight and smell. But I refused to let her eat any of the organs because one time I'd found a worm inside. So instead, I placed them into a coconut bowl and threw them back into the sea. Every time I did that, within seconds, the calm waters would become frenzied with fish of all shapes and sizes battling it out for the bloody guts.

By the time I was ready to start cooking, the fire was just right, crackling with deep orange coals. I pierced the fish with water-soaked cooking sticks and then leaned them over the weakest flames. A moment like that—with the aroma of cooking food wafting in the air, the perfect breeze, the sand trickling through my toes as Bambi curled up next to me—should have made me content.

But it didn't. I was still lonely for my family. For Mom and Dad. For Isa, my Star Sister. Would I ever see them again?

Awww. Awww . . . , Bambi whined as if she knew I was sad. I patted her on the neck and under her chin. "Is there anyone you miss, Bambi?" I asked her.

One of her ears stood, and she tilted her head. Poor thing must have had a human family in the past. It was obvious by how friendly she was, that she'd felt love and given love. I was sure of it.

"I'm sorry, girl. But we have each other now."

While the fish cooked, I took stuff out of the survival kit, making sure everything was clean, working, and in good order. Thankfully, it was all in tip-top shape. One by one, I put the items back into the waterproof bag, except the notebook and pen. I held them in my hand, flipping through the blank pages, clicking the metal tactical pen.

"So . . . *you're not going to forget to write to me, huh?*"

I heard Isa's voice loud and clear. The smell of cooking seafood, the bonfire, the sand on my feet. If I closed my eyes and tried really hard, I could take myself back to Pebble Island, to our lobster-clam bake on the beach.

I'd made Isa a promise. And we never broke our promises.

I opened my eyes, clicked the pen, and turned the notebook to the first page.

Dear Little Star,
Let me start off by reassuring you that I'm alive and well...Okay, maybe that's a bit of an exaggeration. I'm not well, well. But I'm more or less okay. After the boat went down, I washed up on a deserted island. I know, I know. Crazy, huh? I always thought that these kinds of things only ever happened in movies. But, nope. Here I am, stranded in the middle of nowhere, all by myself. Well, not totally alone. Would you believe it if I told you that I had a dog? Believe it! Her name is Bambi, and besides you, she's pretty much the best friend I've ever had. I really think you'd like her, and she'd like you. In fact, you're quite alike! Ha! Don't get mad!

I'm not comparing you to a female dog or anything. Um, well, actually I am. But not in the way you think. Wink, wink. Bambi is awesome. I'd probably be dead by now if it weren't for her.

I wonder what you're doing right now? Are you at work, making a billion and one cappuccinos? Are you restocking the pastry display? Are you eating some of your mom's day-old adobo on a giant mound of rice? Yummm...I'm not going to lie. I'd give anything for one of your cappuccinos, a fresh-out-of-the-oven chocolate croissant, and three or four servings of adobo with as much rice as I can stomach. When I get home, that's the first thing I want to eat. Oh, and a big bowl of chocolate-covered blueberries, too.

Anyway, I know it's probably pointless for me to tell you this, but try not to worry too much. You know Mom and Dad taught me all that wilderness stuff over the years. I'm going to be fine. I promise. And you know that we never break our promises.

Soon, Isa. Soon. We'll be together again. Okay?

Love you to the end of the universe and back, my Star Sister.

Take care,
Coral

Phew. I kept my promise. I tucked the notebook and pen back into the survival kit. For whatever reason, writing all those words exhausted me. I lay down and curled into the fetal position. *Sizzle, sizzle.* The fish was beginning to steam, and in a minute or two, it would be ready. But as hungry as I was, all I wanted was to go to sleep and dream. Dream of being rescued. Dream of seeing Mom and Dad and Isa and her parents again. Dream of Bambi coming home with me. Dream of croissants and adobo and freshly baked bread and pizza and ice cream and french fries with mayo and ketchup.

And for a second or two, that's what I did. I closed my eyes and dared to dream. Because dreams were pretty much the only hope I had left.

THIRTY-FIVE
Isa

HAAAAHHHH... DAD'S FRUSTRATED SIGH WAS THE
first thing I heard when I walked into my house. I peeked
into the living room and found him on the sofa bent over
his ancient laptop with the coffee table scooched too close
to his legs. His knees were bent at a ridiculous angle, so
they almost touched his chest.

"Dad?" I said to get his attention.

He flinched, as if he was surprised to see me. "Oh,
hey, honey."

"What are you doing?" I said, glaring at the clunky
laptop that he usually avoided like the plague.

He sighed again. "The question should be, what am
I *not* doing? Because I cannot figure this machine out."

I grinned, trying not to crack up, because Dad was
pretty much the only person I knew who called a computer a "machine." I walked over to the sofa and inserted
myself next to him. "Let me help. Move over."

Dad made room, shoving the laptop closer to me.

"I'm trying to download a file and open it up, but the machine just won't cooperate . . ."

In Dadspeak, "won't cooperate" basically meant he had no idea what the heck he was doing. He may have been an expert on fishing, boats, and anything sea-related, but when it came to technology, he was a hopeless klutz.

I began tapping away at the keyboard, accessing his email, downloading the files, and launching them with the correct software, which, of course, was completely out of date. After a couple of minutes, the files opened up, covering his screen with colorful map images.

"What are these?" I asked.

Dad was staring at the various lines and number configurations, transfixed. "They're images generated by a software called Search and Rescue Optimal Planning System. It simulates a drift trajectory of lost objects, in this case, Uncle Jack's sailboat."

The numbers and symbols on the screen may as well have been hieroglyphics. None of it made sense to me. "But, like, how do they know where to start looking?"

"They start the trajectory from the last known point of origin. Then they factor in currents, wind, and weather and come up with all the possible scenarios," he explained, pointing his finger at a red dot. "Right here is where Uncle Jack checked in last."

I stared at the red dot so hard my eyeballs felt as if

they were going to pop out of their sockets. "And this is supposed to work?"

Dad leaned back, collapsing onto the backrest. "Well, ideally . . . But with over ten thousand trajectories, and other numerous factors, it's sort of like finding a needle in a haystack."

Suddenly, I understood why Dad was so frustrated. I stood, abruptly, almost knocking the laptop off the table. "Uh. Sorry. I—I have some stuff I have to do."

Dad nodded. Something about the way his eyes looked told me that he understood me, too. "Thanks for your help, honey."

I backed out and ran up the stairs fast, hoping I made it to my bedroom before I totally lost it. Once the door was closed, I leaned up against it, hyperventilating.

Like a needle in a haystack.

It was a stupid metaphor. I mean, who the hell would ever lose a needle in a haystack. *Stupid. Stupid. Stupid.* But as angry and frustrated as I was, the tears just wouldn't come out. Was it possible to run out of tears?

I leaned back even harder, forcing myself to calm down. That's when I felt the lump in my back pocket. The postcards. I reached in and pulled them out. The brown paper bag was crinkly and moist, but the postcards inside were fine—stiff and glossy and ready to be written on.

I went over to my desk, swept aside the piles of magazines and catalogs and rando junk, and sat. With my hand, I spread out the postcards as if they were a deck of cards and stared at each one. Of all of them, the one that stood out the most was the landscape of Sea Glass Point and the surrounding cove, with the lighthouse jutting toward the sky, which was the exact color of an orange Creamsicle.

It was *the* lighthouse. The one Coral had almost killed herself in when we were kids. Mom had banned us from exploring that part of the island because she said it was dangerous. But of course, we never listened.

"*Pfft. Dangerous-schmangerous,*" I'd say whenever Coral reminded me.

I was around nine or ten that fateful day when we decided to disobey Mom, once again. We walked down the long dirt road and across seemingly endless grassy dunes until we reached the crumbling lighthouse, which was probably glorious in its heyday. But now, all that was left was a structure covered in peeling red and white paint, rusted railings, and shattered glass panes. Discarded liquor bottles, cigarette butts, and odd clothing items were scattered around. It was a place forbidden by most of the island's parents, which meant that kids would go there as often as possible to search for treasure, to play pirate games, or to see if they could spy on teenagers smoking or messing around. What we never, *ever* dared to do was climb up the rickety spiral stairs, for fear that the whole thing would just collapse on us.

The night before, at our after-dinner bonfire, Uncle Jack had told us about Sir Edmund Hillary and Sherpa Tenzing Norgay, the first people to reach the summit of

Mount Everest. Something about that story got Coral all riled up.

"*Tomorrow, we're going on our own adventure*," she'd said to me with a glimmer in her eye.

As soon as we got to the lighthouse, we ran around screaming like banshees. Coral jumped on a half-collapsed wall and proclaimed, "*This kingdom is mine. I shall climb to the highest peak and plant the Bituin-Rousseau flag!*"

I glared at her disapprovingly. "*Coral, it's one thing coming out here to play . . . But you better not be thinking about climbing to the top! If something happens to you, my mom is going to kill me.*"

Coral brushed off my comment. "*Oh, c'mon, Isa. You worry too much*," she said, skipping toward the dark and dusty entrance.

My cheeks twitched, because more than anything, I wanted to blurt out another warning. But I knew Coral wouldn't listen. When she had her mind set on something, there was nothing I could do to change it. I was the one who was always afraid, even though I tried to act cool. It was all my mom's fault. Her paranoia had rubbed off on me. I mean, clearly, I couldn't get the Ebola virus from a paper cut. But by the way Mom acted, anything was possible. If she could, she would have permanently cushioned me with two layers of bubble wrap and slapped a gazillion FRAGILE stickers on me.

But before I could say or not say anything, Coral

skipped inside. "*See you at the top!*" her voice echoed from the darkness.

After a few seconds, I followed her in, because the least I could do was keep an eye on her. The interior of the lighthouse was a few degrees cooler. Here and there, the sunrays gleamed through holes and cracks, forming a web of sunlight that showcased a dense layer of floating dust.

I looked up and counted eight rotations to the top. The railing was rusty and covered in filth, and standing there with a solid grip on it was Coral. "*It's all good,*" she yelled at me.

"*You better get down from there!*" I yelled back.

Coral waved, pretending she didn't hear me. Then she climbed even higher, skipping over the broken steps until she was about halfway up. Every time she moved, there was a creak or a thud or a squeak that pulled at my insides. I was afraid—afraid for her *and* afraid that I'd get in trouble.

"*Coral, c'mon. Can you just get down from there already?*" I begged her.

But all she did was smile and climb higher. Just when she was about to complete the sixth rotation, a loud cracking sound cut through the silence. I felt my heart drop. "*Coral!*"

A step had collapsed under her feet. She fell, for a moment looking weightless. Then, *boom!* Both of her legs got jammed in the hole where the step had been. I was stunned, frozen.

"*Isa, help!*" she screamed, her hands gripping the side railing so her body wouldn't slip through. "*Isa, please help me! I don't think I can hold on for too long!*"

That's when I snapped out of it. "*I'm coming, Coral!*" I said, scrambling up the stairs with my heart pounding in my chest. It was all just so fast. A blur. But I managed to reach her without cracking my skull open.

I jammed my hands underneath her armpits and pulled, huffing and puffing, until, finally, she was safe. "*I've got you. I've got you . . . ,*" I mumbled over and over.

For a long while, we held on to each other. It wasn't until I smelled the coppery scent of blood that I realized Coral was hurt. From her ankles to her knees, bits of skin were ripped off, blood weeping out of every single cut and scrape. "*We better go back home,*" I said, swallowing the lump of fear in my throat.

I'm toast. Mom is going to kill me for sure.

We descended the stairs together. By the time we reached outside, the shock was beginning to wear off. My legs were still wobbly. But at least my heartbeat was back to normal.

"*Let's go,*" I said, somehow managing to half-carry Coral, who was double the height of me.

As we made our way home, with our dusty hands and

arms and shoulders intertwined, only one thought stuck out in my mind.

Coral could have died. But she didn't.

And this time, she would make it back home, too. I was sure of it.

I flipped the postcard over and began scribbling fast.

Dear Big Star,

I know you're out there, somewhere, just like one of those constellations you love so much. Nerd. Lol. Anyway, I figured, maybe for now, we can just write to each other until they find you. I'm sure you'll have lots to tell me. I mean, getting lost at sea is pretty epic. Even for you. And, well, on my end, everything is just as boring as usual, except the part about you and your mom and dad. Don't you worry, they are going to find you. Wherever you are, don't lose hope. Because Dad is practically living in two time zones. Every single day he's talking to, like, a gazillion people, diplomats, government officials, the Indonesian Coast Guard, scientists, you name it, he's doing it. So just hang in there, okay? Just remember that day you almost got yourself killed at the lighthouse. Remember? Even after you got hurt, you just brushed it off like no biggie. Well, this is going to be one of those times. You're going to be just fine. And one day, we're going to be sitting out on the docks throwing chocolate-covered blueberries into each other's mouths while laughing about this whole thing. I'm here waiting for you. Don't ever forget that.

Love you to the stars and back,

Isa

I straightened up and stared down at my chicken scratch. Then I ran the tips of my fingers across every single letter. *Coral, wherever you are . . .* I lifted the postcard up in front of my face and blew on the words as if I were blowing on a dandelion. *Wherever you are, I hope you can read this . . .*

THIRTY-SIX
Coral

MY ONLY CLOTHES WERE DRYING UNDER THE SUN. Until they were dry, I'd have to walk around in my birthday suit. When I was a little kid, I loved running around butt naked. But on the island, it was a painful reminder that I was withering away. Every part of me was ravaged by the sun, the wind, and the salt water. My once long, soft hair hung down my back like clumps of straw. Both my hands and my feet were calloused, blistered, and scarred from the rocks and sharp corals. I didn't even know it was possible to be this sunburned. My skin was charred beyond recognition. Even my body was just a frame of what it used to be, I was so skinny.

It wasn't only me withering away, either. The fabric of my T-shirt was practically see-through, worn in parts where my skin had rubbed against it too many times. Every day there was a new hole; threads kept on unraveling as time passed. The sewing kit I had was pretty much useless, because when it came to sewing, I was hopeless. My stitches were sloppy and weak. Whatever I did was just a quick fix.

I leaned back and stared at the entrance of my cave. The sunlight grew brighter and brighter, its rays stubborn, penetrating the blackest of shadows. I held up my hand to the light; my fingers were thin like twigs. The way my body was deteriorating made me wonder how the mysterious villagers managed to survive on this island.

I thought about what life must have been like for them. Their days probably started at the crack of dawn. Huts were cleaned while a simple breakfast of fish or meat was prepared. Children frolicked outside; nature was both their school and playground. Maybe Bambi even joined in, racing the kids down the beach, nipping at their heels while they laughed. Hunting and fishing were a way of life. The shoreline and jungle were their version of supermarket shelves. *God, what I'd give to be able to walk into the IGA supermarket . . .*

When I finally shuffled out of my cave, I felt kind of antsy, but I couldn't figure out why. I stretched out on the ledge. In front of me, the sea shimmered from the brightening sun. Like clockwork, Bambi meandered up the incline with a big bird hanging from her mouth, its head and neck almost drooping to the ground. I patted her on the scruff as she placed the day's catch at my feet.

"Nice, Bambi! This one's nice and meaty!" I said in a high-pitched voice.

She wriggled her butt, overjoyed by my praise. I bent down and studied the bird's unusually long neck and fine white feathers. It looked like a species of heron. Strange, because I'd never seen one like it on the island before. So much time had passed, maybe there was a migratory cycle I wasn't aware of. Perhaps a new flock of birds had arrived from some faraway place to seek refuge. They were castaways, too. But by choice. If only I could grow some wings and fly away whenever I wanted.

Wishful thinking.

Bambi licked my shins and whined.

"Okay. Okay. I'm going," I said, retrieving the bird so I could take it to my beachfront kitchen. I trudged down the incline toward the shoreline. The morning breeze swept the bird feathers into the air as I plucked them, reminding me of winter's first fluffy snowflakes. I shivered, not because it was cold or anything, but because, for the first time since being marooned, I realized that eventually I'd have to learn how to hunt. I couldn't just rely on fishing and the meat that Bambi provided. If I was going to survive, I'd have to work harder, do more, *be* more.

Back home, I used to think hunters were just a bunch of gun-toting dudes. But on the island, it was different. Hunting and fishing were about my survival.

I pushed the thoughts aside so I could finish my dirty work. I lit the fire, stoking its flames till they crackled and roared. It was ready. I slid the bird carcass onto a stick and lay it over the heat. Almost immediately, it sizzled, releasing a heavenly aroma.

But Bambi was too preoccupied to even notice. She was on the beach poking her nose at an irate hermit crab, not to hunt, but to play around. Like a little kid chasing an overexcited kitten. It had become a daily habit, watching her entertain herself with crabs and butterflies and her favorite sticks and makeshift balls. Yet all this time, I had yet to see her hunt at night.

Hmmm. How come I'd never gone hunting with Bambi before? I mean, she was a great huntress. There wasn't a day when she didn't come back with something. I should've been learning to hunt. And she was the only teacher I had on the island.

My mind was a jumble of ideas, but through it all, I could hear Dad loud and clear. "*Coral, you can do anything. I believe in you.*"

"Thanks, Dad . . . ," I said under my breath.

That night, I'd hunt.

What would I do if Bambi got hurt? If she couldn't go out and bring us fresh meat? Could I really survive on my own without her by my side? I really didn't want to think about that possibility. Because in a short time, I'd come to love her. Bambi wasn't just any dog. She was my friend, my family, my guardian angel.

Tears stung my eyes. I blinked fast, trying to make the wetness retreat. Just the thought of losing Bambi made my gut ache. *I'm not going to lose her* . . . I shook my head, trying to fling the thoughts from my mind. But I couldn't stop thinking.

While I carved up the cooked bird, I planned our hunting expedition in my head. I would need: my flashlight, my knife, water, and my first aid kit. I considered taking my poncho for protection against bugs but decided against it. The noisy rubber might scare off potential prey.

The excitement inside me bubbled. It was that same giddiness I used to get whenever Mom and Dad promised me a new adventure, something I'd never done before, an opportunity to learn, to be inspired all over again.

It made me feel alive.

THIRTY-SEVEN
Isa

"ISABEL..."

I snapped my back upright. Mom had caught me slouching *again*. I didn't really know what she had against slouching, but every time she caught me doing it, she acted as if I were decapitating a teddy bear or something.

"Sorry," I muttered under my breath.

Mom widened her eyes and pursed her lips real tight. "Anak, if you're not careful, you're going to ruin your posture for good."

I exhaled. Because what she really meant was that if I kept on slouching, I'd end up even shorter than I already was. Short and squat and chunky were no-nos in her book. I mean, she herself was short, but the way she stood, as if she was the most confident person on earth, made her seem six feet tall.

But I wasn't about to argue with her. So I imagined that I was as stiff and straight as a pencil, rearranging coffee cups to make myself look busy. For a second, Mom watched me. But after a moment, she waltzed off to the back of the store, presumably to boss around some other unsuspecting employee.

"Hey, Isa!"

I whipped my head around, and there was Ada in one of her getups—a black calf-length dress with flowy sleeves, a giant red bow headband, red ballet flats, and an orange messenger bag. Resting around her neck was one of those black cat Beanie Babies, and in her grasp was a small, twiggy broom.

Oh-kay . . .

"Hey," I said with an awkward wave and wide eyes.

Ada grinned and held up her broom. "Kiki's Delivery at your service!"

"Uhhh . . ."

"Ooops. I forgot. You really have no idea, do you?" she said.

I shrugged. "Sorry."

"No worries. We can watch that one next." Ada placed both of her hands flat on the counter and leaned toward me with a dead serious look on her face. "But right now, I'm on a mission, and I need your help."

"*My* help?" I said with a frown.

"Yes, *your* help."

I glanced at the clock. In fifteen minutes, my shift would be over. But I wasn't a hundred percent sure I wanted to help Ada with whatever she wanted me to help her with.

"Um . . . help with what?" I asked.

Ada's shoulders slumped. "My mom took the ferry over to the nearest IKEA to buy some house stuff, and she put me in charge of grocery shopping . . . One, I don't have a bike yet, and two, the last time I walked into the IGA, everyone stared at me like I was a serial killer or something."

I laughed, and then I covered my mouth with my hand to stop myself from cracking up even louder. "I-I'm sorry. It's just people around here aren't really used to your, um, you know . . . your kind of fashion sense."

"Humph." Ada crossed her arms over her chest, her thick and dark eyebrows connecting like one long, hairy caterpillar. "Well? Will you come with me or not?"

I glanced at the clock one more time and then at the back of the store where Mom was. "Sure. Meet me outside in ten," I said.

"Great!" Ada practically jumped with excitement. She ran out the door, past the side of the building, and up the stairs to her apartment.

Thud. Thud. Thud. Her feet were heavy. I could hear her steps echoing through the deli's ceiling. I couldn't help but wish those footsteps belonged to Coral, instead. The guilt immediately crept up my chest into my throat. I coughed. None of what had happened was Ada's fault. Of course it wasn't.

I should be a better friend . . .

I swallowed hard. The pain. The sadness. The guilt. Why did it have to feel like I was betraying Coral?

✳ ✳ ✳

The IGA was the typical small-town supermarket. From the outside, it still looked like it belonged in the 1970s, with its beige and wood cladding and retro signage. Inside, it was a combo of basic grocery items and gourmet-ish foodstuff, with a sprinkling of gluten-free and vegan choices for weekenders. The people who worked there were, for the most part, locals—teenagers and really old folks who needed part-time jobs.

As soon as we walked in, heads turned. Numerous sets of eyeballs gave Ada the once-over. But I just tried to ignore the jerks, hoping she wouldn't notice. "So, do you have a grocery list?" I asked.

"Yup!" Ada fumbled with her messenger bag, rifling through her wallet until she found it. She handed me a semicrumpled and moist neon pink Post-it Note.

I scanned the list. Most of it was just the regular, garden-variety grocery kinds of things, like orange juice, toilet paper, and mayonnaise. But closer to the bottom were a handful of things we would never find there in a billion years.

"Lumpia wrappers, annatto seeds, glutinous rice flour, champorado mix . . . ," I read them out loud, pausing to frown at her.

Ada cringed. "Too weird?"

"Yup. Too weird for *this* place." I grabbed a shopping cart and motioned for her to follow me. "Let's just get the basics. I'll take you and your mom to the Asian Market in Riverhead on my day off . . ."

For a second, I wanted to let go of the cart and stuff my shoe into my mouth. What was I thinking inviting myself to show them around? Now Ada would for sure think that I wanted to be her new bestie or something. And that was the last thing I wanted. Because I was pretty sure I'd disappoint her.

We wandered up and down the aisles.

Soy milk: *Check!*

Granola: *Check!*

Sliced whole wheat bread: *Check!*

Next on the list was sliced turkey cold cuts. We approached the deli section. I tore off a number and flagged down the dude behind the counter, whose name was Nick or Rick or something like that. He was a local kid home from college for the summer. Underneath his blue apron he had on a SUNY T-shirt and jeans. His dirty blond hair was overgrown and shaggy, as if he was trying to hide the spattering of zits on his face.

"Yeah?" he said with an impatient scowl.

Ada smiled. "Hi, can I get a quarter pound of sliced turkey cut thin, please?"

"Thin?"

"Yes, thin like iceberg lettuce thin."

The dude proceeded to slice the hunk of turkey. One slice. Two slices. He held up a slice and glanced at Ada. "This thin enough for you?"

Ada tiptoed higher so she could see better. She frowned and said, "Uh. Could you make it a bit thinner, please?"

He exhaled loudly as if he was annoyed. Then he adjusted the machine and made another slice. "This good?" He held up another slice.

I looked over at Ada, who had this pained expression on her face, jaw stiff, eyebrows all wriggly, cheeks hot pink. "It's just that my mom likes it *really* thin," she said in a somewhat squeaky voice.

He exhaled and rolled his eyes dramatically. "*Huh*. I didn't know that bi—I mean, witches—were so picky about their turkey . . . ," he muttered under his breath.

He wasn't even talking to me, yet my face burned with anger. I pushed my chest out and slammed the glass counter with my hand. "What did you just say?" I spat out.

"Nothing." He avoided my gaze, instead slicing the turkey real thin and then wrapping it up in white deli paper.

"Yeah. That's what I thought."

Ada side-eyed me. But she stayed quiet and waited. When the dude slammed the package of sliced turkey on the counter, he made a point of turning his back to us. But I wasn't having any of that attitude.

"She's my cousin. Don't mess with her again." I swiped the turkey, shoved it into the shopping cart, and stomped off.

Ada scrambled to catch up with me. "Thanks," she said softly.

"Don't worry about it," I said, swatting the air like no biggie. "C'mon, let's hurry so we can get out of this dump."

I mean, truthfully, I wanted to have nothing to do with Ada and her mom. But they were family. And nobody messed with *my* family.

THIRTY-EIGHT
Coral

THAT NIGHT I SLEPT ON THE BEACH. BAMBI WAS curled up beside me, snoring softly, her legs twitching as if she was chasing something in her dreams. I tossed and turned. In the sky, the stars were like millions of pyrite fragments reflecting the moonlight.

It wasn't until the darkness began to shift from black to blue that Bambi woke up with a start, her upturned ears a signal that it was time to go. I pushed myself up onto my elbows and rubbed the blurriness out of my eyes. It took a good minute or two of squinting to get my night vision in focus.

"Ugh. I'd kill for a cappuccino right about now," I mumbled.

Bambi gave me the once-over, surprised to see me awake. I reached over and scratched her on the neck, that sweet spot below her chin that sometimes made her leg jerk involuntarily. Her tail slapped the sand, as if she was confused and excited.

"What? You think I'm going to let you have all the

fun? C'mon, let's see if you can teach this girl some new tricks." I stood and brushed the sand off my shorts. I gathered my supplies, pulling the flashlight out before slinging the survival kit over my shoulder.

As usual, Bambi led the way. Her stride was quiet, and her head low. I tried to be as stealthy as possible—short, silent steps, the flashlight used only in the darkest of shadows. There was something completely terrifying about wandering into the jungle in the dead of night. Everything that was lush, green, and vibrant in the daytime transformed into the eerie unknown. Noises snapped and crackled from time to time. The deeper we went, the more claustrophobic I started to feel. Things seemed to close in on me. The darkness, the sounds, the unknown, screwing with my head.

Finally, we reached a small clearing. The moonlight penetrated through the trees, so it was bright enough to see without the flashlight. At the edge of the clearing, Bambi looked over her shoulder at me and wagged her tail—it was her way of telling me to follow. She knelt and crawled on her haunches toward a thicket of small trees and ferns.

Okay, girl. I'll do what you do. I nodded and crouched down on all fours so I could squirm my way into the bushes. From what I gathered, we were supposed to hide, to camouflage ourselves and wait. And that was exactly what we did. Wait. And wait. And wait some more. It was a true test of patience. Any little movement or sound could make or break us. My breaths became shallower. Every limb and muscle went limp. We stayed that way for god knows how long.

Finally, after what seemed like hours, I spotted something. It was barely a movement, more like a twitch between two mossy rocks. But then I saw it again. An enormous rodent scurried from one side of the clearing to the other.

I shifted my eyes, studying Bambi as she stalked the rat with her gaze. She was like a sniper zeroing in on her target. The minutes were long and torturous. But just when I thought it would never end. *Bam!* The moment we were waiting for.

The rodent darted to the middle of the clearing. Its nose sniffed the air as if it had caught a whiff of us. *Crap. What if it runs off?* I scooted closer to Bambi, anxious for her next move. There was this glint in her eyes. Her chest and neck and haunches tensed as she readied herself. Even though I knew what was coming, I flinched. She leaped out of the bushes as gracefully as a cheetah, running so fast that it seemed as if she were hovering over the ground.

Growl! Snap! Bark! Shriek! I wasn't prepared for the rapid onslaught of violence echoing into the silent night.

I gripped my knife tight, knuckles pale. I had no idea what I was getting into, but I jumped into the clearing anyway. Through the blur of the scuffle, I saw Bambi take one last ferocious bite. *Chomp*, she bit down hard on the rodent's neck. And then she dropped it on the ground. Dead.

"Whoo-h—" I was about to cheer and do a victory dance when something strange happened.

Growl . . . Bambi stared right at me, her stance on attack mode. I took a step back, confused.

"What's the matter, girl?" I said.

But for whatever reason, she seemed even more agitated, snarling and frothing at the mouth. She took one low-lying step and bared her fangs. Panic seized me. My muscles twitched, but I was frozen in place.

Before I could figure out what was going on, Bambi charged at me. "Bambi!" I screamed, ducking to the side and landing on the ground. There was a buzz in my ears. Then silence.

I spun around, my cheek scraping the ground. Finally, I spotted her. She was cowering, tail between her legs. A vile-looking snake loomed over her, hissing as if it was getting ready to strike.

"No!" I screamed again.

Without hesitation, I leaped forward and stomped my bare foot on the snake's tail. I sliced it in half with my knife and let out a satisfied grunt. Stab. Stab. Stab. I kept on attacking it until all that was left was a scaly mess of flesh, blood, and bone. *Thump-thump. Thump-thump.* My heart was beating uncontrollably. Bambi whined.

Oh no. Oh no . . .

I knelt over her, pumping the flashlight, searching for

wounds. *Crap*. There were two clean bite marks where her front leg met her chest. The holes were deep and already swollen, almost pulsating to the touch.

"Nooo!" I shouted.

What was I supposed to do? If that snake was venomous, she'd be gone within hours. If not, she might die anyway. Because in a place like this, an infection could be just as deadly. The pain inside me was unbearable. My heart squeezed tight, guts twisting around until it felt as if I were being strangled from within.

Breathe. I bent over to stroke Bambi's scruff. "You're going to be okay, girl. I promise . . ." My words lingered as I tried to convince myself that what I was saying was true.

THIRTY-NINE
Isa

THE NEXT DAY I GOT UP AT THE CRACK OF DAWN.
Earlier actually, since it was technically still dark outside.
I wanted to spend some time at the abandoned house
before work. But when I went to the kitchen to make some
coffee, Mom was there cooking something that smelled
supergingery.

"Oh. You're still here." I halted by the doorway, surprised.

Mom frowned. "Don't sound so disappointed."

"No. I mean, it's just that you're usually at the bakery
by now," I said, feeling my cheeks get warm.

"I know." Mom stuck a spoon into the pot she was
stirring and tasted what looked like soup. "I'm making
some lugaw for Ada."

I went closer to the stove and peeked into the pot.
"For Ada? Why?"

"Tita Jo messaged me last night that Ada was feeling
under the weather. I thought I'd bring over some lugaw . . .
You know it cures everything, right?" Mom smiled, and

then she covered the pot. "Give it another five minutes and then you can put some in a big thermos and take it over to her? I've got to run. Emmet is waiting for me." She took off her apron and hurried away.

Huh. Weird. Ada seemed fine when we went to the store yesterday. She didn't look even a bit sick. Maybe it was just one of those mysterious twenty-four-hour bugs or something. Yeah, that was probably it. I shrugged it off and proceeded to make my coffee while the lugaw finished cooking.

Once I was properly caffeinated, I filled our largest thermos with as much lugaw as it could hold and took off. It wasn't even seven yet, and it was already oppressively humid. It didn't help that I had the piping hot thermos of the rice porridge in my backpack, which radiated heat. Sweat dribbled down my neck, face, chest, even the backs of my legs. At least I'd worn shorts. And thank god I always packed an extra T-shirt; otherwise, I'd reek of BO the rest of the day, which wasn't exactly ideal when you were trying to sell coffee and yummy pastries to customers.

Finally, I rounded the corner and turned left onto Main Street. It was still pretty desolate, other than a couple of shopkeepers opening their stores. As much as I wasn't an early-morning person, I loved how peaceful it was in town when there weren't any tourists around.

Cring! Cring! I rang my bell at Jean, the owner of the hardware store, who was cleaning her storefront with a spray bottle of glass cleaner and a squeegee. "Good morning, Isa!" she said with a wave.

I pulled into the parking lot by the bakery and left my bike where I usually did. Then I climbed the stairway to Ada's apartment and rang the doorbell. I waited. But nobody answered. So I rang the doorbell again. Still, nothing. *Strange.* I reached out and turned the doorknob. The door opened. "Hello?" I said softly, taking a couple of tentative steps inside. "Anyone home?"

I peeked into the kitchen and living room. The room was empty. "Hello?" I repeated a bit louder.

"In here!" It was Ada's voice, but she sounded weak and kind of hoarse.

I followed her voice to her bedroom and knocked on the door. "Ada?"

"Yeah. Come in," she said.

I went inside. It was kind of dark and gray, but a bit of sunlight shone through the semisheer curtains. Ada was in bed. She blinked as if the light was painful for her eyes. "Don't worry; I'm not dying or anything," she said, pushing herself up to a sitting position.

I took the backpack off and retrieved the thermos from inside. "I brought you some of my mom's lugaw. It's still hot," I said, placing it on her bedside table.

"Thanks. Have a seat." She moved her legs aside and made room for me.

I sat on the bed, trying not to stare too much.

The Ada sitting in bed was nothing like the Ada

from the day before. She was sweaty—so sweaty that her T-shirt was sticking to her. And her skin was pale, her eyelids looked kind of swollen and bulging, and her lips were dry and cracked. Something about her looked weak, too, as if her muscles were just hanging limp from her bones.

"Are—are you sure you're okay?" I asked.

She took a raspy breath and nodded. "Yeah. It looks worse than it is. I have an autoimmune disease called Graves'. It affects my thyroid. Sometimes I forget to take my meds, and if I exert myself too much in the heat, my body will sort of crash for a few days. I just need to rest and hydrate, and I'll be good as new," she said with a weak smile.

I frowned. "Are you sure? Because Graves' disease sounds, I dunno . . . It sounds kind of serious."

"It can be. But I promise I'm fine. I've been taking meds for over a year now. The heat can just zap all the energy out of me. That's all."

I nodded. And then we sort of just sat there for a moment, me staring at the paisley pattern on her quilt, she wringing her hands nervously. I glanced at her again. I mean, I guess she didn't really look like she was dying or anything.

"I swear. It's not terminal, and I'm not going to drop dead at the end of the summer," Ada blurted out.

It was as if she were reading my mind or something. "Good. I'm glad," I said, relaxing my shoulders and exhaling. "You need anything? Water? Juice? I can set up your laptop for you if you're bored."

"No. It's okay. Watching something will just make my eyes more tired. They're kind of sensitive to light sometimes. But I could use a water refill, if you don't mind," she said, gesturing at the empty glass on her nightstand.

"Sure. No prob." I took the glass into the kitchen and refilled it from the pitcher in the fridge.

When I got back to her room, she had one of those pill organizers opened on her lap. I gawked at all the pills inside. "That's *a lot.*"

She chuckled. "It is. But they're mostly supplements. It's only this one and this one that are actual medicines," she said, holding up a tiny white-and-pink pill. "This one is to prevent my thyroid from producing too much hormone, and this one helps my heart calm down since it tends to beat too fast when my levels are off."

"Got it." I refilled her glass and handed it to her.

I didn't want to sit there and watch her swallow dozens of pills. Something about seeing all that medicine, and seeing her look so sickly all of a sudden, made me anxious even though she said she wasn't going to drop dead of anything. Was she downplaying her illness? Was it more serious than she was leading me to believe?

"Uh. I have to go to work now. But I'll come by and check on you on my lunch break. Okay?" I said.

Ada smiled. "Yeah. Sure. That would be nice."

"Cool. Later 'gator," I said, leaving her room with a wave.

As soon as I got outside her front door, I whipped out my phone and googled "Graves' disease." My heart was beating like crazy. I scrolled through the results. *Thump-thump. Thump-thump.* I clicked on the WebMD page and read as fast as I could.

Once the Graves' disease has been correctly diagnosed, it is quite easy to treat. In some cases, Graves' disease goes into remission or disappears completely after several months or years.

Oh, thank god, thank god, thank god. I was so relieved. If I lost someone else . . . *no. I don't even want to think about it.*

All that mattered was that Ada was going to be okay.

FORTY
Coral

I CARRIED BAMBI BACK TO THE CAVE, CRADLING her in my arms like a baby.

Don't die. Please don't die, I repeated frantically in my head.

There was no way for me to know if the snake was venomous. No magic X-ray for me to see if poison coursed through her veins. The only thing I could do was make her as comfortable as possible. To ease her pain with whatever I could find in my first aid kit.

I fumbled with medicines, ointments, and bandages. With a cotton ball, I swabbed her bites with iodine, and then I applied antibiotic cream, wrapping the wounds when I was done.

Bambi whined softly, her tail wag temporarily subdued. I studied several packages of medicine, some with familiar names, others not so much. I popped one of the capsules out of its package labeled "antibiotics" and slid it into a piece of meat. When I offered it to Bambi, all she did was sniff it, uninterested. But with a little coaxing, she obliged. She gazed at me with sad puppy dog eyes, and then she chewed and swallowed.

Now all I could do was wait and see.

Seconds, minutes, hours passed. I was glued to Bambi's side. With every twitch, every whine, I freaked out. Just the sight of her feverish and trembling body made me nauseated. My stomach twisted and turned in knots. So much so that, after a while, I ran out to the ledge and puked my guts out.

A day later, she was still alive. *Still* being the key word. She was in bad shape—weak, her skin hot to the touch. I had to force her to eat and drink. It became even more challenging to get her to swallow her meds. All I could do was encourage her with gentle pats on the scruff. "Bambi, you have to eat this; it'll help. I promise you'll feel better soon."

All she did was whine weakly.

It didn't work. So I was forced to stick my fingers into the corner of her mouth, jamming the medicine-laced meat down her throat until she gulped it down. I hated myself for doing it. Whenever she gagged, it was as if I were gagging, too. I was suffocated by the uncertainty.

Will she live? Will she die? Will she live? Will she die?

The only times I left the cave were to catch fish or fetch water. Otherwise, I was trapped inside—trapped by the fear of losing the only thing that made my existence on the island bearable. Bambi was my lifeline, and if she died, I might die, too. Maybe not right away, but eventually, my mind and body would wither away like a dying star.

The next forty-eight hours, Bambi went in and out of consciousness, trembling hot, cold, and everything in between. When I wasn't tending to her wounds or trying to force-feed her, I lay down beside her. Maybe my heat, my life force, would somehow seep from my body to hers.

But as hard as I tried, nothing happened. Bambi's eyelids twitched. It was almost as if she was comatose or something.

I blew on her face, gently, reminding her that I was still here. "Bambi, don't leave me," I whispered.

She didn't reply, though.

I didn't know what else to do. Exhaustion took over. So I closed my eyes, hoping, praying that when I woke up, some sort of miracle had happened.

✳ ✳ ✳

Sweat dribbled down my face. I forced my eyelids open. There was an empty space next to me. Bambi was gone. I sat up, my heart beating wildly in my chest.

"Bambi?" I called out.

Then I saw something. By the entrance of the cave. A ghost. A mirage. No. It was Bambi. Her tail wagged limply as she walked toward me.

"Oh, girl. You—you look better . . . You're okay!" I exclaimed.

All I could do was cry. Teardrops pooled in my eyes, making everything blurry. Bambi stuck her muzzle into the crook of my neck, not minding the tears dropping onto her fur. I wrapped one arm around her, leaning my chin on her scruff. An overwhelming relief filled my heart.

"Bambi, you're okay. You're *really* okay," I said over and over again.

After a long embrace, Bambi lay back down. I could tell she was still weak. Clearly, she wasn't back to her old self yet. I placed a bowl of water in front of her, and she lapped it up. As much as I wanted to stay with her, I had things to do. I needed to be strong for Bambi so I could take care of her.

I tiptoed outside. Dawn was like a somber curtain, pulling apart to reveal the promise of sunlight. I stretched my sore muscles and then went to the beach. The bonfire needed reigniting. So I got down to it, preparing my tools, adding more wood and pieces of kindling. Within minutes, the golden flames seemed to meld with the sky—streaks of orange and pink and blue welcomed the rising sun.

It was beautiful. But as tempting as it was to just stand there and watch the colors change, watch the sea shimmer to life, there was a dull ache in my hollow stomach. Hunger pulled at my sides, reminding me that I'd forgotten to eat. Foraging in the tide pools would have to do for now. I was still too exhausted for anything else.

So I walked toward the shoreline. At the perimeter

of the tide pools, my feet prickled, sharp pieces of rock scraped bits of dried skin from my calloused soles. I stretched my limbs again, trying to smooth out the cramps and kinks, loosening my tense muscles by reaching for the clouds.

But then something caught my eye—a sparkle in the sea. Whatever it was, it stood out from the usual shimmer of waves. I squinted, placing my hand over my brow to block out the glare of the sun. Again, there was a split second of sparkle before it vanished.

Huh. What could it be?

I waded into the sea. When I was waist deep, I dove underwater, pushing against the current. One stroke, two strokes, three strokes, four. My breath was starting to push against my lungs. I swam to the surface and broke through. I inhaled and wiped the salty sting from my eyes. With more steady strokes, I made headway, the sparkling object getting closer and closer.

I was almost there. The glare of the sun blinded me for a split second. I blinked. Little white dots made my vision hazy. But then the sun retreated behind a cloud, and I could see clearly again.

What the . . .

At first, I thought I must have been seeing things. There, a few feet away, was a single white flip-flop floating along like a toy boat or something. I blinked. There were sparkly gems on its strap, winking as it bobbed up and down.

No. It can't be . . .

My blood rushed to my head, the realization of what it was making me dizzy. One of Mom's favorite flip-flops. Her *princess tsinelas*, as she liked to call them.

I wanted so badly to believe that it really was Mom's flip-flop. But I knew I would have to see it up close to know for sure. With quick strokes, it didn't take long for me to reach it. I treaded water, almost too scared to touch the flip-flop. When I did, a shiver trailed down my spine. My index finger circled the exact spot near the center of the strap where one jewel was missing—the jewel that had fallen off when Mom tripped on a cleat and stubbed her toe. I remembered that precise moment when the tiny gem bounced on our boat's deck, bouncing and bouncing until it dropped into the sea, disappearing forever. Dad had helped Mom back up, tendrils of her hair escaping from her French braid as she slipped her flip-flops back on. When she noticed the missing jewel, she just shrugged it off. "*Bahala na . . . I suppose they're more unique now*," she'd said with a grin.

Now I held on to the flip-flop for dear life. Then I made my way back to shore. With the sandal close to my chest, I walked to the bonfire and rummaged for the other flip-flop, the blue one I'd salvaged from Bambi's village. Like a bedraggled Cinderella, I slipped my foot into it and dropped Mom's sparkly one on the sand, slipping my other foot in. I wiggled my toes, a big grin plastered on my face.

Thanks, Mom.

FORTY-ONE
Isa

LATELY, DINNERS HAD BEEN EVEN MORE QUIET than usual. Only the sounds of our cutlery scraping the plates, of our glasses clinking the table, of our biting and chewing could be heard.

We were all too preoccupied with our own thoughts. It was almost as if we'd decided not to mention anything that had to do with Coral, Tita Alma, and Uncle Jack's disappearance.

That is, until tonight.

I took one last bite of my fried bangus and rice and pushed the rest aside. "Thanks for dinner," I mumbled, standing to take my plate to the dishwasher.

"Isabel, wait . . ."

I put my plate down on the counter next to the sink and turned to look at Mom. Her food had barely been eaten. Her black hair was dull and unkempt. Her skin was paler than usual, except for under her eyes, where there were puffy, dark circles. It wasn't until that moment that I'd noticed how tired and sad she looked.

"We should talk," she said in a softer tone than usual.

I glanced over at Dad. He didn't look all that different. Maybe a bit thinner, his cheeks more sunken in, his shoulders slumped as if he was too tired to hold them up.

Dad cleared his throat. "Sit, Isa."

I didn't want to sit. My feet were stuck to the floor as if they'd been superglued there. "Did—did something happen?" I said, leaning back for support.

Dad stared at the kitchen table. Mom glared at the empty chair beside her. I stumbled forward and somehow made it back to my seat. *Creak.* The wood shifted underneath me. I waited for one of them to say something. Anything to break the silence.

"No. Nothing has happened. That's the problem," said Dad.

I frowned. "And why would that be a problem?"

For a second, he didn't respond. But then he clenched his jaw and placed his hand on mine. "Time, Isa . . . time is not on our side."

I felt my cheeks tingling, my neck burning, my eyeballs stinging.

Time is not on our side.

What did he mean, exactly?

"I'm sorry. I—I don't understand," I said.

Dad exhaled. "When someone or something gets lost, the chances of finding them get slimmer and slimmer with every day that passes . . . They've been gone almost three months, honey. We have to begin accepting that maybe—"

"NO!" I pushed my chair back and slammed my hands on the table. "They're okay. Coral is okay. I can feel it."

"Anak . . ." Mom's face looked like a crumpled, discarded tissue. "We have to accept that maybe . . . they're gone."

"NO!" I stood.

"Isa, honey. I'm so sorry. There's nothing more we can do. They're calling off the search." He got up, reaching out to hug me.

I stepped back. "But they can't . . . It-It's not up to them. They're *our* family!"

"I know, Isa. I know. In situations like this, though, it really isn't up to us. It costs a lot of money to continue the search. And at this point, they've decided that the chances of finding any survivors are slim to none. I'm sorry," said Dad with tears in his eyes.

I fumbled for my pocket and pulled out my wallet. "We can pay. I—I can pay. All my money. You can have it," I said, trying to force Dad to take it.

He grabbed hold of my arm, closed my hand around my wallet, and pushed it back toward my chest. "No, honey. It's just not enough. We don't have enough."

Mom got off her chair and embraced me. "They're gone, Isa. We just have to accept that they're gone."

I pushed her away. "NO!"

"Honey . . ."

"NO!"

I was under the doorway. My hands were shaking. My neck and arms were numb. My stomach was churning as if it wanted to hurl out the dinner I'd just eaten. "NO! I'm not giving up . . . ever!" I screamed and ran out as fast as I could, stumbling up the stairs to my bedroom.

When I was inside, I locked the door. *Breathe. Breathe. Breathe. Breathe.* But I couldn't. The air felt heavy, too hot. I was dizzy. Everything started spinning, first slowly, then faster. I stumbled toward my desk and collapsed into my chair.

Close your eyes, Isa, and breathe. I repeated the chant to myself. After a minute or two, I opened my eyes. The spinning stopped. But I still felt as if I'd been run over by a garbage truck.

A gust of wind blew in through the open window, making the sheer blue curtains dance. The stack of postcards on my desk shifted. Almost immediately, my gaze zeroed in on one of the postcards—a beach, a calm blue sea, three little girls in swimsuits running and jumping and splashing one another. Just as Coral and I used to do.

My eyes welled up with tears. I wiped them away with the backs of my hands. And then I flipped the postcard over and grabbed the nearest pen.

Dearest Big Star,

Remember that day on the beach when you showed me how to fly like a bird? I watched you run and leap across the sand, thinking that you really did look like you were about to take off. I was so hopeless! Me and my stubby legs couldn't keep up with you. Every time you leaped, I tried to do the same. But instead, I ended up dropping like a sack of potatoes. After a while, you told me to imagine I was actually a seagull or something. So I did. When I tried again, you cheered me on, shouting, "Look at your shadow, Isa! You're flying!" And when I glanced at my shadow on the sand, I was taller, my legs and arms were longer, and when I leaped again, it truly did look like I was flying.

Now it's your turn, Coral. Wherever you are, I want you to imagine that you're a strong and powerful bird. I want you to take off and fly. Don't stop flying until you're home. Until we're together again.

You are a survivor. I believe in you.

I'm waiting. Always and forever.

Love,
Isa

FORTY-TWO
Coral

I PUSHED MYSELF UP ONTO MY ELBOWS. A BLURRY twinkle greeted me—Mom's flip-flop.

I whispered, "Hey, Mom . . . ," feeling a tightness in my chest thinking about her. And even though my thoughts were on Mom, a vision of Tita Sunshine appeared in my mind. She was staring up at the sky, arms outstretched as if she were catching something. "*It's a sign, Coral. Heaven-sent,*" she kept on saying.

I didn't really believe that heaven existed. But I did think that somehow it was a sign. To give me hope. To make me feel less lonely. To remind me that I was loved.

I love you, too, Mom, Dad, Isa, Tita Sunshine, Uncle Henry . . .

I stood. My body complained, creaking with every tiny movement. Even my head wouldn't shut up. The questions kept barging into my consciousness.

How did Mom's flip-flop make it all the way to this island?

What were the chances of my finding it?

If I had a map and a computer, I'd take a stab at tracing its route, studying the ocean's tides to see exactly how it happened. If Dad were with me, we would draw a chart, design some experiments, come up with some sort of hypothesis.

But Dad isn't here.

I poked my head out of the cave. The clouds seemed even grayer than usual. The wind tousled my hair, swirling it around my face and neck as if it were angry at me. I swept my hair aside, forming a loose braid down my back. Bambi was already on the ledge, watching the horizon.

"What's the matter, girl?"

She whined and glanced at me with her droopy doe eyes. I wasn't sure why she was so agitated. So I bent down and caressed her scruff reassuringly. "C'mon, let's go get some breakfast," I said, hoping that the mention of food would make her tail wag.

Nope.

I shrugged. Maybe she still wasn't 100 percent recovered yet. Or maybe she just didn't sleep well or something. Since recovering from her near-death experience, Bambi had attached herself to me like a piece of Velcro, stuck to whichever part of my body was closest. I scaled down the rock face, slapping my leg for Bambi to follow. At first, she hesitated, gazing at the horizon again with a worried frown. But eventually, she caught up to me with her tail tucked between her legs. When we got to the beach, she seemed to relax more. Her thrill for the hunt seemed to have waned. Other than the occasional bird, we mostly relied on the fish I caught. Some days my catches were plentiful, hauling several fish at once. Other days, I was less fortunate, only one or two little ones flopping in my net.

Hunger became a reality again, clawing out from the depths of my gut. I had no choice but to sleep with an empty stomach some nights. By my calculation, it had been three months or so since I'd washed up on the island. On the days I remembered to, I'd scratch lines on the wall of my cave with a sharp stone. There were ninety-seven lines the last time I'd tallied them up. But those ninety-seven lines felt more like thousands of lines. An eternity.

I ignited the fire, then busied myself with preparing a simple breakfast—fish leftovers, seaweed, and coconut water. Bambi sulked, her muzzle tucked between her front paws while she gazed at me. I could tell she was hungry. Her nose wriggled while I scooped her share into a bowl. As soon as I placed it in front of her, she gobbled it up. Not even a few seconds had passed, and she was done, peering over her bowl, eyes darting back and forth nervously.

Hmmm . . . Something wasn't right.

It wasn't until the sky went dark and a deafening boom of thunder almost knocked me off my feet that I understood. The clouds whirled as if there were a fire in the sky, as if all the anger in the world had been sucked up and spewed out.

Bambi ran around in circles, spooked.

Boom! It happened again. This time so intense that the ground vibrated. Was it an earthquake?

I searched the sky for answers, and it screamed back at me, *Run! Run! Run!* I stumbled back and gawked at the horizon. My heart felt as if it were about to burst out of my chest. The clouds were no longer white. They'd turned black and monstrous, looming right above us. For a second, I was frozen, unsure whether I should study this freak of nature or run from it. Dad had warned me about such storms.

"Coral, you've got to run to the highest ground you can find. If there's a tsunami, you can't be anywhere near the shore," he'd once told me.

Bambi's teeth nipped at my fingers, breaking me out of my trance. She zoomed down the beach, her bark unrelenting and urgent.

"Hold on, Bambi!" I screamed, rushing toward the cave to retrieve my survival kit. I ran, kicking off my flip-flops to scale the rocks faster. But just before the landing, I slipped. Both of my knees were bloody and raw. It was an excruciating pain, yet I kept on going. The storm could hit at any moment.

Finally, I reached the cave. It was dark, but I managed to find the survival kit. I crawled on the ground searching for my poncho, hands scraping the rocks until I felt it.

"Thank god," I mumbled, placing it over my body before leaping down to the beach again.

Bambi barked as soon as she saw me again. When I reached her, my chest seized up. The fishing net! The knife! I couldn't leave them behind. They were both precious tools I couldn't afford to lose. Even though I was breathless and scared, I backtracked to the bonfire.

Whoosh! Slam! The wind slapped my face with a force I didn't think was possible. But I pushed my body against it until I was able to yank the net off the tree branch and slip the knife into my bag.

I ran back to Bambi, falling to my knees and stumbling from the fury of wind behind me. My bloody knees were caked with sand, throbbing as if they wanted to pop and explode. By the time I reached the edge of the jungle, sheets of rain assaulted us. Within seconds, we were completely soaked. Even the plastic poncho couldn't protect my body from the rivulets of cold water cascading down my neck and back.

Bambi led the way into the dark, wet jungle. Heavy rain pelted the leaves like bullets; our steps cracked branches in our path. It was hard to keep up, but somehow I was able to follow the furry blur in front of me. I dodged the endless maze of trees, trying to match Bambi's frenzied pace.

Keep on going, Coral!

Rain pooled in my eyes, and the mud under my feet made it almost impossible to move at a steady pace. The sounds of splitting wood, the thunder, the rumbling, the vibrating ground made it feel as if we were in one of those disaster movies.

It seemed like we'd been running for a long time, until finally, just as the storm intensified, Bambi halted. A strange-looking cliff appeared through the trees. It almost looked as if a bunch of square and rectangular boulders had been piled over one another. I scanned the area. We seemed to be somewhere unfamiliar. The cliff was intimidating, but at least it faced away from the storm.

Woof! Woof! Bambi turned her head to find me, as if she was reassuring herself that I was still there. Then she began to climb, hopping from boulder to boulder. I struggled to keep up, my mud-caked fingers slipping every time I grasped something. But with Bambi barking and gazing at me from above, I was able to plod on.

With every single movement, I made headway even though my muscles were burning. I climbed and climbed, crawling over the geometric-shaped rocks until my limbs were completely numb. Eventually, my fingertips touched a ledge. I made one last push. Bambi clamped down on my poncho with her teeth, helping me over. I exhaled, relieved to have my back on flat ground. The rain started falling even harder. A never-ending slew of buckets pouring right on top of us. Even then, I just lay there, too drained to even care.

It wasn't until I heard Bambi bark that I bothered pulling myself up to look around. What appeared to be a ledge jutting out from the cliff was actually the lip of a cave. Unlike my cave back on the beach, this one had no end in sight. Desperate for shelter, I crawled over to the entrance. I whipped out my flashlight and cranked it for a few moments before turning it on.

The beam sliced into the shadows, illuminating several feet ahead of us. When I felt something at my back, I almost dropped the flashlight, startled by the unexpected movement near my calves.

"Bambi?" my voice echoed eerily.

Woof!

It was a relief to feel the brush of wet fur and the thump-thump of her wagging tail. Bambi whined softly, calming my nerves. She circled around my legs like she was telling me to follow her.

"Okay. C'mon, then," I said.

Bambi went ahead, directly in front of me, so the flashlight could brighten her path. A few minutes went by. Then we rounded a corner into an even larger chamber. I gazed upward and noticed these weird black clumps above us. I pointed the flashlight toward them.

I flinched. The clumps began to twitch and move. *Holy crap.* Hundreds of bats hung upside down. Bambi followed my gaze, seemingly unperturbed. Slowly and quietly, I walked underneath them with my head slightly bent, just in case any of the bats decided to drop and fly my way.

After passing the corridor of bats, we reached an open area where the ground was as smooth as marble. Its surface was covered with a collage of old mats, similar to the ones I'd seen at the abandoned village.

Huh. Now, it all made sense. Bambi knew where to go because people had shown her. This place was some sort of storm shelter. I collapsed, my body sagging like a tired, old sofa. The mats were brittle and scratchy, but having a barrier between my wet body and the cold stone floor was comforting. Bambi uttered a sound somewhere between a whine and a groan as she huddled her sopping wet body next to mine.

The only sounds were our breaths and the distant howling of the wind.

FORTY-THREE
Isa

IT WAS MY DAY OFF. SO I SLEPT IN AND SKIPPED breakfast. I wanted to avoid Mom and Dad for as long as possible. I didn't need them lecturing me about moving on and whatnot.

Let them move on if they want to. Last I heard, I was free to believe what I wanted to believe.

When I finally got the energy to drag my sorry butt out of bed, I grabbed the cleanest clothes I could find off the floor—a ribbed white tank top, denim shorts, and my trusty canvas sneakers, perfect for riding my bike into town—and got dressed. When I was upset, the only thing that would make me feel better was stuffing my face at Melville's Diner.

Outside, the weather was weird. In a way, it kind of matched my mood—overcast, gray, and windy. I preferred it to the usual cheery and sunny summer day. The other added benefit of a cloudy day was that I could ride my bike all the way to town without sweating buckets. By the time I reached Main Street, I did have a sweat mustache, but other than that, I was fresh as a daisy. Well, as fresh as I could be, having been in too much of a rush to take a shower. So maybe more like a day-old, slightly wilted daisy.

Good enough.

I leaned my bike against the wall facing the blue neon smiling whale sign that was supposed to depict Moby Dick. The owner of the diner was a distant relative of the author Herman Melville, so of course, the diner was fishing/boating/sea-themed. Instead, though, it looked more like the interior of the Krusty Krab restaurant from *SpongeBob* rather than a serious literary masterpiece.

But whatever. The food was good, so I was willing to ignore the giant harpoon hanging from the ceiling. I pushed the door open and immediately spotted my favorite window seat. Even though it was too late for breakfast and too early for lunch, the place was bustling with customers. The interior echoed with chatter, the sizzle of the grill, and the gurgling of the coffee machine.

"Hey, hon. Grab a seat and I'll get to you in a jiffy," said Peggy, the middle-aged waitress who'd been working there since forever. She handed me a menu and disappeared into the kitchen.

I dodged a bunch of tables and then plopped down into the teensy-weensy booth facing Main Street. Despite it being a weekday, there were still swarms of bikers, tourists strolling with their kids and dogs, and expensive-looking SUVs fighting for parking spots.

"Hey!"

I looked up expecting to see Peggy. Instead, I found Ada in one of her usual I'm-going-to-an-anime-convention outfits. Her shaggy bangs were covering her face, so all I could see were her bright yellow blouse, red schoolgirl uniform, white boots, and a gray stuffed toy creature in her grasp that looked an awful lot like Totoro. Surprisingly, she didn't even look sick anymore, except for her eyelids, which were still a bit swollen.

"Oh, hey," I replied. "You look better."

She smiled. "I am. You'd be surprised what a thermos full of lugaw, a gazillion cups of ginger tea, and a whole lot of sleep can do."

Both of us glanced at the empty seat across from me. There was an awkward silence. She waited for me to say something while I waited for her to say something. Then we both chimed in at the same time.

"Uh. You can sit if you, um, want."

"Is it okay if I join you?"

We giggled. Ada slid into the leatherette seat and situated the stuffed toy beside her. "I hope you don't mind if Totoro joins us," she said with an exaggerated wink. Then she peered at the menu on the table. "Mom is working her shift at the deli, and I'm a hopeless cook. So I figured I'd give this place a shot. What's good?"

I shrugged. "Pretty much everything. I'm ordering a bunch of stuff if you wanna share."

"Cool," said Ada.

Peggy appeared with a plastic pitcher of ice water and

two glasses. She placed them on the table and poured us some. "Hey, ladies. Are you ready to order?"

I handed the menu back to her. "Yeah. We'll have a cheeseburger with fries, an order of onion rings, a BLT with extra mayo, a chocolate milkshake, and . . ." I glanced at Ada.

"A strawberry milkshake for me," she said.

Peggy nodded and jotted everything down on her notepad. "Be back in fifteen," she said, rushing off.

After she left, we stared out the window for a couple of seconds. We didn't really know each other well enough for a comfortable silence or a conversation that flowed easily. Ada might have technically been my cousin, but it still felt kind of weird. As if some alien spaceship had beamed her down out of nowhere, expecting us to get along just because we were both human.

I peeked at her from the corner of my eye. "So, um, I've been meaning to ask . . . Ada . . . your name. Is it, like, Filipino or something?"

"Yeah, it comes from the Spanish word *hada*, which is spelled 'ada' in Tagalog. It means 'fairy,'" she explained, flapping her arms as if they were wings.

"Like fairy, as in the fairy godmother in Cinderella?"

"I guess. But I think my mom meant it to be more of a tiny fairy, you know, like Tinkerbell. Because I was born premature, so I was way tinier than most babies."

"Well, it's pretty unique. It suits you," I said.

She perked up at the mention of unique. "Thanks."

"Anyway. So you just bummin' around today or what?"

Ada frowned. "I guess? I mean, what else am I supposed to do? I can't stay in bed anymore. The boredom was driving me crazy."

"Ha! No surprise there. This island gets boring *real* fast."

"Well, the tourists seem to like it," she said, pointing at the crowd on the other side of the window.

I smirked. "That's because they can leave whenever they want."

"True."

And then it was silent again. Our eyeballs wandered like scattered marbles. I tapped the Formica table with my fingers.

"Do you miss Jersey?" I blurted out.

Ada gazed into the air, thinking. "I guess, sometimes. It was cool being able to take the train to Manhattan whenever I wanted. You know, not being stuck on an island and all. But it's nice here . . ." All of a sudden, she looked up and squinted. "Wait. Is that a harpoon on the ceiling?"

I chuckled. "Yeah. After a while, you won't even notice it's there."

"Here you go, ladies!" Peggy sidled up to our table with a humongous tray in tow. "Cheeseburger, fries, onion rings, a BLT with extra mayo, and two milkshakes," she recited while arranging the plates of food on our table.

"Thanks, Peggy," I said with a smile.

She saluted us and wandered off toward another table.

Ada gawked at all the food, which pretty much covered our entire teensy-weensy table. "We might be here for a while."

"Nah." I scooched close to the edge of the table and plucked a french fry from a plate. "I'm starving."

"Me too!" said Ada, plucking her own french fry and dipping it into her milkshake. "The only good thing about Graves' is that it makes me hungry all the time. And of course, I *love* food."

"Ohhh . . . good call on the french fry–milkshake combo," I said, doing the same with another fry.

Ada cut the cheeseburger exactly in half, and then she took half the BLT, and a handful of fries and onion rings onto one plate, before giving me the other. She made sure to pile everything neatly, giving each of us the same number of fries and onion rings. She even rearranged the curly parsley garnish.

Despite looking like a character from a zany cartoon, Ada had this way about her, as if she were an organized and precise scientist arranging all her lab equipment.

"Thanks." I took my plate and began to devour my food.

By then, the diner was crammed with people eating and waiting for tables. This hum of conversation echoed off the walls and ceiling. It was kind of hard to hear each other, but between bites, we somehow managed to chat about all sorts of random stuff.

"Don't you just love Zach King's TikTok account? I mean, who doesn't like watching cats fighting with light sabers. And oh! Did you see his flying on a broomstick video? I wish I could do that dressed in my *Kiki's Delivery Service* outfit! How cool would that be?" said Ada.

"Uh. Zach King who?"

Ada giggled. "Okay, okay. I get it. TikTok is not everyone's cup of tea."

"But I do like *actual* tea and coffee," I said, staring at her with squinty eyes. "I'm guessing you're more of a tea person than a coffee person. Am I right?"

"Yeah! How can you tell?"

I shrugged. "Dunno. It's just one of my many talents. Next time you come by the bakery, I'll make you my signature matcha latte. I use an authentic ceremonial matcha powder that comes all the way from Japan."

"Ohhh. I love matcha anything," said Ada.

Surprisingly, even with all the chatter, we managed to finish the food, slurping our milkshakes until our straws made that obnoxious sucking noise.

"Ahhh . . . that hit the spot," I said, slumping back.

Ada cradled her belly. "I need to walk this food off. Otherwise, I might puke it all up."

After paying and leaving Peggy a nice tip, we wandered outside through the sea of bodies lingering by the entrance. In the time we'd been eating, the sky had gone from overcast to dark gray and menacing. The air smelled of humidity, salt, and rain.

I looked out at the horizon. "It's going to start pouring any minute."

"C'mon, then," said Ada, grabbing my arm.

We strolled down Main Street, passing the hardware store; the fancy-schmancy seafood restaurant, which only opened from April to October; the rinky-dinky, only-one-movie-showing theater; the tiny scented-candle shop; and a boutique with expensive swimsuits and cover-ups.

Boom! Crack! Bang!

When we reached the Pebble Island Art Gallery, it was storming. The sky had gone from dark gray to nearly black. Sheets of rain fell. The crowds scattered as everyone ran for cover.

But not Ada and me.

We just stood there, allowing the rain to soak our clothes, our bodies, our hair, our shoes. It took only a minute before we were completely drenched.

Ada gazed at me, her expression somewhere between amused and horrified. "Is even your underwear wet?" she said, widening her eyes more.

"Uh, yeah," I replied.

Boom! Boom! The thunder was so loud it felt as if someone had crashed cymbals between my eardrums. *Ahhh!!!* We screamed at the same time. And then we dashed down the street, jumping in and out of puddles, all the while laughing hysterically. It didn't matter that we were soaked, that our stomachs hurt from eating too much and laughing, that passersby were staring at us like we were a couple of weirdos. All that mattered was that we were having fun and that, for the briefest of moments, all our worries were forgotten.

FORTY-FOUR
Coral

BROKEN BEAMS OF SUNLIGHT PENETRATED THROUGH piles of debris—rocks, branches, vines, and leaves. The cave entrance was impassable.

Oh no . . . There was no way out.

Bambi hopped and twirled in circles, yipping as if she was desperately trying to tell me something. Maybe she had a plan? Maybe she knew another way out? Her eyes darted toward a narrow corridor, barely wide enough for me to fit through.

"Should we go down there?" I asked her.

I pointed my flashlight, hoping to see what was on the other side. But it was too dark. My insides fluttered with fear, doubt, panic. I did my best to ignore those emotions. Because Bambi was a reliable guide. I needed to trust her.

I shimmied into the rock corridor, scraping my knees and elbows along the way. The pathway narrowed with each twist and turn. But I tried not to worry. Bambi's paws *tap-tap-tapped* ahead of me. The deeper we went, the more humid it became.

Drops of water fell on my head, neck, and back, mingling with the sweat on my skin. As the corridor widened, the darkness seemed to shift, as if I were staring through a kaleidoscope. A soft glow bounced off the ceiling, diffusing light over our heads. Even the rocks changed colors, from gray to orange to white. Shallow neon green pools appeared where the rocks dipped, forming natural basins.

A noise, somewhere between a buzz and a hum, echoed off the walls. We rounded a jagged bend and then *whoosh*—a wall of sound and light surrounded us. The sudden brightness momentarily blinded me. I squinted until my eyes adjusted. In front of us was a waterfall. But instead of gazing at it from the outside, we stood on the other side. From within.

I'd never been inside a waterfall before. But as much as I wanted to *ohhh* and *ahhh* in amazement, I knew there was also a major *uh-oh*. We were stuck. Trapped. With nowhere else to go.

I looked down at Bambi for answers, but all she did was bark—loud and fast, as if she was revving her engine. I frowned. "What's the matter, girl?"

No reaction. Instead, she sprinted toward the sheet of water.

"No! Bambi, don't!" I screamed, lunging for her.

But it was too late. She was already far ahead, her gait confident and powerful, every muscle tensed for action. I sucked my breath in, knowing that, at any second, Bambi would leap through.

"Bambi!" I screamed again.

It was no use, though. She soared through the air. I froze. My heart, my breath, even my muscles wouldn't move. As soon as she disappeared through the water, I exhaled and stumbled forward. "Bambi!"

All I could hear was the waterfall. I listened harder, leaning my ear as close to the edge as possible. Seconds felt like hours. But then, something broke through— barking. Thank goodness. The sound was muffled, but it was definitely there. I breathed in deep. But the relief was only temporary.

It's my turn now. I gulped.

I approached the barrier of water. It was there, right in front of me. Everything vibrated—the air, the walls, the ground beneath my feet. It was powerful, maybe too powerful. I reached out and touched the liquid wall with my fingertips. It stung on contact, as if someone had thwacked me with a hard metal ruler.

"Ouch!" I yanked my hand back. My knuckles were throbbing and red. But I knew I had to act fast. If I didn't go right away, I might lose my nerve.

All right . . . you can do this. I took five paces back and then ran. A few inches from hitting the water, I shut my eyes and jumped.

"Ahhh!"

The force hit me hard—a flash of pain, and then it was gone. I was soaring and falling. I opened my eyes— *splash!*—and landed feetfirst in a lagoon. My body sank for a couple of seconds before catapulting back to the surface. I broke through and swallowed big gulps of air. Stunned.

"Holy crap!" I screamed as loud as I could, following the waterfall back up with my gaze.

Awww. Awww. Awww.

I spun around. Bambi dog-paddled toward me and then licked my shoulder, my arm, my neck, my cheek. "Bambi. Thank god!" I pulled her close. Even her musky, wet-dog smell couldn't dampen my spirits.

We swam to the edge and pulled ourselves out. Then I dipped my hand into the lagoon, scooping handfuls of water so we could take turns drinking from my palm. It felt great to be outside, breathing fresh air, drinking water to quench our thirst.

After a minute, we collapsed on a mossy spot and rested in silence. Even the jungle seemed abnormally quiet, as if every living being was recovering from the storm. Branches were scattered all over. Small trees had been uprooted, balancing on one another like a pile of pickup sticks. The jungle floor, normally covered with ferns, had an extra layer of debris—a mixture of twigs, fruit, and seedpods.

Oh no . . . I bolted up, panicked all of a sudden. The shoreline was probably just as battered, if not even worse. There was a possibility that the strong wind and waves could have destroyed the home I'd made for myself. My cave. My makeshift kitchen. They might be gone. The urgency of the situation forced me to my feet. I swayed and stumbled, reeling from that sick feeling crawling in my stomach. Dread. The last thing I needed was to have to start from scratch. Having to build another camp somewhere else on the island wasn't just an inconvenience. It threatened my survival.

"Come on, girl, let's go home," I said, my voice croaking.

Bambi squinted one eye open. And then she rolled over and stretched into a downward dog yoga pose.

Woof! she barked with an enthusiastic tail wag.

This time, I led the way. We trekked through what was left of the jungle. The damage looked even more severe the closer we got to shore. It was as if a crazed *Tyrannosaurus rex* had stomped through, ripping vegetation with its teeth and spitting mouthfuls out where they didn't belong.

I scrambled up onto a fallen tree and surveyed what was left of the shoreline. Almost every square inch of sand was littered with debris. There was everything from plastic bottles, rubber car tires, and random flip-flops to giant clumps of seaweed, coconut husks, driftwood, and a surprising number of fish—some dead, others flopping on the sand.

It was a disaster.

Nothing was familiar to me. It was like I'd fallen asleep and woken up to a living nightmare. As I wandered through the mounds of stuff, tiny crabs scuttled by my feet. They seemed to be the only ones going about their usual business, digging their holes, darting in and out as if nothing had happened. I envied them. They had no real home. Every hole in the sand was just as good as the next one.

Even though I was in shock, my stomach wasn't. It growled. My last meal was nothing but a forgotten memory. I scanned the beach, searching for Bambi. She was probably busy scavenging.

Bingo! Just as I suspected, she'd already cornered a fish trapped in a shallow pool. Her paw smacked its wiggling body. Then, *chomp!* She ripped its head off with one bite. My mouth watered, the prospect of a meal—even a raw one—made the hollowness in my stomach grumble.

I walked across the wasteland, pulling the knife out of my kit in preparation. Several more fish were trapped, most likely a school caught in the storm surge. Their silver scales shimmered under the sun, daring me to try to catch them. As I approached my first victim, I watched it struggle in the shallow water, gills moving too fast. Its eyes met mine. I knew it was suffering. So I knelt on the sand, ready to put it out of its misery. With one swift movement, I stabbed it with my knife, holding it down to prevent an escape. A trickle of red stained the salt water. And then it was dead.

I slid the knife off the fish and then scraped all the scales off with the edge of the blade. The slickness of blood made it difficult to handle; it slipped from my grasp several times. I wiped the sweat from my forehead. I caught a glimpse of Bambi, her teeth bared as she devoured another fish.

Huh. Something clicked inside me. I was just too exhausted, too hungry to bother. I dropped the bloody knife. And then I brought the fish up to my mouth and bit into its succulent pink flesh with my teeth. I swallowed the barely chewed flesh. With each bite, I became more and more exhausted.

But still, I managed to eat two more fish. Afterward, all I wanted was to sleep. I dragged myself to the edge of the beach and collapsed under the shade of a leafy tree. The sand shifted around my body, embracing me, welcoming me.

You're home.

It was quiet. Finally, I could rest.

✳ ✳ ✳

The sand nearby moved. I blinked and wiped the warm sweat off my neck. Bambi was beside me, sniffing the air. Her ears were pointed at full alert. I pushed myself up onto my elbows and scanned the perimeter.

Nothing.

Bambi began nervously circling the mounds of debris. Occasionally, she'd sniff the air again. I stood and watched her. But still, nothing was out there, except for the mess that I'd already seen. Unfortunately, nothing seemed to have fixed itself during my nap. In fact, everything looked even worse. I gasped for air, suddenly overwhelmed.

You did it once. You can do it again.

But should I set up farther inland? Surely it might be safer to do so. The only problem, though, was if a boat or airplane passed by, I could miss it. No. I couldn't let that happen. We would stay on the beach. It was decided. My first task was to clear as much of the debris as possible, starting with the area where my kitchen used to be. I was able to locate the clearing where my bonfire was. The rocks I'd arranged were in a circle, visible under mounds of seaweed, driftwood, and a neon orange buoy. First, I tackled the piles of seaweed, doing my best to untangle and toss them aside. Sweat poured from my scalp to my ankles. I retrieved my knife and then began to hack away at the mess.

Just as I was making headway, Bambi trotted over with a battered rubber duck in her mouth. She dropped it on the newly cleared area. And then she proceeded to gnaw on it. I chuckled, her antics distracting me from the task at hand. Not for long, though. I got back to work, collecting some sticks and kneeling on the sand so I could re-create my fire-lighting tools.

Grrr . . . My body tensed. I looked over my shoulder, searching for Bambi. She was farther down the beach. The rubber duck was discarded at her feet, forgotten. Her body was rigid. Her nose was pointed up. Her eyes were fixed on something I couldn't see. Her fur was standing on end as if she was scared.

And if *she* was scared, *I* was scared.

I gripped my knife, frozen with fear.

FORTY-FIVE
Isa

ADA AND I WALKED INTO THE BAKERY WITH OUR rain-soaked clothes dripping everywhere. Normally, Mom would have thrown a hissy fit and commanded me to mop the floor before anyone slipped and broke their neck. But that didn't happen. All Mom did was stand there, stare at us, and clutch the cordless phone to her chest. And then she gasped and said, "Susmaryosep," with her hand covering her mouth. The color suddenly drained from her skin; it was almost like watching someone pour too much half and half into a cup of black coffee. With every second that passed, she turned paler and paler.

"Mom?"

She heard me. But it was as if my voice went in one ear and out the other. The last time I'd seen her like that was when we got the phone call about Coral, Uncle Jack, and Tita Alma. *Oh god.* My knees went weak. My insides twisted and turned. I had this sudden urge to puke up everything I'd eaten at lunch.

Tita Jo went over to Mom and placed her hand on her

back. "What happened, Ate Sunshine?" she asked with a concerned frown.

"No. No. No." Mom shook her head back and forth.

Ada and I glanced at each other.

"Here. Let me take that," said Tita Jo, prying the phone out of her grasp.

For a moment, Mom wouldn't give it to her. But then she let go. Her arms went limp, and she sort of fell back on the counter behind her. "The phone . . . ," she mumbled.

Tita Jo dragged a stool over and positioned it behind her. "Why don't you sit?" she said.

Mom did as she was told without even looking where the stool was. Thankfully, Tita Jo was there to help her. A long minute passed. We just stood there, awkwardly. Nobody seemed to know what to do or say.

But then, without even thinking about it, I moved toward her. One step, two steps, three. The words just tumbled out of my mouth. "Mom. Did something happen?"

"Y-Yes," she said, finally seeing me.

I gasped and held my breath. Every muscle in my body tensed as if they were bracing themselves for bad news. Of course it was going to be bad. Why else would Mom act like that?

"Th-They found the boat . . . They found . . . ," Mom's voice trailed off.

I stepped closer to her, my hands curled into fists so tight it hurt. "WHAT?" I yelled.

"Uncle Jack . . . and . . . and . . . Tita Alm—" Her face sagged just as the tears began to gush out of her eyes.

I looked at Tita Jo. Her face was blank. Clearly, she didn't know what was going on, either. I didn't want to think about the worse-case scenario.

No. It can't be . . . What if I'd been wrong all along? What if they were all gone? Just the thought of it made my knees buckle. I almost stumbled and fell. But I caught myself and shuffled over to Mom. When I was right in front of her, I placed my hands on her shoulders and gazed into her tear-filled eyes. "Mom, *please*. Tell me," I pleaded.

She heaved. But after a couple of raspy breaths, she finally came out with it. "Some fishermen spotted a sailboat grounded on a small island. They found them . . . inside. Th-They're gone . . . They're gone . . . ," she whispered.

I felt a lump in my throat, but the words pushed through. "Coral too?"

"I—I don't know. Only two bodies were recovered."

Two bodies. Uncle Jack and Tita Alma.

"She could still be alive?" I muttered softly.

Mom wiped her tears away with her apron. Then she stared at me so hard I could have sworn I felt a stabbing pain in my eyeballs. "Anak, I'm sorry. But we have to accept that they're gone. *All* of them."

"No." I stepped back. "I'm not giving up on Coral."

"Anak. Please."

"No."

My face burned. So did the back of my head, as if too many people were staring at me. I spun around and found Ada. Her eyes were red-rimmed. Why was she so upset? She didn't even know Uncle Jack, Tita Alma, and Coral. For whatever reason, seeing her that way made me angry. "I'm sorry, Isa," she said, reaching out and grazing my arms with the tips of her fingers.

I yanked my arm away. "She's not dead!"

Ada blinked. Her face went still and splotchy, as if I'd slapped her or something. "I—I didn't mean—"

"Just shut up! All of you!" I screamed.

Everyone gawked at me. I backed all the way to the door and then fumbled with it until I was outside.

My bike . . . I need my bike . . . It was still at the diner. So I ran.

"Isa wait!"

I looked over my shoulder. Ada was on the sidewalk looking like a trampled-on weed. But I ignored her and kept on running. Because I was going to look for Dad and persuade him not to give up on Coral.

❋ ❋ ❋

I found him on the deck of his all-black fishing boat, *Star Daughter*, named after his one and only kid—me. He was leaning on the railing, staring off into the horizon.

There was this dazed, exhausted look about him, as if he'd stopped sleeping and aged a decade in mere months.

"Dad?"

For a split second, I thought he hadn't heard me. His eyes were still lost somewhere out in the sea and sky. But then he looked over his shoulder, his sea glass–colored gaze faraway and watery.

"I-I'm sorry, Dad . . . ," my voice cracked.

He turned all the way around and held out his arms. "Give your old man a hug."

I ran fast, hitting his chest with the side of my head and shoulders. His arms held me tight, and I finally felt safe enough to let it all out. All the tears, all the sadness, all the anger, all the frustration. *All* of it. It was like a waterfall of emotions gushing out of me, wetting his shirt, my shirt. Tears. Saliva. Snot. I was a hot mess.

"Oh, honey," he said.

I looked all the way up, past his chest, past his chin. There were tears in his eyes, rolling down his cheeks, clinging to the wiry hairs of his overgrown beard. "Dad, I'm not ready to give up on Coral."

He pulled me into an embrace again. I could hear his heart beating in my ear, loudly. His breaths made his chest push against my cheek. I knew he was thinking. Or maybe he just didn't know what to say. But after a minute or so, he cupped his hands over my cheeks and gazed straight into my soul.

"I'm not ready to let go, either. But—"

"No." I smacked my hands over his. "We have to try one more time, Dad. *Please*. She might be stranded somewhere, waiting for us to find her. If it was me out there, I know Coral wouldn't give up . . ."

He exhaled and gazed at the horizon again. I watched the hue of his irises shift to a deeper greenish-blue that matched the color of the Long Island Sound. After a long moment, he nodded. "One more week, Isa . . . I'll ask them to search for one more week."

I jumped up and down, nearly trampling his feet with mine. "Thank you, thank you, thank you," I said over and over.

"But please, hon. Try not to get your hopes up. Okay?" he said in that deep voice he used whenever I got too excited about something I wasn't supposed to be excited about.

"Dad. They're going to find her. I just know they are," I said.

"We'll see . . ."

I could hear the uncertainty in his tone. I could feel muscle spasms under his shirt. I could sense his entire being hesitate. Because he didn't want me to get hurt. Of course he didn't.

But I knew in my heart that this wasn't the end of our story.

The Star Sisters would be together again.

I'll see you soon, Big Star.

FORTY-SIX
Coral

BAMBI'S FUR BRUSHED UP AGAINST MY LEGS AS WE walked down the beach. It was scary, going toward something unknown—a potential threat. I had no idea what to expect when we rounded the bend. But I had my knife in my hand and Bambi at my side. So I tried to stay calm.

Breathe in. Breathe out.

The light was a monochromatic gray, making everything around me seem as if it were covered with a layer of dust. For whatever reason, the island felt different. Its tropical brightness was muted. The trees leaned sadly, the flowers drooped to the ground, the translucence of the sea was replaced with murkier greenish-blue water. Everything washed up on the sand was starting to decay. The stench was almost unbearable.

I gagged and coughed, halting for a moment to catch my breath. Bambi looked at me, her ears and tail pointy and stiff. "It's okay, girl. I just need a sec," I said.

Grrr . . . Bambi growled again. The fur on her scruff ruffled. Her eyes were fixed on something I couldn't see, something that scared her. I gripped my knife and brought it closer to my hip.

"C'mon," I said, stepping forward lightly.

It took us only a couple of minutes to reach where the sand ended. A large, craggy boulder was obstructing our view. I inhaled and then signaled for Bambi to follow me. We crept around the boulder, keeping our bodies close, in case, god forbid, someone was on the other side. As much as I was desperate to see other people, I wasn't ready for any surprises. It had been too long since I'd set eyes on another human being. Inch by inch, our progress was painstakingly slow, but finally the other side was there. I moved my head to the side and peeked through a gap in the rock.

What the . . . For an instant I thought I was seeing things. But then I blinked several times. My vision cleared. It was there. It was really there. Posing on the sand like in some touristy postcard was a small outrigger dinghy, its hull a faded blue with a stripe of what must have been bright orange on its side.

A boat! I could hardly believe it. But where had it come from? Boats didn't just appear out of nowhere.

I peeked again, looking right and left, searching for signs of life—for a person or persons. There was nobody, though. Absolutely no one. *Huh.*

Bambi kept on looking at me, then at the boat, and then at me again. It was almost as if she was asking for my permission to go. I placed my finger to my lips, hoping she could figure out I was telling her to be quiet. "*Better safe, than sorry*," Dad always liked to remind me. Even though it seemed as if nobody was there, we still had to be cautious. The thought of people was both exciting and nerve-racking. I wasn't sure if the locals would be friendly.

But what if they could help me?

My heart was beating uncontrollably. As nervous as I was, though, my curiosity propelled me forward. I stumbled toward the dinghy, eager to see it up close. When we were about two feet away from it . . . *Woof!* Bambi went berserk.

"Shhh. Be quiet, Bambi," I whispered to her.

But she just wouldn't stop barking and growling. At what, I wasn't sure. But there really wasn't a single person around. I ignored her and went closer to the boat. Until finally, I was there, right beside it. My fingers brushed its wooden contours, tingles of excitement radiating across my arm.

The homesick feeling that had been dormant inside me rushed back. Familiar faces popped and burst in my mind like Fourth of July fireworks. The realization that I might have a chance of seeing my family again made me dizzy. All the fear and despair I'd felt vanished, replaced by something I hadn't felt in a long time.

Hope.

I leaned into the interior of the boat, and that's when I saw it. Or rather, saw him. A man. I startled and jumped back.

Woof! Woof! Woof! Bambi leaped toward the boat, scratching the side of it with her claws as she kept on barking and snapping. But the man was still, unmoving, as if he was passed out . . . or dead. I inched closer again. The man was old, like, *old* old, and frail-looking. He was wearing a frayed pair of shorts. His shirt was wrapped around his head instead of his torso. If he was dead, he hadn't been dead for long, because his skin was a shiny, deep brown under the sunlight. The way he was positioned, at the bottom of the boat, curled up as if he were taking a nap, made it seem as if his limbs were not yet stiff or anything.

"Hello?" I said, loud enough so he could hear me.

But the man didn't move a muscle. Surely, he would have heard Bambi's barking and woken up. Right?

So I did the only thing left to do. I leaned toward him with my arm outstretched, reaching until my hand touched his wrist. His skin was warmish yet somehow clammy. When I placed my fingers over where his pulse would have been, I felt nothing. I clutched his shoulder and shook him. Still, he didn't react.

He's dead. Gone. Maybe a heart attack or something.

I felt shivers down my spine. The man was dead. It was only at that precise moment that I fully absorbed it. A dead person. The hand that had touched him went numb. I held it up and stared at each finger one by one. My stomach was suddenly queasy. I wanted to puke, but there wasn't much to puke up. *Cough. Cough.* Except maybe there was. I leaned over and spewed slimy strings of saliva, and bile, and bits of raw fish onto the sand. After a minute, the nausea passed. I stood and wiped my mouth with the back of my hand.

The man might have been dead, but the boat was still there. I studied it from tip to tip. From what I could tell, it was in decent condition, most likely beached after the man had keeled over. But inside, near the bottom, I noticed a hairline crack with some sort of pinkish-colored putty in it. As if it had broken and been repaired a bunch of times. It didn't seem to be leaking water, though. So maybe it *was* seaworthy?

Where would I even go, though? The dinghy wasn't motorized. Could I just set off and hope that somewhere nearby there was a place with people who could help me? I thought and thought. But the thinking was useless. There was no way for me to know what would happen until I tried it. I had to take a risk.

But first, I had to move the body. Even though I knew he was dead, I approached him with caution. He was really small and thin, so his body probably wasn't all that heavy. Still, he was dead, and deadweight was likely heavier than I imagined. And the thought of carrying a corpse wasn't exactly all that appealing. I cringed. My insides got all queasy again. But I had no choice. I just had to suck it up and do what I had to do.

Here goes nothing. I reached out and placed my hands under his arms. There was hair in his armpits. I gagged at the sensation of coarse hair against my skin and at the pungent aroma. I held my breath and closed my eyes for a second to let it pass. *Okay, keep going, Coral.* So I huffed and puffed and pulled and pulled. It took a lot more effort than I anticipated. But after a few minutes, I was able to drag him off the boat and onto the sand.

Seeing him there on the sand was almost worse. He looked even more lifeless. Like he was one of those washed-up fish. Except he wasn't a fish. He used to be a person—someone's father, someone's grandfather, someone's brother, someone's husband. He probably had a family that was missing him, like I was missing Mom and Dad and Isa and Uncle Henry and Tita Sunshine. I leaned over and threw up again. But not much came out, only the bitterness of bile in the back of my throat.

Now what?

I didn't have a shovel, so I couldn't bury him. And I couldn't just leave him there to rot like a piece of discarded meat. It was too undignified. I glanced all around me, searching for an answer. As soon as my gaze landed on the sea, *boom!* An idea popped into my head. I could drag his body to where the water was deepest. I mean, if it were me, I would much rather be laid to rest in the sea, becoming part of what Dad loved so much, instead of rotting under the sun, waiting for the flies and maggots to eat away at my flesh.

Phew. You can do this, Coral. I grabbed hold of his ankles and pulled him toward the shoreline. After several minutes of pulling and resting, I was halfway there. Bambi kept on circling us, sniffing at the man's head, at his face, at his limp arms, until she was satisfied that he wasn't a threat.

I dropped down on the sand with my back facing him and wiped the sweat off my brow. The exhaustion was overwhelming. But I had to carry on, because I knew that the searing hot weather would decompose the body in no time. I pulled my knees up and hid my face between them, taking a moment to myself.

Get it done, Coral. Soon you'll be off this island . . .

I held my head up high and took a deep breath. My view of the ocean changed. The clouds shifted to let the full sun through, making the water shimmer. It was almost as if it were calling me.

I stood and resumed the task at hand. This time, I took hold of both feet, tucking them under my armpits while I gripped both ankles, my face pointed forward so I could see where I was going. I was able to go much faster, and within a few minutes, I reached the edge of the water.

I waded in and kept on pulling. One hand held on to his leg, the other hand I used to paddle and swim. The buoyancy made it possible for me to drag the body along. But as soon as the shallow water became deeper, the body just drifted off and dropped like a sinking anchor. The tide would finish the job for me.

Phew. Thank goodness. I swam back to shore. My strokes were tired and sloppy, but somehow I managed to get back on dry land. When my knees touched sand, I collapsed forward with the ripples of seawater rolling over me. I could have laid there with my stomach on the sand for hours, listening to the sound of the waves. But I didn't. Because I had one night left on the island.

Then I would set sail and hope for the best.

FORTY-SEVEN
Isa

I SPENT AN HOUR ON GOOGLE LOOKING UP STORY after story of people who had been lost at sea and rescued. It was a rabbit hole that I had fallen into and couldn't get myself out of. There were two articles I kept going back to. One about six boys who'd escaped from a Tongan boarding school in 1965 and ended up being marooned on a deserted island for fifteen months before being rescued. Fifteen months! The other one was more recent, in 2010, about three teenage boys from a Pacific island named Atafu, who were lost at sea in a fourteen-foot dinghy for fifty-one days without food and water, until they were rescued by a commercial tuna-fishing boat from New Zealand.

As I read the words, my eyes began to sting, my nerves prickled with excitement, my stomach twisted and turned and churned with anxiety. It was possible to survive. I wasn't being silly. Coral could be somewhere out there . . .

No. She *was* out there. *She's alive.*

But the search would continue for only another week.

Please. Please. Please. I closed my eyes, clasped my hands together, and pointed my face up toward the ceiling. *Please, god . . . if you're out there, please bring Coral home . . .*

I didn't really believe in god, but I was desperate. If there was the slimmest chance that he did exist, I was going to beg for him to help her. I had to try everything and anything. Even if it meant that an almighty being might strike me dead with a bolt of lightning for doubting their existence.

I opened my eyes.

Nope. Still here.

It was almost midnight, but I was too wired to go to sleep. So many scenarios whirled around in my head. I kept imagining how Coral would be rescued:

1. A low-flying airplane would spot an *SOS* sign on a beach, and soon after they'd see Coral jumping up and down, waving her arms at them.

2. A fishing boat would happen upon a neon orange dinghy with Coral onboard, who'd somehow managed to survive on raw fish and rainwater.

3. A scientist studying the plant life of the remote Indonesian forests would find Coral deep in the jungle living with a troop of fruit-eating monkeys.

As the minutes passed, each scenario I thought of became more absurd. When I reached the Coral-was-going-to-build-a-paraglider-with-scrap-wood-and-leaves-and-fly-back-home stage, I sighed and banged my forehead on my desk. I was losing it. Big-time.

Ping! My messenger notification alerted me. It was a note from Ada.

Hey, Isa . . . Are you awake?

For a moment, my hand hovered over the laptop keyboard. I didn't need anyone distracting me from what was most important—making sure Coral made it home. But I knew she knew that I'd seen her message, so I couldn't very well just ignore her. I mean, what if she told her mom and what if her mom told my mom?

Ugh. Crap. Then I'd never hear the end of it. So I started typing and wrote:

Yeah.

There, at least she couldn't accuse me of ignoring her. I watched the dots in the chat box move as she typed her reply. *Dot dot dot dot dot dot dot . . .*

Are you okay?

I typed another response:

Yeah.

There was a long pause before I saw the moving dots again. *Dot dot dot dot dot dot dot dot dot dot dot . . .*

You want to hang out tomorrow? I finally got a bike. I could go to your place, or you could come over here, if you want. We could watch another movie. And, I've got leftover flan in the fridge.

Dang. Flan *was* tempting. But I had to resist. I stabbed at the keyboard again:

Sorry. I'm kind of busy this week.

Dot dot dot dot dot dot dot dot dot dot dot dot dot dot dot dot dot . . .

Oh yeah, of course . . . I'll see you around at the bakery, then. Good night!

I could almost hear the disappointment oozing off my computer screen. There was this flutter of guilt in my stomach. It wasn't like I didn't like her or anything. Ada was cool and all. But Coral was my priority. And until she came home, nothing and nobody would get in my way. I could not afford any more distractions.

One week . . . it was all the time that Coral had left.

I reached for the keyboard to type "good night."

Blip.

But Ada had disappeared.

If I could sense the disappointment oozing off my screen, then maybe she could sense my lack of interest. I just hoped she wouldn't rat me out. The last thing I needed was a lecture from my already distraught mother.

Sigh. Double *sigh.* Triple *sigh.* There weren't enough *sighs* in the world to show how utterly frustrated and afraid and desperate I was. I banged my forehead on my desk again and left it there. Because all of a sudden, it felt too heavy to lift back up. My eyelids drooped. My vision blurred. My mind was spinning black with glittering stars.

Big Star . . . Where are you?

Saliva drooled out of the corner of my mouth right before I passed out.

"*I'm coming, Little Star. I'm coming . . .*" It was Coral's voice loud and clear. She wasn't whispering, she was yelling as if she were standing right there, next to me with a bullhorn pointed at my ear.

I bolted upright at my desk. The pile of postcards scattered. One was just a couple of inches from my hand. It was a photo of a gorgeous fiery-orange Pebble Island sunset with a woman on a horse riding toward it.

Riding into the sunset, happily ever after. The end. It was a sign. I flipped the postcard over and grabbed the nearest pen.

Big Star,
You have one more week for them to find you. Please do whatever you can to make sure you're out there in the open so they can see you. Please, please, please. This is your last chance, Coral. If they don't find you now, then they might never find you. Get out there! Make some noise! Shout! Jump! Swim! Because I can't imagine this place without you. I'm waiting, Big Star. Come home.

Love,
Isa

I stared at my nearly illegible chicken scratch. No matter. The words were there, and I was sure Coral would hear them. I slid the postcard off the desk and onto my chest and hugged it. I closed my eyes and imagined all my love, all my strength, all my hopes, drifting out of me into the air, into the postcard, drifting all the way to wherever Coral was.

You can do it. I believe in you, Big Star . . .

FORTY-EIGHT
Coral

THE SUNLIGHT WAS ALREADY SIZZLING HOT BY THE time I woke up. My body must have really needed the rest, because I couldn't remember the last time I'd slept that long or that soundly. When I moved, my joints creaked like stepped-on twigs. My stomach gurgled. Bambi lifted her chin and opened one eye to gaze at me.

"Morning, girl," I said with a yawn.

She opened her other eye and wagged her tail.

I slurped some coconut water and then scooped its flesh before taking the last few bites of some leftover fish. If I ever got back home, I'd gladly never drink coconut water or eat fish ever again. The idea of some hot tea or coffee or fresh orange juice with one of the bakery's warm ham-and-cheese croissants made my mouth water.

Until then, I'd try my best to push those thoughts out of my head. They felt too distant, too unattainable. I had faith that somehow I would make it off the island. But I had to take it step by step instead of getting ahead of myself.

I stood over the items I had gathered for my journey: a bottle of fresh water, a couple of coconuts, the fishing net, the knife, my survival kit, and my poncho. Hopefully, these would be enough to tide me over as I paddled from island to island, searching for signs of civilization.

I opened the survival kit one last time, just to double-check that its contents were complete. The notebook and pen caught my eye.

Hmmm . . . What if . . . ? I shook my head. No.

But what if something happened to me? What if I died? I had to write to Isa one more time. Just in case.

I sat on my favorite fallen coconut tree, and with the notebook on my lap, I tried to verbalize everything I was thinking.

Dear Little Star,

It's been over three months now (I think!), and finally there's a sliver of hope. A dinghy washed up on the island with a dead guy in it. I know, I know . . . I'd rather not talk about all the gory details. But let's just say I had to do some things I didn't want to do. But now I've got this boat, and well, I'm going to try to get off this island with Bambi. If all goes well, we will find someone to help us. But if not, I want you to know that I gave it my all. Not a single day has passed when I haven't thought about you, Uncle Henry, Tita Sunshine, and <u>home</u>. God, I really miss home. I miss you, Isa. If something goes wrong, though, if for whatever reason I don't make it, I want you to promise me something. I want you to live, Little Star. Don't shut yourself out of life. Don't shut yourself away from people. Don't shut yourself from the possibilities in your future. There are so many more people and places beyond Pebble Island. And I know that if you put yourself out there, you'll do amazing things. I might not be there with you. But I'll always be with you in spirit. Star Sisters are forever. Don't ever forget that. I hope to see you soon, Isa. Wish me luck. Cross your fingers, toes, and whatever else you can cross.

I love you always,
Coral

I read it out loud a couple of times, and then I snapped the notebook shut and tucked it back into the survival kit, making sure the waterproof bag was good and sealed.

There. I was ready.

Even though I was beyond excited to be leaving, there was this pang of sadness. Looking out at the horizon in front of me, I was still mesmerized by the beauty of this place. Everything seemed to shine; the colors were even more vibrant and alive, as if it had been covered with a fresh coat of paint and a sprinkle of fairy dust. I took one last look before loading my supplies into one neat bundle that I could sling over my shoulder.

I walked across the beach, my stride purposeful. Not once did I turn back. And neither did Bambi. *Woof! Woof!* she barked excitedly, as she did every time we set off to do something fun.

As soon as we rounded the bend, I sighed with relief. *Thank goodness.*

The dinghy was still there, waiting for us exactly where we left it. Its faded orange stripe was like a welcoming smile.

Hey, Coral. Let's go on an adventure, it seemed to be saying.

I dumped my stuff inside the boat, tucking it into the space in front of the wooden slat that I'd be sitting on.

"C'mon, Bambi!" I said, patting the dinghy's hull. Bambi hopped up on her hind legs. I leaned over and carried her onboard. She pranced from one side to the other, wagging her tail a million miles a minute. For a split second, I had this vision of her sticking her head out of a moving truck, watching the trees and the birds and the people zoom by like all the other dogs on Pebble Island. I grinned.

"Okay, settle down, girl . . . Let's get this show on the road," I said with a deep breath.

I climbed out of the dinghy and then positioned myself at the back, resting my palms on both sides of the hull. *Push!* With all my strength, I thrust the boat toward the shoreline. It was a struggle at first, but as soon as the momentum kicked in, the dinghy started to slide with its own weight.

We reached the water. I'd have to get in before it got too deep, so I pushed off as hard as I could and leaped back in. My sudden weight wobbled the dinghy from side to side before I regained my balance and took my seat.

We were on the boat! In the water! *Whoo-hoo!*

Bambi was near the bow, posing with her snout straight ahead like a figurehead on an ancient ship. I grabbed the wooden oar and dipped it from side to side, catching my rhythm as I paddled away from the shoreline. One paddle, two paddles, three paddles, four . . .

At first, it seemed easy. The dinghy glided forward with each push, skimming the smooth turquoise sea until the island began to shrink behind us. Though I didn't really want to look back, I found myself cheating. For a quick moment, I peered over my shoulder for one last glimpse.

Goodbye, island. Thank you for keeping us safe.

But as we got farther away, my arms began to throb, the numbness setting in from my shoulders all the way down to my abdomen and back. My strokes slowed until I was forced to put the oar down. *Ouch . . .* A series of agonizing cramps attacked my muscles. At least I was far enough from the island that the current worked in my favor. The vessel drifted toward the neighboring islands while I regained my strength.

Bambi settled beside me, laying her head on my lap.

I was pretty sure she could sense something was wrong. But having her there with me made me feel hopeful and excited.

Time passed, and I started feeling a bit better, except for the sun—its rays burned my skin as if I were being roasted alive. The only thing I could do for relief was dip my hand into the ocean and pour the cool seawater over my head and body. But the water just sizzled, evaporating after a few seconds.

God, why couldn't it have been a cloudy day?

I leaned forward, moving my feet lower to steady myself, so I could grab my bundle of supplies. The desperation for something to quench my thirst was real. But my feet landed in a puddle. *Huh?* There was a lot of seawater at the bottom of the boat—about three inches swishing back and forth over my feet.

I glanced at the spot where I'd seen the crack in the hull. Most of the pinkish putty stuff was gone. And water was gushing in at an uncontrollable speed. *No! No! No!*

Bambi started pacing nervously on the wooden seat. I glanced at the gushing water again. It was impossible. The logical part of me knew there was nothing I could do to fix it. Absolutely nothing. The part of me that was in denial decided that scooping the water out with my hands would do the trick. So I did just that. It felt silly. But what else could I do?

Woof! Woof! Bambi's barks became louder.

My heart was beating too fast. I tried to catch my

breath. But I couldn't. Panic was setting in. Fast. My feet were submerged in about six inches of water.

I just sat there, petrified, while the dinghy filled with more and more water. What was the point of scooping out the water? It was futile. Hopeless. Before I could even think of a plan B, the dinghy started sinking, leaning to the side as the seams creaked under pressure.

"Bambi! Jump!" I screamed.

I only had time to grab the survival kit and place it around my neck before hurling myself out of the sinking ship. *Splash!* My body slapped the surface, and then I sank underwater. A stream of salty liquid burned my sinuses. I coughed. I choked. I swallowed a lot of seawater. My arms flailed, and I kicked my legs until I broke through the surface, sputtering up water, saliva, and snot.

"Bambi!" I screamed again, whirling around and around, trying to find her. Finally, I spotted her a few feet away, dog-paddling toward me.

Creak. Crack. Whoosh . . . The dinghy was almost completely submerged, only the very tip of it was sticking out of the surface. Its blue-painted hull seemed to meld with the ocean as it sunk.

What now?

I treaded water, trying hard not to panic. Bambi was behind me, clawing at my back, frantically. "It's okay, girl. We're going to make it . . . ," I said, my voice raspy from all the seawater I'd swallowed.

I turned around and stared off at the island. It was

too far to swim back. The neighboring islands were a bit closer. But still, a twenty- or thirty-minute swim. Maybe even longer if I factored in resting and cramps and not having water to drink. But we had no other choice.

I wrapped my arms around Bambi and positioned her with her front legs over my shoulders so she was piggy-backing me. The only thing left to do was push off. *One, two, three, four.* I counted every stroke as a distraction from the blazing heat.

Bambi was whining softly in my ear.

Minutes passed. I lost count of my strokes. Bambi was slipping off my back. Then my muscle cramps returned, tiny spasms running from my shoulders down to the arches of my feet. Even though I was determined to stay strong, it wasn't long before my body started shutting down. I grew weaker and weaker. Flashes of light blinded me. Moments of clarity were interrupted by sparks of confusion.

Where am I?

Who am I?

Why am I in all this water?

Is this a dream?

My eyeballs twitched. My shoulders stiffened. The most intense pain came from my burning calves—so intense it felt as if my flesh were melting off. Despite the pain and exhaustion, my body kept on moving, one sloppy stroke after another.

Awww . . . Awww . . . Even Bambi's whining was quieter.

The island ahead of us was close enough for me to get my hopes up. But the bright flashes in my eyes intensified. A searing pain squeezed my head, making my arms and legs almost completely limp.

"Isa, can you hear me?" I said, my voice barely a whisper.

At that moment, something occurred to me.

Maybe I'm dying. This is it. The end.

I gazed over my shoulder. The silhouette of the island, *my* island, loomed in the distance. I hugged Bambi close, but she was going limp, slipping away.

"Bambi . . . no . . . don't leave me . . . ," I gasped.

Between moments of blindness, of weakness, of confusion—a beam of sunlight broke through the clouds, shining down on a majestic white boat—its yellow-and-white flag with a dolphin on it billowing as it glided toward me.

It's not really there. It's just a figment of my imagination.

Didn't people see things right before they died?

For whatever reason, my mind and body felt at peace. I blinked at the boat.

Could it be Mom and Dad? Have they come for me?

At that moment, Bambi's body went limp. I tried to hold on to her. But I couldn't. My arms, my hands, my fingers wouldn't work.

No! Don't go, Bambi! Wait for me!

I struggled to stay afloat, but my attempts were useless.

Shoulders, neck, head, one by one they were submerged. I was underwater, sinking. Above me, the surface darkened. Slowly, my air ran out. I was drowning. Dying.

This is it. Goodbye, Little Star . . .

But then, something happened. The surface of the water went from black to blue again. Beams of sunlight broke through, illuminating everything above and below. There was a splash. Bubbles spiraled, then scattered, revealing a pair of brown eyes, like marbles zooming toward me. Hands, arms, pulled me back up. I was fading, losing consciousness, yet somehow I could breathe again.

Gasp. "Bambi! Bambi Bambi!" I screamed.

FORTY-NINE
Isa

TWO DAYS...

That was all the time we had left to find Coral. I'd been up most of the night, tossing and turning. My nerves making my arms and legs so cold and numb that it was impossible to fall asleep.

The last week, Dad had been on the phone a lot with the Indonesian Coast Guard and the US Embassy, getting updates and trying to get them to expand their search grid. Every time I would eavesdrop, my nerves would fray even more whenever he would sigh or cry or slam his laptop shut in frustration.

Mom, on the other hand, was going about her usual business acting as if nothing were wrong. It didn't even seem as if she were grieving or anything, as if she didn't care one bit that her sister and brother-in-law were dead, as if it didn't matter that Coral could still be out there.

It pissed me off. Like, *really* pissed me off.

I couldn't stand being around Mom, because her

casual attitude angered me to the point that I couldn't even look at her. Dad had explained, *"Everyone grieves in different ways, Isa . . ."*

But she could have at least taken one day off from work to cry a little. Instead of pretending work was more important. Making money was more important. Anything and everything were more important than her own sister, her own niece, her own brother-in-law who was really more like a brother.

Not only that, but she forced me to go to work, too. Supposedly, it wasn't healthy for me to stay cooped up in my room with my nose glued to my computer. Yeah, well, at least I was doing something. Even if it was just looking up the same stuff on Google until my eyes blurred.

"Uh. *Hello?* Can I order, or what?"

I was spaced out, leaning on the counter with my hands and elbows holding my head up. At the sound of the lady's voice, I flinched, my chin dropping and hitting the wooden counter. *Owww . . .* My butt slid off the stool. "Oh, yes. Of course. What can I get for you?" I said, brushing my apron as if I'd been busy all along.

The lady pursed her pink glossy lips at me. She was one of those too-blond wives with a glowing tan, "natural" makeup, and activewear that cost hundreds, maybe thousands, of dollars. "I'll take an almond latte, *almond* not *soy*, with half a packet of brown sugar, and a gluten-free muffin. You're sure it's gluten-free, right?"

I rolled my eyes. I'd actually meant to turn my back,

then roll my eyes. But I was tired, and when I was tired, I tended to get real sassy and sarcastic.

"Excuse me? Did you just roll your eyes at me?" said the lady, whose name was probably Karen-Schmaren.

I shrugged. "No."

She squinted at me with her piercing blue eyes. I walked over to the espresso machine, hoping she would cool off while I made her *almond* not *soy* latte. But clearly, she was not in the mood to let it slide.

"That's too much foam. I asked for a latte, not a cappuccino," she said, shaking her head.

Ordinarily, I ignored those kinds of people. But I was exhausted. And that turned me into a moody, temperamental, generally unpleasant version of my normal self. So I rolled my eyes and handed her the unfinished coffee. "Well, I guess you know way more about making coffee than I do, Karen. So why don't you just go ahead and make your own stupid *almond* not *soy* latte?"

The lady huffed and then slammed the coffee cup down on the counter before stomping off. I could have sworn she was just going to leave. But nope. She wasn't quite done. Instead of leaving through the front door, she marched over to the back, yelling, "Hello? Is there a manager around here? Hello?"

Great. I ducked under the counter to hide.

"Yes, can I help you?" I heard Mom say.

Crap. Crap. Crap.

And then the lady went on some tirade, screaming

about caffeinated beverages as if she were the captain of the coffee police force, and whining and complaining about my eye-rolling and my lousy attitude. I covered my ears with my hands, but it was no use. Her shrieking was too loud.

Finally, after what felt like eons, the shrieking stopped, and I heard the door slam closed. *Phew.* Except my relief didn't last very long, because I could feel Mom's eye lasers burning the top of my head.

"*Isabel!*" she said through her teeth, which may as well have been fangs.

I gazed up at her with my best puppy dog impression. "Sorry . . ."

"Sorry? That's all you have to say? Sorry?"

I gulped the lump in my throat. "Sorry, *Mom?*"

She sighed and then slumped her shoulders. "Anak. I know you're going through a lot. We all are. But we still need money to eat. To live. You can't treat the customers that way. Even the annoying ones."

"So you admit the lady was annoying?" I said, pulling myself out from under the counter.

"Well, of course she was annoying. I do have eyes and ears, Isa."

I slumped on the counter with the sulkiest sulk I could muster. "Fine."

"Good," she said, glancing at the wall clock. "It's not too busy today. You can clock out early if you like."

"Really?"

Mom nodded. "Sure. Why don't you go home and rest? The next few days are go—"

I grabbed my backpack and hurried off without letting her finish her sentence, because the last thing I wanted to hear was about "the next few days."

Besides, I knew exactly where I wanted to go, and it wasn't home to get some rest. There was another place—one that might give me the hope I so desperately needed.

The old lighthouse was like a rusty, old nail poking from a piece of discarded lumber. It served no purpose, yet it was still there—a derelict hazard of a structure that should have been torn down years ago. This was where Coral almost killed herself when we were little kids. The memory of that day was forever imprinted in my mind. It was as if it were yesterday. If I closed my eyes, I could picture it so vividly, I could hear all the creaks and echoes and shouts, I could smell the mustiness of the lighthouse, the coppery smell of the blood dripping from Coral's legs. But as much as I remembered the sights and sounds and smells, the feelings I'd had were so distant.

I stood several feet from the lighthouse's entrance, trying to recall all the emotions I'd had that day—fear, panic, anger, horror, regret, relief, happiness, love. Not necessarily in that order. I closed my eyes and pretended I was there, years ago in that precise moment when I grabbed Coral and pulled her to safety. That moment when I realized she was going to be okay. But I just couldn't feel anything.

Zilch. Zip. Nada. Maybe I needed to go inside.

I hadn't been in there since . . .

Go on, Isa. Don't be such a chicken.

Even though my feet were heavy, hot, and numb, as if they'd been dipped in molten steel, I managed to shuffle toward it. When I reached the doorway without a door, I halted and breathed in the dusty, damp air. It smelled like beer and piss and mold and rust.

I stepped into the darkness. My gaze followed the spiral staircase all the way up, squinting at the rays of sunlight peeking through the broken glass windows at the very top. Despite looking even more rickety, with its missing steps and completely rusted railing, I began my ascent.

It took way longer than I expected, because every few steps, I would stop and grip the banister without looking down, because if I didn't, everything would spin and blur and I might have lost my balance.

Finally, after several minutes, I made it to the spot where Coral had tripped. There were still smudges of dried brownish blood on the displaced wooden plank.

Coral . . .

I could almost see her there with her legs jammed through the broken step, her knuckles pale as she held on tight.

"*I'm coming, Coral!*" I'd screamed.

I bent down, just as I had that day, and pretended to tuck my hands into Coral's armpits, pulling and pulling until she was safe. We embraced each other tight, my heart radiating warmth as I squeezed her.

The warmth I'd felt at that moment was truly what I needed now. A warmth filled with hope, love, relief. One that reassured me everything was going to be fine.

Coral could have died. But she didn't.

And she wouldn't die this time, either. I would see her again. I knew I would.

I sat down on a step and wrapped my arms around myself, imagining she was there. Safe. It started in my heart, the heat spreading across my chest, to my shoulders, down my arms, to my legs, to the tips of my fingers and toes, until every part of me was as toasty and gooey as a freshly roasted marshmallow.

FIFTY
Coral

CONSCIOUS. UNCONSCIOUS. FRAGMENTS OF DARK-
ness and light. I was sinking. I was floating. Whispers—I
could hear words in English and in another language, far
and close. Even closer.

"*Coral. Coral, can you hear me?*" The voice hovered.
Was it real? My heart stopped. And then it quickened—
beating way too fast.

Was I dying? Was I dead?

Something crackled. "Mayday. Mayday. Mayday.
This is Captain Suwarno."

Silence.

It was as if I were swimming in a sea of liquid black
velvet, searching for something I couldn't find.

Mom, Dad, where are you? Isa are you there? My
words echoed. But nobody answered.

In the distance more crackling—louder this time.
"Mayday. Mayday. Mayday. This is Captain Suwarno.
We found a girl. She matches the description of Coral

Bituin-Rousseau. I repeat. We found a girl. She matches the description of Coral Bituin-Rousseau. She's alive. Over."

Wait. What?

I'm alive?

I'm alive . . .

I'm alive!

FIFTY-ONE
Isa

I WAS DEAD TIRED. TOO TIRED FOR PAJAMAS. ALL I managed was to walk to the edge of my bed and drop like a fallen tree. *Timber!* My body landed with a bounce. I curled into the fetal position, sweaty T-shirt, dusty jeans, dirty sneakers, and all. It didn't even matter that I smelled, that I probably should have taken a shower. Within seconds of my head hitting the pillow, I conked out.

Hours passed. I was in that deep stage of sleep where everything was black, and it felt as if I were cocooned in a nest of feathers and air and fluffy cotton balls, when suddenly, I heard a distant voice.

"Isa . . . wake up," it said.

Was I dreaming? I tossed and turned and curled up into a tighter ball, hoping that the voice was in my dreams.

But then, I heard it again. "Isa, honey. Wake up."

I moaned in protest. Something touched me. Hands. Big, meaty ones touched my upper arms, gently.

"Honey. It's important," said the voice.

Hmmm . . . uhhh . . . mmmm . . . ahhh . . .

Even though I was still half asleep, I managed to swat the hands away and turn so I was facing the other side. Nothing was going to get me to wake up from my delicious slumber. Absolutely nothing.

"It's Coral," said the voice, louder.

Coral?

I bolted off my pillow as if a firecracker had exploded underneath it.

"What?" I said, squinting at a blurry someone who looked an awful lot like Dad.

A few seconds went by, and my vision focused. Dad was kneeling by my bed, tears streaking his cheeks even though he had a stupid grin on his face.

"Dad?" I said, confused.

That's when he lost it. His face crumpled, and a bucket of fresh tears poured from his eyes while his chest heaved uncontrollably. "Oh, hon . . . ," he croaked out, and then leaned over to hug me.

My heart was beating as if I were riding an out-of-control bike down a hill.

"What happened?" I asked.

Dad pulled away, and his stupid grin was back. "They found Coral!" He grabbed me and held me tight. "She's alive . . . She's *alive!*"

I gawked at him. "Are you sure?"

"I'm sure."

For a moment, I just let it sink in. Months and months had gone by. I'd hoped and prayed and wished for some miracle to happen. And there we were, saying the words out loud, like no biggie.

"She's alive," I whispered.

Dad stood. All six foot three of him started jumping with his hands in the air like an oafish cheerleader. "She's alive! She's alive! She's really alive!"

I laughed and giggled and shrieked. And then I hopped on my bed and joined Dad in his cheering. "She's alive! Holy crap! She's alive!"

FIFTY-TWO
Isa

I WAS IN BALI. I COULDN'T BELIEVE IT. ALL THOSE years of wishing I could travel somewhere far, far away, and it finally happened. The moment Mom and I walked out of the airport, the first thing I noticed was the heat and the humidity, which kind of felt as if the air were constantly being blown by an overheated hair dryer. It also smelled different than home, of damp earth and dried salt and coconuts and spices and flowers I'd never smelled before.

"We welcome you to Bali with this Jepun flower," said the lady at the reception desk of our hotel. She placed a necklace of superfragrant yellowish-white flowers around each of our necks.

"Thanks," I said with a smile.

Mom closed her eyes, inhaling deeply. "Oh, these were my favorite when I was a little girl. We call them Kalachuchi flowers in the Philippines."

I gawked at the lobby while Mom checked us in. The hotel was perched on a cliff facing the Indian Ocean. It was modern, with lots of wood and glass and ginormous tropical plants and flowers, with waterfalls and pools adorned with Balinese statues and carvings. Mom couldn't find us a room in a more affordable hotel on such short notice, so there we were, slumming it in a five-star resort.

"Sweet," I mumbled under my breath as I gazed out the window at the white sand beach and the turquoise-blue water surrounding us.

"Let's go freshen up," I heard Mom say.

I turned around and scrunched my nose at her. "Can we go straight to the hospital? Please?"

Mom grinned. "Okay. I won't make you wait any longer."

"Yes! Thanks, Mom!"

She guided me back to the entrance. "I guess we can try to catch one of the hotel shuttles."

After Mom told one of the hotel staff where we were going, a sleek gray van pulled up to take us. Except, well, we didn't know the BIMC hospital was less than a mile away, so we were literally in the van for five minutes.

The hospital didn't look like a hospital at all. It looked more like a resort, with a terra-cotta tiled roof, tropical landscaping that included palm trees and orchids and those birds-of-paradise flowers, and a fancy-schmancy lobby.

As soon as we approached the information desk and mentioned Coral's name, several nurses shrieked and smiled from ear to ear.

"We are so honored to have Ms. Coral in our hospital. What an amazing young lady, to have survived such an ordeal," said a youngish Balinese woman with ponytailed black hair and scrubs in this cool blue-and-red batik print.

I grinned because the lady was not only sweet and kind, but she was also right. Coral *was* amazing. "Can we see her now?" I asked, my feet itching to run down the corridor even though I had no clue where her room was.

The lady tapped on her keyboard a couple of times, squinting at the computer screen. "Dr. Surya would like to talk to you first. He'll be out in a moment," she explained.

I plopped onto a nearby leather couch and exhaled impatiently. After a couple of minutes, an older doctor with salt-and-pepper hair, wire-framed glasses, and a crisp white coat came over to us. "Hello, Ms. Sunshine and Ms. Isabel. I'm Dr. Surya, Coral's attending physician."

At first, Mom just shook his hand. But then she accosted the poor guy, hugging him as if he were Coral, not Coral's doctor. "Thank you for taking care of my niece!" she said to him.

He chuckled and hugged her back with one arm. "Now, I just want to brief you on all the latest, so you know what to expect when you see her . . ." He glanced at the clipboard in his other hand. "The first couple of days, Coral was in a medically induced coma. She was in shock, and her body was extremely weak from malnutrition and from nearly drowning. But this morning her vitals are looking much better, so we decided to take her out of the coma. She's been fairly unresponsive thus far. Which is normal. Her body might be healing, but her mind is still in shock."

"Does she know anything about her parents yet?" said Mom with a concerned frown.

"No, we thought it would be best if the news came from family."

Mom nodded, nervously clenching her jaw.

"So can we see her now?" I asked, taking a step toward the corridor.

"Yes. But there's one more thing," said the doctor.

Mom and I glanced at each other.

"I don't think anyone has informed you yet, but there was a dog rescued with Coral. It's at a vet clinic just down the road. The veterinarian is asking what will happen with it?"

Mom's eyebrows arched up. "A dog?"

"Yes. It nearly drowned. But like your niece, it seems to have a fighting spirit," said the doctor with a grin.

"Huh. Well, I don't know . . ." Mom shrugged.

I glared at her. "Mom. We can't just leave it here. Coral has already lost so much. If she wants to bring it home, we need to bring it home."

"Fine," Mom grumbled. I could tell she wasn't all that pleased with the idea. But *whatever*. She'd just have to deal. For Coral's sake.

"All right, then. Let me take you to her room," said the doctor.

We followed him up a set of stairs to the second floor. Then down a long hallway with framed abstract paintings and potted plants. When we reached the end, he knocked on a wooden door and stepped aside. Nobody answered. Mom turned the doorknob gently before opening it.

The first thing I saw was sunlight shining through the closed window blinds. It made the room kind of golden, despite the rows and rows of stripy shadows on the wall. And then I saw her. Coral was lying in bed with her eyes closed. There were white sheets and a baby blue blanket over her, so I couldn't see her that well. But it was her. Except she was different. Her hair was a dry, tangled mess; her skin was peeling and burned to a crisp; and her body was frail and gaunt. It was as if she'd grown out of her body and left it behind, lifeless—like a discarded snakeskin.

"Coral?" I whispered.

Her eyes fluttered.

I should have been excited. But instead, I was afraid.

FIFTY-THREE
Coral

MY LEGS TWITCHED UNDER THE COVERS. *HELLO, we're still here*, they seemed to be telling me. They creaked like rusty, old gates when I tried to bend them. I pushed the blanket aside and gasped. I'd forgotten how frail I was—just skin over bone, a violent pattern of scars and bruises trailing all the way down to my shins. I traced the purple, red, and pink lines. Each one had a story. But I was too exhausted to think, too sad to reminisce about the island.

Bambi. Thinking about her made my eyes sting.

You almost made it, girl . . .

A tear snaked down my cheek. I stumbled out of the bed and held on to the mattress, teetering slightly as my foot inched forward. A gentle breeze drifted in through the window, blowing past the opening of my hospital gown. I hadn't felt this cold in a while. Goose bumps sprouted all over my sunburned skin.

Eventually, I made it to the bathroom, gripping the doorframe while pressing the light switch. The room glowed with a bluish incandescence. So blue that, for a second, the mirror shimmered—like the sea when the sun used to illuminate it. I shielded my eyes and placed my hand over my heart. I stepped closer, and it became a mirror again.

My god . . . The face staring back couldn't be me. The girl in front of me was ghoulish. Like a horror-movie version of myself. I looked away, trying to remember what the old Coral looked like. But it was no use. It had been too long. My fingers grazed the wall, searching for the light switch. *Click.* It was dark again. The mirror disappeared.

I shuffled back to the room and collapsed onto the bed. Sleep. It came and went like the tide. My eyes blinked nonstop. A sense of unease kept nagging me, poking me, pulling me in.

What is going to happen to me?

Am I going to go home soon?

When am I going to see Isa?

The room was bathed in shadows, elongated stripes were projected onto the white walls. It was quiet. Except for the cawing of a bird outside—cawing that somehow took me back to the island. Just thinking about it made me feel tired again. I closed my eyes and allowed myself to go limp.

An image of Dad's head poking out of the cabin flashed in my mind. I pressed my eyes closed even tighter. It didn't work, though. Another image appeared: Bambi struggling to stay afloat, dog-paddling like her life depended on it. Well, it did.

Bambi! Bambi! Don't think about it, Coral . . .

I focused on the blackness behind my eyelids.

Go to sleep . . . Go to sleep . . . Go to sleep . . .

Finally, everything got heavy and hazy, and my body felt as if it were sinking into the mattress. My eyes fluttered again. I heard the door swing open, ever so slowly.

No! No more doctors and nurses.

Through a slit in my eyelids, I spotted a silhouette peeking in. I pushed myself back against the pillows. Trembling. Why was I so scared? So nervous?

The light shifted, revealing round cheeks, narrow shoulders, wide hips. My skin prickled, but I didn't make a sound. I wanted to say something, to gasp, to sigh, to groan, to make some sort of sound to acknowledge whoever it was. But the scratchy steel wool lump in my throat prevented me from doing so.

"Shhh." The person stepped into the sunlight. "It's just me," they said softly.

Me, who? I squinted and focused on the person's face, which was oddly familiar.

"We came straight from the airport to see you—" That crooked smile, that whiff of cinnamon and vanilla.

"Isa?"

"Yeah."

I focused on the warm pools of caramel in Isa's eyes. For a second, we just stared at each other. I could tell she was holding in the tears, her apple-shaped cheeks twitching just like when we were kids. The words. I couldn't make any words come out. My chapped lips moved, but only the faintest of sounds escaped.

But then Isa threw herself onto my bed. Her arms wrapped around my shoulders, her head burrowed into my collarbones, her top bun poked me in the face as it always did.

I had dreamed of this moment for so long. Yet I felt numb, hollow. A hum was vibrating out of my ears, drowning out Isa's crying. I could hardly hear her. Only the wetness of her tears reminded me that she was actually there.

My Star Sister.

Isa in the flesh. Not the imaginary Isa that had kept me company all those months. I shifted, trying to find that groove where Isa belonged. That groove that we had carved out over the years. But I couldn't find it. Everything was misaligned. Maybe it was me. Maybe I was the one who didn't fit anymore.

"Oh, sweetie . . ."

I looked up. Tita Sunshine was at the foot of my bed, her eyes red-rimmed, her lip quivering.

My god. She looked just like Mom.

"Hi." It was all I could manage to say.

Isa finally pulled herself off me. Her top bun was leaning to the side, making it look as if she had a giant mushroom growing out of the side of her head. I covered my mouth and giggled. *Huh.* I'd forgotten how much Isa made me laugh.

"What?" said Isa.

I pointed at her mushroom bun. She yanked her hair tie off and redid it so it was on top again. Then she side-eyed me with her signature Isa smirk. "Girl . . . I'm not the only one in need of a makeover."

"Isabel!" Tita Sunshine hissed through her teeth.

I held up my hand in protest. "It's okay, Tita. I know I look, um, terrible."

"No. Of course not!" She dragged a chair next to the bed and sat in it. "We should talk, Coral."

Isa stiffened. I knew because the mattress bounced slightly. And her gaze drifted toward the window.

"Okay," I mumbled, pulling the blanket up to my neck as if it could protect me from whatever she was going to say.

Tita Sunshine sighed. "This isn't easy for me to say . . ." She shifted in her seat and cleared her throat. "A-About a week before they found you, some fishermen spotted a sailboat beached on an island. Your mom and dad—they were . . ."

She couldn't even finish before she broke down in tears. That was when I knew they were really, truly gone. The entire time I'd suspected it. But now I knew. For sure.

Mom and Dad were gone.

I nodded slowly. Tita Sunshine reached out and placed her hand on mine. Isa scooched over and hugged me from the side. I didn't know what I was supposed to say. But feeling their skin, their flesh, their warmth, somehow made me feel a little less alone. I might have lost my mom and dad, but I still had family. I still had Isa.

We sat like that for a moment. In shock. After several minutes, though, Tita Sunshine squeezed my hand and got up. "We should let you rest, Coral. I'll talk to the nurses and see if we can visit again for dinner. I'm sure you'd like to eat something other than hospital food."

I tried my best to smile, but it felt forced, as if my lips were rubber bands stretching in opposite directions. "Thanks."

Isa stood to follow her, but she halted and stared at my collarbones. "You still have it," she said under her breath.

I touched my star pendant. And then Isa touched hers. The Star Sisters were together again.

Isa bent down so her forehead was on mine. "I never gave up on you, Big Star. I knew. I just *knew* you were alive."

"Thanks for believing," I whispered back.

"Anak," said Tita Sunshine.

Isa pulled away and walked toward the door. With every step, she'd look over her shoulder like she was making sure I was still there. "We'll be back later."

"Okay."

But right before she left, she stopped, so sudden her sneakers squeaked on the floor. "Oh. Wait," she said, the wide-eyed look she had every time she remembered something. "The dog."

A dog?

My heart skipped a beat. My breath felt as if it had been sucked out of my lungs. I stared at her, too afraid to say anything.

"There was a dog with you when they found you. It was rescued. It's in a vet clinic near here," Isa explained.

Bambi? Oh my god! She's alive?

FIFTY-FOUR
Isa

CORAL MADE ME PROMISE TO VISIT BAMBI AT THE vet clinic before it closed. But I was going to do something even better. Luckily, Mom cooperated in the bestest sense—passing out right after her shower.

As soon as I was sure she wasn't going to wake up, I changed into a clean pair of denim shorts and a tank top and flip-flops, which to me was an unassuming, blending-in-with-the-crowd look. And then I stuffed another clean set of clothes into my backpack.

I glanced at Mom one more time, snoring softly under the fluffy hotel duvet because the air conditioner made the room feel like an igloo. Hopefully, she would stay asleep, because if she found out what I was up to, she would surely kill me.

When I got to the lobby, I tried to look like all the other guests, milling around before dinner, chilling in the lounge with fruity cocktails, admiring stuff at the gift shop. Nobody seemed to think that I stood out or that I was some dumb kid about to do some dumb thing. So

I strolled over to the entrance where the shuttle buses were lined up and asked one of the drivers if he could drop me off at the hospital.

"Of course, young lady. Get in," said the mustached driver with a smile.

At the hospital, I greeted the uniformed man at the front door and sort of hid behind a group of people in the waiting area. When I was sure that nobody had noticed me, I sneaked down the corridor, up the one flight of steps, down the corridor again, until I was standing outside Coral's room.

Knock-knock.

"Come in," I heard Coral say from inside.

I opened the door and entered. Coral was in bed, exactly where we left her. She looked even weaker, but still, she managed a slight smile. "Hey," she said, looking behind me. "Where's your mom?"

"Passed out." I tossed my backpack onto the foot of her bed. "Get dressed; I have a plan."

Coral's eyebrows arched. "A plan?"

"Yup. Hurry!" I said, nervously glancing at the door.

Usually, Coral would grill me before agreeing to anything, but clearly, her weakened state had also affected her judgment, because she crawled out of bed without asking questions.

She unzipped my backpack and pulled out the clothes I'd brought—yoga pants with a drawstring waist, a long-sleeved T-shirt so that her scars and sunburned skin would remain under wraps, a Pebble Island baseball hat to hide her tangled hair, and a pair of sandals that I knew would be too small.

For a second, I thought she would go into the bathroom to change. But she didn't. Of course she didn't. Ever since we were babies, we'd always been comfortable being naked in front of each other. It had never really mattered before. As soon as she took off her hospital gown, though, part of me wanted to turn around and give her some privacy. It seemed intrusive, seeing her bony, frail body like that. As if all her deepest, darkest secrets were out in the open.

So I did the next best thing and stared at my sneakers.

"Ready," she said, spreading her arms out as if I was supposed to admire her outfit. "I look ridiculous . . ."

"No, you don't."

Coral looked down at the sandals, with her toes sticking out comically, at the yoga pants, which, besides being way too big, were way too short, and at the baggy T-shirt, which was meant to be long-sleeved but just reached past her elbows, at the hat, which made her look as if she were hiding a bird's nest underneath it. "I may have been stuck on an island for months, but I think I still remember what counts as ridiculous."

I covered my mouth, but the snort-chuckle still managed to slip out. "Okay. I'm sorry. You do look kind of ridiculous."

Coral rolled her eyes. "I thought so."

I grabbed her hand. "Don't worry. Nobody is going to notice," I said, trying my best to reassure her.

At the door, I put my finger to my lips before opening it a crack. I poked my head through to see if any doctors or nurses were in the hallway. But there were none.

"C'mon," I said, pulling her along.

We sneaked toward the staircase, trying to look all casual, but probably looking more like a couple of suspicious shoplifters. When we reached the last step, I craned my neck to the right and then to the left. The lobby and waiting area were still pretty crowded, and the lady at the reception desk was busy talking on the phone. I stared right into Coral's hazel eyes and mouthed, "Just. Act. Normal."

She nodded.

I took the lead once again, striding past the receptionist's desk, laughing as if Coral had just finished telling me a joke. "Ha, ha, ha! That's hilarious!" I said loudly but not too loudly.

Coral laughed, too. "Yeah, can you believe it?"

"For real! Let's go get some dinner, and we'll come back later," I suggested at the entrance.

The uniformed guy at the door glanced at us. For a split second, I thought he was going to remember me or recognize Coral under her ridiculous getup. But all he did was open the door for us and say, "There's a wonderful café just down the road called EAT Local. I highly recommend you ladies check it out," he said, pointing to the left.

Coral looked him right in the eye. "Thank you!"

My heart felt as if it were tap dancing in my chest. I didn't know why I was so nervous. I mean, it wasn't like I was breaking someone out of prison or anything. But just the thought of Mom finding out made me all sorts of nervous.

When we were a good fifty feet away, I stopped to catch my breath. "Oh god. I thought that guy was totally on to us!"

"I know!" said Coral.

I looked up and down the street, trying to get my bearings. Reading maps wasn't exactly my forte since I'd never really had the need for it before. But one thing I knew for sure—we had to move fast.

"Hurry. The vet clinic is going to close any minute now," I said, yanking Coral's arm.

✳ ✳ ✳

Well, technically, the vet clinic was closed. But it had only *just* closed, and after I explained who Coral was and that she had to see Bambi because her recovery depended on it, they unlocked the door and let us in for a quick visit.

The vet technician dude led us to the boarding area, which was basically one big room at the back of the clinic with a bunch of dogs yapping in steel cages as if the world were ending.

"She's very quiet and very scared. But she has a good

appetite," said the technician dude. He halted at a large cage in the corner.

I heard Coral's breathing stop. She approached the cage slowly and whispered, "Hey, girl. It's me."

She unlocked the cage door. It squeaked open. Coral knelt on the floor. She didn't do or say anything. All of a sudden, a skinny reddish-brown dog with spindly legs hobbled out of the shadows. Her amber-colored eyes were droopy; her face and body were nicked with scars; her tail was tucked between her legs. So this was Bambi.

For a moment, Bambi stared at Coral, and Coral stared at Bambi. It was as if they were reading each other's minds. Then Bambi blinked once, twice, three times before moving closer. Until finally, she rested her face on the crook of Coral's neck.

Huh. Just as we used to do.

Except they seemed to fit better, like two peas in a pod. I felt this squeezy, twisty feeling in my stomach. Guilt. Jealousy. Whatever.

Get over it, Isa. She's just a dog.

I looked away, trying to push that horrible feeling out of me. But I couldn't look away for too long. Coral held Bambi as if she'd just been reunited with her long-lost best friend or something. And Bambi, well, after a few minutes, she lifted her tail into a sort of, kind of wag.

Woof! Woof! she barked, and then she stood on her hind legs and licked Coral all over her face.

"I'm happy to see you, too, girl!" said Coral, laughing

and crying and gasping for air. She turned to gaze at me. There were tears in her eyes like sparkly quartz crystals. "Bambi saved my life, Isa. I wouldn't be here if it weren't for her."

I nodded because I didn't know what else I was supposed to say. The cat got your tongue. Except in this case, it was the dog that got my tongue.

"Come here," Coral said, waving me over.

I stepped toward them.

Grrr . . . , Bambi growled, and bared her teeth.

"It's okay, girl. It's only, Isa. Remember? I told you all about her."

Miraculously, she stopped growling. I inched forward with my hand outstretched. When the tips of my fingers were an inch away from her moist doggie nose, I froze.

Don't bite me. Don't bite me. Don't bite me.

Bambi sniffed me for a good ten or twenty seconds. And then, well, she did the last thing I expected her to do. She licked my fingers and wagged her tail so fast that it blurred. Coral smiled and giggled. And so did I.

"It's nice to meet you, too, Bambi."

FIFTY-FIVE
Coral

One week later.

I WAS FINALLY HOME. THOUGH PART OF ME HAD stayed behind in Bali. We were forced to leave Bambi there. I could have sworn my heart literally shattered when I'd hugged her before we left for the airport.

"*I'll see you in two months, girl,*" I'd whispered in her ear.

Two months because there were all sorts of requirements to bring a dog from Bali to the US, and only a pet-transport company could fulfill them. So despite being relieved and happy and excited to be home, I couldn't help but wilt a little on the car ride from the ferry to the house. I sat in Uncle Henry's truck and imagined that Bambi was already with us, sticking her head out the window, tongue hanging out, ears flopping in the wind.

I glanced at Tita Sunshine and at Isa and at Uncle Henry, who was blabbering about how excited he was to see us, about all the seafood he'd caught for my "Welcome Home" brunch, about some people named Jo and

Ada who were supposedly some aunt and cousin I'd never met before.

To be honest, though, it was all a bit overwhelming. I had missed Pebble Island so much, but being here without Mom and Dad, knowing they would never take part in our epic lobster-clam bakes, our birthday pig-out celebrations, our family game nights, made me feel hollow and numb inside. It was bittersweet—no, bittersweet was too polite of a word. It was a horrible feeling. So horrible, I felt sick to my stomach.

The reality was that every time something familiar passed us by, a memory of Mom and Dad would pop into my head. Seeing the entrance to the Mashomak Preserve reminded me that it was Mom's favorite place to go biking. How many Sundays had we spent riding our mountain bikes through the maze of oak and beech trees? Driving past Melville's Diner reminded me of my impromptu lunches with Dad. How many meals had we spent chatting about our future adventures over crab cakes and lobster rolls and milkshakes? Would I ever be able to go to any of those places without this tightness in my chest? Without memories plaguing my brain like an inoperable tumor? There was no way for me to know. But I guess I'd have to wait and see.

So the rest of the drive home, I just stared at my lap and avoided looking out the window. It was better that way. Less painful.

"We're home!" Uncle Henry pulled onto the long gravel road leading up to the house. But after twenty feet or so, he slammed on the brakes.

Tita Sunshine glared at him. "Susmaryosep!" After a second, her eyes widened as she gazed at something through the windshield. "Susmaryosep . . . ," she said again, but that time it was more of a shocked kind of whisper.

I leaned forward and craned my neck. There was some sort of commotion. All the way down the road was a line of news vans parked one after the other. Reporters were gathered by the house like ants clustered around a discarded cupcake. A couple of police officers were making a hopeless attempt at cordoning off the entrance of the house, trying to form a barrier between the front door and the press.

"Holy crap," said Isa.

I looked at her and then at Tita Sunshine and Uncle Henry. "Are they here for me?"

Uncle Henry sighed. "Must be. They weren't here before, but someone might have tipped them off. This is a pretty big story, after all."

An intense feeling of claustrophobia overwhelmed me. Everything seemed so real, so in my face.

Coral Bituin-Rousseau, the lone survivor . . .

If I was with Mom and Dad, it would have been different. We would have faced the reporters together as a family. Instead, it was just me. The girl who'd survived on a deserted island, rescued only to find out her parents were dead. I was just another news story that would be long forgotten in a day or two. Captain Charlie would probably use those old newspapers to absorb the excess grease off his fried seafood.

"Let's get this over with," I said through gritted teeth.

The truck moved forward slowly. The sound of the wheels crunching on gravel heightened my nerves. When the swarms of reporters spotted us, they rushed the truck, jostling one another, screaming out questions, pointing cameras at me through the window.

I tried to ignore them, focusing on the house and the sea beyond it. The sky was gray. And the wind was forcing the sea to spew out white frothy waves. It was almost as if the weather matched my mood.

Uncle Henry pulled up right by the front door. That was the moment when everything exploded, and I mean *everything*. There were people shouting, car doors slamming, tires screeching, shoes stampeding on the gravel driveway. All the reporters crowded around the truck as if a celebrity were hiding inside. The police officers tried to push them away. But their attempts were futile.

I wheezed, unable to catch a full breath. This was not the homecoming I'd wanted. Me, sitting in the car, petrified. A bunch of strangers waiting to bum-rush me. But there was no other way but through. I just had to go out there.

Before anyone could do or say anything, I unlocked the door and opened it. "Coral! Coral! Coral!" they all screamed in unison.

I stepped outside. It was as if a hundred eyes were burning holes through me. The camera flashes intensified. Each flash blinding me. Each flash making my heart beat even faster. Each flash weakening my knees until they were almost too wobbly to stand.

"Coral, hurry!" Tita Sunshine swooped in like a ninja. She grabbed hold of my elbow and guided me up the stairs. All five foot one of her, elbowing reporters along the way. When we reached the landing, she nudged me with her other arm until we were inside. Isa darted in behind us. And then the door slammed closed.

Huh. Huh. Huh. We were hyperventilating.

"Please, leave our property!" Uncle Henry yelled from outside.

I was shell-shocked. I leaned my head into the crook of Tita Sunshine's neck. She was warm, safe. For a moment, I closed my eyes and pretended she was Mom.

I miss you so much. I coughed and heaved and whimpered. The tears gushed out.

"It's going to be okay, Coral . . ."

I looked up into Isa's eyes, which were darker than their usual caramel brown, as if whirls of espresso coffee were mixed in. Her hand curled into mine. I knew she was trying to comfort me—trying but failing. Because even though I was surrounded, I couldn't help feeling totally and utterly alone.

We stayed like that for a while, until eventually my cries and whimpers became gentle sniffs. By then, Isa's hand was limp. I lifted my head and gazed at her through puffy eyes. "Can—can you take me to my room?" I whispered.

She nodded.

Tita Sunshine loosened her grip on me. "Yes, I think that's a good idea. I'll make a statement. Hopefully, they'll go away afterward."

Isa looped her arm through mine and led me down the hallway. The door to the ground-floor guest bedroom, otherwise known as "Coral's home away from home," was already open. We entered. Thankfully, all the curtains were shut, so nobody could see us. The moment we were inside, I let out a sigh of relief. Seeing the familiar seashell bedspread, the framed watercolor sunsets, the windowsill with potted cactuses and succulents, the turquoise-blue sofa chair and ottoman where I used to read before going to bed made me feel all warm and fuzzy.

"I never thought I'd see this place again," I said, my eyes wandering around the room.

Isa pulled the curtains even closer together so that the room was cocooned. There wasn't a sliver of sunlight coming in. She went over to the small desk, picked up a pile of something, and handed it to me. "I know it's kind of silly, but I wrote you these when you were missing."

I stared at the pile of Pebble Island postcards and then flipped them over. Isa's handwriting, well, more like a bunch of chicken scratches, was scrawled on the back.

I know you're somewhere out there . . .

I miss you, Big Star.

Come home, I'm waiting for you.

All the words. All the sentences. I read them over and over again.

"It's not silly," I said, my voice quavering. "Thank you, Little Star." I wrapped my arms around her shoulders and squeezed her tight.

"I hope, somehow, you heard me speaking to you," she whispered.

"Yes. I knew you would never give up on me, Isa."

We pulled apart.

Isa spotted my blue batik backpack, still on my back. "Here, let me get that for you," she said, pulling the straps off my shoulders.

"Wait!" I blurted out, suddenly remembering something. I retrieved the backpack and placed it on the desk so I could unzip it. Inside, I found the little notebook and pen from the survival kit. "Here. I wrote to you, too," I said, handing it to her.

She grinned and held it against her heart. "Thanks, Big Star."

I kicked off my shoes and sat on the bed. Every muscle, every nerve, every bone in my body was sore and tired. All I wanted was to lie down and sleep until I couldn't sleep anymore.

Isa lingered by the doorway. "I should go."

"Don't leave," I said softly, patting the space next to me. "I don't want to be alone right now."

I scooched closer to the pillows and curled myself facing the wall. And then the mattress bounced. Isa placed herself on the other side of my body, her face so close I could feel her warm breaths on my neck.

FIFTY-SIX
Coral

Two months later.

TODAY WAS THE DAY. MY REUNION WITH BAMBI WAS finally here!

We'd offered to meet the pet-transport service at the Pebble Island ferry to make things easier, because there were hardly any street signs on the island, and newcomers always got lost.

I stood by the pickup area, my legs cramping from standing on my tiptoes for so long. The ferry was about fifty feet away from docking. I watched the sea froth around its hull. I watched people scurrying on deck to get into their cars. I watched the seagulls gliding up above, watching out for scraps of food.

"Coral, staring at the ferry isn't going to make it go any faster," said Isa with her signature snarkiness.

I looked over my shoulder and rolled my eyes at her.

"Oh, just let her be excited!" Ada shoved Isa playfully.

I chuckled. Ada had become the fulcrum to our balance scale—she managed to keep everything even Stephen when it came to mine and Isa's nonsense.

"She's here . . . ," I heard Uncle Henry announce from the driver's seat of his truck.

The ferry bounced off the rubber padding a couple of times before it slid into the docking area. Almost immediately, the car ramp locked in place and vehicles began driving off. I stepped forward, craning my neck to get a good look. Car after car passed us. None of them stopped. But just when I was starting to believe that the pet-transport folks must have been delayed or something, a white van emerged, pulling over right by where I was standing.

My heart pounded.

Will she still recognize me?

A tall and strong-looking woman wearing a navy-and-white uniform got out of the van. "Hey, y'all! I'm Pat Monroe from Pet Transport International. I'm assuming you're this fur baby's family?" she said with a toothy smile.

"Yes!" I said, bouncing in place.

The woman slid the van door open and then lugged out a large dog crate with all sorts of official-looking stickers on it. "Bambi did great on the trip . . . But she's understandably pretty nervous and scared. It might take her a while to adjust. Just try to be patient," she said, setting the carrier down in front of me.

I didn't even bother replying. Instead, I knelt on the ground and peeked through the carrier grate. Bambi was scooched all the way to the back, her body pressed awkwardly against the hard plastic walls, her face burrowed between her two front paws. "Hey, girl. It's me. Don't be scared. You're home now," I said softly.

But Bambi didn't budge. I knelt even closer and noticed her scruff was trembling. "Shhh . . . it's okay, girl. You're going to be okay."

Nothing. My stomach dropped.

What if . . . what if Bambi's already forgotten me?

I stood. Uncle Henry was next to the Pat lady, signing a bunch of papers on a clipboard. Isa and Ada gathered around me. "Don't worry, Coral," said Isa.

Ada placed her hand on my shoulder. "Yeah. She just needs some time, that's all."

I nodded, trying not to look disappointed. This was supposed to be a happy day.

"Thank you, Pat. We really appreciate it," said Uncle Henry, shaking the woman's hand.

"We're just thrilled for Bambi and Coral. Y'all are going to have an amazing life together," she said.

"Thank you," I mumbled.

She waved, got in the van, and drove off just like that. I stood there, feeling kind of useless as Uncle Henry loaded Bambi's carrier into the truck.

"Coral, c'mon." Isa took me by the wrist and guided me.

We all piled into the truck, Ada up front with Uncle Henry and Isa and me in the backseat with Bambi's carrier between us.

"Let's go on home," said Uncle Henry as he pulled out of the parking area.

Silence.

Nobody really did anything other than gaze out the window. After a couple of minutes, Uncle Henry started to hum some random song.

Awww . . . Awww . . . Awww . . . Bambi started to whine.

I bent over and peeked into the carrier. She'd lifted her muzzle from between her paws and was peering through the ventilation holes with worried eyes. "Don't worry, girl. It's going to be all right," I whispered.

But she didn't look reassured.

Uncle Henry passed Main Street, and then he reached a fork in the road. "Wait!" I said right before he was about to turn. He pressed on the brakes, and everyone looked at me. "I have an idea. Can we make a quick stop at Sea Glass Point?"

"Sea Glass Point?" said Uncle Henry with a frown.

"Yes. Just for ten minutes."

He shrugged. "Sure."

He turned the truck left, and we headed toward the point.

Bambi's whining got louder.

Finally, we reached Sea Glass Point. Uncle Henry pulled into the dusty parking area, right next to the stairway. We all got out, including Bambi's carrier, which Uncle Henry set down on a grassy patch.

I reached into my pocket and pulled out the collar and ID tag I'd ordered online. It was turquoise blue, the same blue as the sea back on the island. The ID tag was a shiny silver with the same exact star engraved on it as the one Isa and I had on our pendants. Except hers had "Bambi" written below it with our home phone number. I bent down and opened the carrier door.

"Shhh . . . I'm just going to pull you out. Okay?" I said, reaching in until my fingers felt fur.

Slowly, I wrapped my hands under her doggie armpits and brought her out. She stood in front of me, her spindly legs trembling. I took the collar and wrapped it around her neck, tight enough so it wouldn't fall off but loose enough that it wouldn't bother her. For a second, she seemed uncomfortable, as if I'd tied a brick around her neck. But then she shook her head back and forth so hard her ears flopped.

"C'mon," I said to Isa and Ada as I scooped up Bambi into my arms.

They looked at each other, then at me. "You sure about this?" said Isa.

"Yup," I said, taking the first step down.

Uncle Henry waved us on. "I'll just wait up here. Ten minutes, all right?"

I nodded. "Okay."

We trudged down the sandy, uneven steps until we reached the bottom. It was nearing lunchtime, so the beach was deserted, except for us and the remnants of the bonfire from the night before.

I went over to it and set Bambi down on the sand. All she did was tremble and wobble some more. But that moment passed as soon as she realized where we were. She lifted each of her paws and stared down at the sand we were standing on. The trembling stopped. She walked around in a circle, sniffing the sand, sniffing the logs, sniffing the bonfire ashes, sniffing the shells. I stepped back to give her some space. Isa and Ada did the same, watching her silently.

A couple of minutes went by, and Bambi's tail went higher and higher, like a flag being raised up a pole. And then, it wagged—tentatively at first—but the more she looked around, the faster her wagging got.

"You see, girl? It's like home. It's just a different island, that's all," I said to her in a high-pitched voice.

Bambi jumped and leaped in happy circles, whirling just as she used to when we were back on the island. I laughed, and Isa and Ada smiled.

The sea and the sky were a calm blue—the perfect blue. I kicked off my flip-flops, my bare feet sinking into the sand. I wiggled my toes, feeling that familiar sensation of sand sliding on my skin. I reached into my pocket again and pulled something out. But I hid it behind me and walked slowly toward the shoreline. Bambi watched me. Her body tensed. Her hind legs readied themselves.

One. Two. Three. Four. Five!

I flung my hand as hard as I could and let go of the tennis ball in my grasp. Bambi leaped into the air, her body floating, flying, soaring. *Thud.* She landed on the sand with the ball in her mouth.

"Good job, Bambi!" I shouted.

Isa and Ada clapped and cheered on the sidelines.

And then Bambi took off running down the beach with the tennis ball in her mouth. "Go, Bambi! Go!" I cheered, running after her.

We all took off. Fast. Bambi in the lead, a reddish-brown blur splashing through the incoming waves. It was weird, because time seemed to slow down. Slow. Fast. Past. Present. It almost felt as if I were running through a flurry of memories and dreams and fantasies. I was racing down the beach, I was a kid, Isa was a kid. Bambi was back on the island, and then she was in the sea dog-paddling, and then she was at the vet clinic in Bali. It didn't really matter that the past was colliding with the present. We just kept on running and leaping and laughing.

"You can run faster than that!" I yelled, and reached back for Isa's hand. She giggled and reached for Ada's hand. We swooped and glided, flying as if we were seagulls. Bambi sprinted toward the sea, faster and faster.

Whoosh . . . A wave crashed in front of us.

I let go of Isa, and Isa let go of Ada, and all of us, including Bambi, cannonballed into the sea.

ACKNOWLEDGMENTS

By the time you're reading this, I hope (crossing my fingers) that the pandemic will be mostly over and that life will be back to some semblance of normalcy. But let me tell you, writing and publishing books during a pandemic has been beyond challenging. There is no way I would have been able to accomplish any of it without a solid support system.

Birthing this third book baby has been easier in some ways and harder in others. I won't go into the nitty-gritty, but suffice it to say that having that support system saved my butt big-time. I'm truly grateful for everyone in my life who's helped shape who I am as a person and who I am as an author.

To my wonderful agent, Wendy Schmalz, who has stuck with me since day one. Thank you for picking my query from the slush pile and taking a chance on me. Thank you for continuing to champion my work. Thank you for your enduring loyalty. I'm excited to work on more books together!

To my editor, Trisha de Guzman. Thank you for

continuing to believe in me and my stories. I truly appreciate everything you do to make my books better—from your thoughtful editorial feedback, to your spot-on vision of book cover illustrations and design, to your overall enthusiasm and excitement. I couldn't have a better editor on my side.

To Joy Peskin, the big boss lady with the coolest glasses. Thank you for taking a chance on an unknown writer from halfway across the world. I'm so proud to have been discovered by you.

To Naira Mirza, editorial intern extraodinaire. Thanks for helping me whip my manuscript into shape! I'm pretty sure you've got a great career in publishing ahead of you.

To the entire team at FSG BYR/Macmillan. Thank you for everything. Not only do you publish some of the most amazing books out there, but you do it with an efficiency and panache that is unrivaled. I'm most especially grateful to my book designers, Liz Dresner and Aurora Parlagreco, for putting together the cover design of my dreams.

To my cover artist and kababayan, Enid Din. Thank you for bringing Coral, Isa, and Bambi to life. They are exactly how I pictured them. Not only did your illustration blow me away, but it surpassed all of my expectations.

To my mom, Helena. Thank you for sharing Mangenguey with the world. Without it, I would not have had the inspiration I needed to write this story.

To my dad, Wahoo. Thank you for always reading